A
DANGEROUS
REMEDY

Peter C. Cavelti was born in Switzerland. He has lived on four continents, pursuing his career as a financial executive and writer. Several of his non-fiction books have been published internationally. This is his first novel.

By the same author from Legacy Editions:

Tuiavii's Way: A South Sea Chief's Comments on Western Society

A DANGEROUS REMEDY

by Peter C. Cavelti

Legacy Editions, Toronto

A DANGEROUS REMEDY

For information contact Legacy Editions Ltd., 3219 Yonge Street,
Suite 220, Toronto, Ontario M4N 2L3, Canada.
legacyeditions@rogers.com

ISBN: 0-9682469-1-5

Library and Archives Canada Cataloguing in Publication

Cavelti, Peter C. (Peter Christian), 1948–
    A dangerous remedy / Peter C. Cavelti

ISBN: 0-9682469-1-5

    I. Title.

PS8605.A92D35 2004   C813'.6   C2004-905575-5

Manufactured in the United States of America

If I had one wish, Christian, I'd want to stand on the porch at the cottage with you. It wouldn't have to be at sunset, nor would the weather matter. Perhaps we wouldn't even talk. Just sharing the moment would count.

But that won't happen, because in the end you did something I could never have expected. The police did their investigation, but all I've learned from them is that you and Claudia disappeared. And that's my burden.

I have loved you like a brother—no, more than a brother! Brothers you get, you don't choose. I chose you and you chose me and that's how we became friends in grade five. In our adolescence our views hardened into opposing ideologies, but by the time we became adults we were closer than ever. Remember our talks at the tavern and our campfires up North? Both of us professionals, but still dreaming of a better world.

Then Claudia came into your life and you became a father. And later, with my help, an executor of justice. I sense we'd both express pain over what we did, but not regret. If we ever brought it up, that is.

Think of it: you are the person in this world I know best. We know each other better than most humans ever get to know one another. And yet, at the height of our friendship, you vanished!

Unless I find out what happened, I'll be damned to always think of you as an enigma. But by searching for the truth, I open myself to worse: if I learn that you perished, how can I live?

Such is my love for you, Christian, and such is my burden.

PROLOGUE

It was his birthday and Paiazzo was his favorite restaurant. He and Claudia had come twice together and it had been at least two years since he'd been here on business. But Gustavo, the owner, welcomed him like a long-lost brother and amazed Claudia by remembering her name. Claudia noticed that they were led to one of the best tables, then were asked if it was acceptable.

Gustavo came over with a bottle and uncorked it. Claudia knew little about champagne, but she recognized the odd shape and unusual label. Gustavo poured, let the fizz settle, poured some more.

"Enjoy…it's on the house," he announced.

"What a nice way to get started," Claudia said. "At this rate we'll have to be carried out of here."

Then, flashes of her life with David. She'd known luxury with him, too, but David had thought nothing of sending back an expensive bottle of wine, sometimes twice, complaining that the quality wasn't up to his standards. The few times Claudia had challenged him, he'd made a scene. Abused a waiter, or demanded to see the chef. Once he'd simply got up and walked out.

She watched Christian chat with Gustavo and thought of how

uncomplicated he was. Everything just took its course, as if the world was designed this way. She never had to be on guard with him.

Tonight would be perfect: spectacular food, pleasant surroundings, unrushed.

"To us," she said. Their glasses touched. "Happy birthday, my love."

Christian let the champagne roll around in his mouth, his jaw moving as though he were chewing on air. He squinted a bit, while the flavors teased his palate.

The meal was exceptional on all counts. The food prepared to perfection, the presentation of each course imaginative but simple, and the service excellent. "What do you have planned for us tonight?" Christian asked, as they were finishing their soft-shell crab.

Claudia giggled. "Let's see. I think it's a safe bet that we'll drink a bit too much. So by the time we're out of here, we'll be in a deliciously serene mood."

"Not a care in the world," Christian announced.

"Not a care in the world," she echoed. And then went on to describe how they'd return home, fall into each other's arms and have each other undressed before reaching the end of the hallway.

The men's room was lavish. Large bluish slate tiles covered the floor and the walls were finished in richly textured plaster. Expensive sconces shed a discreet light on the art. The built-ins were made of a dark, exotic wood. The place was meticulously clean.

Two tall men, built like football players and deeply tanned, were washing their hands and chatting. They were debating whether they should be using the cloth towels piled up on the counter or the paper ones in the dispenser. Christian smiled.

A man wearing a loose-fitting black suit and a black shirt followed him into the washroom. His haircut was among the strangest Christian had ever seen: a black mane down the back, the sides shaved clean and on top a crew cut. Christian glanced at the mirror, but the stranger turned away, moving in the direction of the toilet stalls.

Christian watched the man's back for a moment, wondering what the rest of his party might look like. He stepped over to the urinals. As he started to relieve himself, a hard object was rammed into his lower back.

"Don't move, buddy, or I'll have to hurt you."

Christian's first thought was that he might piss all over his pants. Then he noticed that his muscles had already contracted and that he'd stopped urinating. He knew it was the guy in the black suit. Was that a gun?

An arm came around his neck from the left. A hairy hand with conspicuously manicured nails glided by, then a gold Rolex. No shirt cuffs, just more hair and the black fabric of a jacket, shiny in the light of the sconce above it. The smell of sickeningly sweet cologne.

Christian's brain flooded with a hundred impulses, most of them useless and all hitting at the same time. The embarrassment of being hit in a toilet, the need to remember things, the possibility that it wouldn't matter since he might die anyway. Hope that he might be able to alert others and escape. The likelihood that he'd peed over his suit, after all.

"Pack your dick away and listen to me." Christian noticed an accent: Italian, Portuguese, Spanish?

He thought of Claudia, sitting upstairs. What would happen to her?

He tried turning his head, but the arm around his neck tightened.

"Easy, buddy, take it easy. Nobody's goin' to help you…got another guy in front of the bathroom, see? Look, here's the deal, buddy, you'll be in trouble if you stay with that woman and her kids. You'll leave her before the end of the month. Or you'll get killed, see?" He kept pushing the gun into Christian's back as if to hammer home the point.

"You leave her and you're fine…" the voice again. "She and the kids are fine too. On the other hand, you stay and you all pay. Big time, buddy. We been told to make it plenty painful, see?"

"I get it." Christian surprised himself with how calm he sounded. It gave him confidence. He might escape alive. He was prepared to be knocked out and his muscles tensed up.

The thug relaxed his grip. "Wash up and return upstairs. But first, keep facin' the urinal for a minute…pretend you're still pissing."

Christian listened as the thug stepped away: click, click, click. He'd expected this apparition from the underworld to move with stealth. The door opened, then shut again.

"I wonder what the hell that was about," someone said. "Did you take a look at the guy coming out? Christ, right out of the fucking movies."

"Probably snorted coke in here while his pal covered the door, is what I think," said another voice. "You know what? I think we should check out the stalls." Then to Christian: "Are you okay, sir? You look as though you didn't even notice!"

Christian felt exhausted, realizing that he was free to go. Perversely, he had an overwhelming urge to urinate. "Notice what?" he said and then listened to a whole litany of how they'd wanted to go to the toilet and how a huge, bouncer-type guy had just stood there barring the entrance.

"And I guess you saw the other guy in here, whatever he was doing," they pressed Christian, three of them now standing at the urinals next to him.

"Actually, I didn't look…he must have been back there," Christian nodded toward the stalls. He knew he didn't sound credible. He looked down at his pants and was relieved to see that they weren't stained. *I wonder what I look like?* he thought, as he stepped in front of the mirror. His forehead was covered with beads of sweat and the part in his hair was messed up.

Christian straightened himself up and walked down the hallway and through the throng of people clutching drinks and making conversation. As he climbed the stairs, he remembered the smell of cologne. He felt dizzy.

Claudia saw that something was wrong. "Are you all right, Christian?"

Gustavo rushed over to help Christian sit down. "Is everything to your satisfaction, Mr. Unger?" He placed Christian's serviette on his lap with a flourish.

"I don't feel so well. I think it may be better if we leave, Gustavo." The owner looked disappointed, so Christian added: "Nothing to do with the meal, let me assure you. Everything is exceptional as always."

"Your wife told me it's your birthday, too. An *eau de vie* might restore you. A cognac maybe?"

Christian surprised himself. "All right, Gustavo. Whatever you recommend." He took a deep breath and drank some mineral water.

"What on earth happened?" Claudia asked, taking Christian's hand into hers. "You were down there for quite a while, you know."

Christian said he'd tell her everything…after the cognac, on the way home.

When they left Paiazzo, Christian looked at the cars waiting at the curb. Perhaps the two thugs were waiting for them. But apart from a couple of taxis and private limousines, the vehicles near the restaurant were all empty, with motors running.

A valet held open the door for Claudia. Christian tipped him, then walked around the car, taking a careful look at the other side of the road. There was no sign of the man with the strange haircut.

. . . .

He pulled into the traffic and headed toward Claudia's place in Forest Hill, frequently checking his rear view mirror. After a few blocks, he turned into a side street and pulled up to the curb. He turned the lights off.

"What are you doing?" Claudia seemed anxious.

"Just bear with me for a second, I'll explain." Christian watched for cars that might have followed them, but saw nothing suspicious.

"Okay, my love. I owe you an explanation." He told her what happened.

"What are we going to do, Christian?" Claudia sobbed quietly, pressed against his chest. Then she gripped him hard. "What the hell *can* we do, for God's sake?"

Christian felt far away from his encounter of just an hour ago. Distance made it easier to think logically. "It'll be all right, Claudia. Trust me, everything will be all right." He kissed her on the forehead. "The first thing I have to do when I get home is to write everything down. The time, what I saw...what he looked like. He was short, with a fleshy nose and big lips. And of course that haircut. One of the people coming in afterwards said the guy looked straight out of the movies. Then his black outfit and his Rolex...that might be his trademark."

Claudia exploded: "I just can't believe that bastard! It's David, I just know it. It's exactly what he'd do, that damned coward. He's pissed off with you and he can't get up the courage to face you himself."

"It's got to be him...it's pretty obvious what happened, isn't it?"

"Maybe we should just take the whole family and move away somewhere. It's our happiness which matters and you and I can be happy anywhere. Who cares about Toronto?"

Christian drew her close. They stared at the fogged up wind-shield. "You know I'd move to the end of the world with you, but if they found me in the Paiazzo washroom they can find me anywhere else too. Besides, I'm not even sure we'd be *allowed* to move before you've settled with David."

"Christian, I'm afraid."

"Let's go home and sleep over this. Tomorrow we'll see what we come up with. Maybe we can let David know that *he'll* end up in jail if something happens to us. We'll find a way of getting through to the guy..."

He gave her a long, hard squeeze.

I imagine Christian stayed over at Claudia's that night. They didn't make love like she'd said, but they took comfort in each other's presence.

Neither of them slept much.

The condition of freedom is risk.

GOETHE

PART 1

I think I'll start with Claudia. I only knew her for 14 years, yet I seem to know more about her than Christian. That comes as a surprise, because I've been around Christian forever. I guess once you know someone so well, you relate and accept. You understand everything about the person, or that's what you believe. And so you talk about the Maple Leafs blowing the playoffs again or how the Canadian dollar keeps falling.

At first, Claudia was hesitant to share, but once she opened up there was no stopping her. I made myself vulnerable to her, too. Talking about my disastrous relationship with Hugo and exposing my other failings. So we became each other's confidants.

I gobbled up information about her as fast as I could. I wanted to know her. Out of suspicion, at first...out of a desire to protect Christian. Later, because it had become a habit and felt good.

Even so, I may make the occasional error where Claudia is concerned, especially as I record her days with David. I'll start with what I remember and, where there are holes, I'll have to trust my intuition.

Luckily, intuition is one of my strong suits. It's a facility I didn't know I possessed until my mid-thirties, mostly because my law school professors did such an atrocious job. They taught us to focus on research and process.

While I followed their advice I was moderately successful, but I sensed that something much bigger was always lurking nearby: intuition. To know which way the judge is inclined toward a case. To believe or not believe a key witness. I realized that I had to trust my instincts early on, but the logical part of my mind was so strongly developed that it took me years to conquer it. In the end I succeeded and that's when my career went ballistic. I attribute ninety percent of my success to intuition. Research can easily be delegated and process takes care of itself.

But let me take you back to Claudia and the beginning of the story.

Claudia felt good that morning. She stood at the kitchen counter, slicing sandwiches for the kids' lunches.

She'd feared that this would be a difficult morning, but here were David and the kids chatting and, a couple of times, she heard Jason and Karen giggle. They were playing some game with the jam. *The sounds of a happy family morning,* she thought, as the toaster popped with a loud clatter.

She placed the hot pieces of bread inside the chequered napkin she'd spread over the wicker basket to keep them warm. Strands of her auburn hair kept falling in front of her eyes. Then she walked over to the dining room.

"What's all the giggling about, hmm?"

Karen smiled broadly, as she described how Jason had created a strawberry jam face on his toast and how she was trying to best him. Claudia couldn't believe how pretty she was.

"You shouldn't play games with food, you know."

"Dad doesn't mind," Jason answered.

Claudia looked at her husband. David's expression was neutral. She thought the corners of his eyes revealed a smile. *He's in a good mood, after all.* She noticed that his cup was half empty. "Would you like some more coffee?"

"You know what?" David said, "This morning reminds me of that resort we visited in Jamaica."

"That place near Negril we went to on our tenth anniversary?"

"That's the one…do you remember it?"

"I loved the way it was perched above the sea. And the beach…" She could see the white stretch of sand, forming a gentle arc around the turquoise ocean with bits of reef showing dark. Then her mind flashed to the pain she'd felt when stepping onto the sea urchin and how the resort's doctor had cut into her swollen, purple heel to remove the barb. "I think that was the most spectacular beach we've ever been to—except for the sea urchins, wasn't it?"

Karen was on the verge of asking what a sea urchin was, but her father's voice stopped her. She withdrew to a place where nothing could harm her.

"I wasn't thinking of the beaches or the aquatic life of the Caribbean just now," he said, and all Claudia could think of was how wrong she'd been again.

"Not the beach, huh…?"

"No, not the beach, Claudia."

She wasn't sure whether he had pronounced her name intentionally slowly or whether her mind was playing tricks on her, but each of the syllables, CLAW-DEE-UH seemed to have taken on a life of its own.

"What's the weakest, most tasteless coffee we've ever had? Jamaica! Except they're animals down there—uneducated, half-baked, useless animals, preconditioned by a deficient gene pool and demotivated by slavery. Christ, I get sick even thinking about it. And who, among millions of housewives, serves me the worst tasting coffee since Jamaica? My wife…I can't believe it."

Claudia knew that more was to come. He was merely collecting his thoughts, catching his breath for the finish. She felt faint and her temples had started to throb.

"Besides," David continued digging, "it's *lukewarm*, too." He dragged out the word.

Everything slowed down for Claudia. She'd been here before and knew the feeling.

"I don't get it. After fifteen years of marriage and an unlimited budget, how can you still come up with tasteless, lukewarm coffee?"

Claudia returned to the kitchen, as she'd done on countless occasions. She took the nearly full glass pot from the hotplate, and walked back to the dining room, squeezing by her son's chair to where her husband was sitting.

She lifted the pot to pour. Then, her hands as steady as her voice was firm, she threw the scalding coffee into David's face, saying, "I don't think so." David jumped back and screamed, holding his burned face.

She added, "Tasteless maybe, David…but not lukewarm. It's hot. Scalding, searing hot, you bastard!"

Claudia couldn't hear her own words all that well. There was a ringing in her ears.

When drawing on my recollections of what Claudia has told me about her parents, I have to rely on another resource I've developed: my ability to retain facts. After intuition, it's the second cornerstone to a successful career in law. Of course, you can't retain information without listening, and being a good listener is in my nature. Even the subtlest details don't escape me; I file them away until needed.

On the subject of Kenneth and Harriett Hetherington, let me say that their involvement in this story is peripheral. But their impact on its characters is of consequence, which is why I have to deal with them.

Kenneth Robert Hetherington was an insurance man. He'd started as an insurance administrator and later in his professional life become an insurance executive.

Actually, the term "professional life" was one to which Hetherington took great exception. In his mind, it was a sign of the times that people made a distinction between their professional and private lives. The only private dealings in his years in business had been the few occasions of intimacy with his wife, Harriett. At all other times, he maintained the decorum due an insurance administrator, which meant that he dressed and acted the part of an insurance man. When going out to dinner, at movies and even on holidays.

None of this had ever bothered Harriett, who adored Kenneth. She was aware that such blind devotion was being scoffed at by modern society and she despised her contemporaries for it. To them, devotion was equivalent to dependence—a hindrance to the fulfilment of one's potential. But Harriett understood what today's social image makers could never understand, namely that a wife who subjugated her own ambitions to the unconditional support of her husband would in time share in the glory of his achievements. So what if others felt that she did not have a personality? Her husband's personality and successes were hers, as well. And Kenneth had never once given her cause for anything but pride and respect.

It was a splendid Thursday afternoon in early November: cloudless and crisp, but cold enough to remind one that winter wasn't far off. Harriett had just finished covering her roses for the cold months ahead—first with mulch and then with a few lengths of burlap, as she'd learned from her mother in England a long time ago.

She was pleased. In May, her rose bushes would come alive again in all their glory. They'd delight her and Kenneth and the many neighbors who regularly came by to see their garden.

Harriett was standing at the sink, scrubbing dirt off her hands, when the phone rang. She was annoyed. What if it was her husband? Kenneth did not like it when she didn't answer the phone. She turned off the tap and quickly wiped her hands. She made it on the fifth ring and, slightly out of breath, picked up the receiver, saying: "This is the Hetherington residence."

Harriett was disappointed that it wasn't Kenneth, but Claudia. She always felt slightly uncomfortable with her daughter. Claudia

26 PETER C. CAVELTI

didn't approve of her, she was certain of it.

"Hi, Mom, how are things?"

"They're fine, except you phoned at a most inconvenient time. I was just washing my hands, having prepared the roses for winter."

"If it bothers you to go to the phone, why do you, Mother?"

"Because it might have been your father…he doesn't like it when I don't answer."

"He doesn't, huh? Well, maybe you should get him used to the idea that it's not always convenient to run to the phone. Anyway, Mom, we've been through that before. I'm calling because I need Elliott Wyndham's phone number. There's something I need to discuss with him."

"I'll have to ask your father."

"I'm sure it's written down in that list you keep by your phone."

"You don't understand, Claudia. I'm afraid your father wouldn't approve if you contacted Elliott without his permission."

"Why? It's not that Elliott doesn't know me."

"You know that is not the reason," Harriett said formally.

"I see." Claudia voice rose. "You realize that I can simply look up his firm in the phone book and ask for him. Why did I even call you? I don't need your approval to call a lawyer. You realize that, don't you?"

"Now, now…you're becoming emotional. You know what your father would think about *that*. Why don't you let me talk to him and see…"

"You sound like a damned answering machine, Mother. 'No one can take your call just now, but if you leave your number we'll call you back just as soon as we can.' Except you have to work on your presentation. The machines leave me with a much warmer feeling." Claudia hung up, then looked up the number of Wyndham's firm. She got an appointment for the next day.

. . . .

Claudia told me this story a few years later. Her eyes lit up when she described how her father called the lawyer to find out if and why his daughter had phoned and was promptly rebuffed.

"What do you think he said to him, Jake?" she asked me.

I have a bit of an advantage, in that I know the venerable Wyndham, even though I don't get to meet too many family lawyers. So I had fun imagining what he might have said.

"Come, come, my dear Hetherington, I know you have more honor than anyone when it comes to the maintenance of discretion, and without discretion there can be no honor," I blurted out. "Whatever he said, it must have been a crippling blow to your father's pomposity."

Claudia shrieked with delight.

Claudia knew that Elliott would be asking questions. After all, that's what a lawyer does.

She found it hard to sort through the jumble of emotions that cluttered her mind. Her thoughts were driven by random impulses, flitting from one episode of her life with David to another.

David walking into the family room and, in a fit of uncontrolled anger, kicking at everything that's left on the floor or on the sofa. Toys crushed, a cassette player shattered, school materials damaged.

David throwing me for a loop. A messenger standing at the door with a bouquet of long-stemmed roses and a note saying, "Just to let you know how wonderful you are."

All of us wondering when the cycle would peak and always getting it wrong. The kids so intimidated they do whatever David demands, just to avoid further humiliation.

The final tirade, over absolutely nothing, and always directed at me.

Claudia tried to push out the thoughts of degradation and the rancor with which David had lashed out at her, but she couldn't.

Finally, plunging into the sweet abyss. Letting myself fall and fall…and falling around me, the few remaining shards of my self-

. . . .

esteem. Lying in bed in the dark, welcoming in the catatonic gloom, as the tranquilizers take their effect.

David taking the children on a shopping spree and bringing me back a piece of jewelery, or a little something from one of the better boutiques, telling me how unworthy of me he is. The bastard!

And then yesterday…an ordinary Wednesday. Who could have known that would be the day? Things had started routinely enough. The kids sitting down and reaching for toast, then David joining them. The game they played with their toast and jam.

Then, out of nowhere David's tirade about the worst coffee since Jamaica, and Claudia looking straight at him. Like an actress performing an inconsequential role with which she is completely bored. *What was it Karen told me at breakfast today? "It was as if you were far away somewhere. That was really something, Mom."*

Time had slowed down. David's words broke into syllables that drifted by her, one at a time, like soap bubbles with a menacing hue. And then she was outside her body, looking onto a scene played by others. All sensation was suspended, on her walk to the kitchen and back, the coffee pot weightless and her feet unaware of contact with the floor.

She never consciously thought of throwing the coffee at David. It just happened, an action her nervous system executed independently.

Her voice changed. It was as if each word came from a place further back in her throat than the one before. She would always remember that place. It was where her darkest rage lived.

W̶hat happened next?" asked Elliott Wyndham.

"I told him I wanted him out of the house within an hour. That he couldn't live with me and the kids any longer. If he didn't leave I'd call the police."

"And then?"

"Well, several seconds of silence followed, and then all hell broke loose. David screamed things like 'Why did you do this to me?' and 'Who do you think you are, anyway?' before leaping up. I stood there, overwhelmed. But then something in David's eyes told me that he'd try to beat me."

"So your bet that he'd never physically assault you was wrong?" Elliott looked at Claudia, but kept scribbling on his note pad.

"That's when I ran toward the door leading to the basement. David followed, screaming that he'd kill me."

"Kill you? Are you positive?"

"Positively. That's what he said."

"Did he say anything other than that? At that particular point, that is?"

"No, just 'I'm going to kill you,' once."

"I'm sorry I keep interjecting, Claudia. I know this is difficult and painful for you, but these details are important. And it's vital that we get everything down exactly the way it happened. Please continue."

"I'm sorry....So here I was halfway down the stairs, running as much as falling, and then it occurred to me that I'd be trapped in the basement, completely at David's mercy. And maybe he'd even grabbed a knife or something else. I mean, why else would he say he'd kill me? That's when I screamed and fell."

"Why did you scream, Claudia? Was it because you fell or because you were afraid of being killed?"

"Because I thought he might have a knife...the fall came just after that."

"You're absolutely sure of this?" Wyndham waited for an affirmation, before signaling to Claudia to continue.

"So, as I said, I was lying at the foot of the stairs when everything happened at once. David was right there, pulling me up by my hair, tugging really hard. And the kids were screaming, too."

"How did you fend him off?"

"Not very successfully, Elliott. I couldn't see him, because he stood behind me, so I screamed and kicked and hit in all directions."

"Then what happened?"

"Karen and Jason entered the fray, trying to restrain him as well, holding on to his shirt and pants."

"And that helped?"

"I don't really know."

She recalled the scene in the downstairs family room, where they'd ended up. David had lessened his grip and as she looked up she saw their reflection in the wall-length mirror. She contemplated the sad tangle of bodies and realized that this would be their last family portrait. David's clothing soaked with coffee, his face blotched from the scalding brew and his hair a mess. Tears welling in his eyes.

A few moments later, on his knees and buckled over, he threw up his breakfast. "You bitch…you bitch," he said, over and over, between heaves and blubbering sobs.

Nothing that Claudia had said so far surprised the lawyer, but at her description of these last events he let his pen slide.

"And that's it?" he asked.

"Well, for a few seconds I actually caught myself feeling sorry for him…I mean he looked so pitiful, and in front of the children, too."

Claudia was almost embarrassed relating her feelings now, but when she'd been there her pity for David hadn't lasted long. Anger and contempt had quickly taken over, as she'd reminded herself that he would deal with this episode of his life the way he dealt with everything. David had a unique capacity to blame others for his own misfortunes and to feel sorry for himself.

And she'd been right. By the time he had showered and packed, uttering obscenities and swearing revenge, he'd convinced himself that he was the victim of Claudia's intrigues and that she was about to ruin his life.

Kenneth Hetherington had not become an insurance executive for nothing. He may have been an unimaginative and pretentious bore, but once he was onto something he didn't give up. Claudia's independent behavior and the snub he'd received at the hands of Wyndham had irked him and he was determined to find out more. He phoned his son-in-law at his chiropractic clinic.

"David, I'm so sorry to interrupt you at work. How have you been?"

"Actually, Ken, I'm pleased you're calling and I bet it's about Claudia." Apart from his using the short form for Kenneth, which annoyed him no end, David was more charming than Hetherington could remember.

"I am calling about Claudia…"

"You know, Ken, it's good we're talking. I have no idea what's got into Claudia and I didn't know whether I should bother you with this mess. I know she's been sleeping around for years, but I've been willing to put up with it for Jason and Karen's sake. You know how important the children are to me. They're my whole life, Ken."

Hetherington was speechless.

"Did you hear what I said?"

Kenneth's mind was racing. David must know of things his daughter had decided not to discuss with him or her mother.

"I'm rendered speechless, David. Surely this is all a regrettable mistake, which must be corrected at the earliest opportunity. May I speak to Claudia and call you back?"

Such talk was balm to David's ears. He'd planned to visit Kenneth and Harriett on the weekend, but this was better. If played right, it allowed David to achieve the same results on his own terms. He pressed his advantage. "I'd appreciate that, Ken. You have no idea how wounded I am by Claudia's irrational behavior. I really hope you can do something—for the children's sake. I guess if you fail, I'll have to take custody of them. She really isn't fit to be a mother and, besides, our courts take a dim view of adulterous mothers." And then David hung up.

Kenneth didn't hear the monotonous shrillness of the dial tone. He just sat there, hearing David's words, repeated over and over. What on earth should he do? Talk to Harriett? Confront Claudia? Hetherington had never faced a situation like this.

Claudia was puttering in the kitchen, waiting for her parents. Like bits of celluloid, episodes from the past few days paraded through her mind.

David throwing things, slamming doors, and finally leaving. The kids in their rooms, brooding and feeling sorry for themselves.

Claudia had gone to see Karen twice and Jason three times. Jason accused her of breaking up their family, while Karen predicted that they'd all have to pay for what her mother had done. "He'll make our lives so miserable we'll all want to commit suicide," was how she put it.

"Have you ever thought of my position?" Claudia responded. "My life has been miserable since you were two years old. And do you realize that this will benefit you, too? Don't tell me you didn't suffer each time your dad lost it. I guess you know nothing else, but believe me what you experienced isn't usual, sweetie." Claudia hugged Karen and viewed it as a good sign that she got hugged back.

Jason was a different matter. Claudia's first two visits to his room were demoralizing. Her attempts to put her arms around him failed. He tensed up completely and accused her of selfishly destroying their family. The third time he wouldn't even let Claudia in.

The next day, she sent the kids back to school and went to see Elliott, who gave her at least some hope regarding Jason and Karen. If David decided to fight her over custody, the choice would most likely be the children's, he said. Most judges would accept the decisions of an eleven- and a fourteen-year-old. But which way would the kids decide?

"My experience is that mothers have a very good track record…they usually know their children well." Elliott's words may only have been that—words—but they made all the difference.

Harriett seemed in an enormous hurry to take Jason and Karen to Ricardo's for pizza. The grandchildren knew what was up and tried to stay. Their parents' problems would be discussed.

When Claudia was alone with her father, she took refuge in a ritual to which she resorted whenever they were together. She made a pot of his favorite Oolong tea.

"I suppose by now Elliott has told you all there is to know, Dad," she opened. "How I threw the scalding coffee in David's face, kicked him out and told him I'd call the police if he showed up again. That's why you wanted to see me, isn't it?"

Kenneth had dreaded the talk with his daughter, knowing that he was hopeless in handling any confrontation, but now he felt better. Her assumptions of what he'd learned from Elliott were plainly wrong. "No, my child, that's not how things are. Even though

Wyndham has been in our employ for three decades, he refused to give me any information."

Claudia ignored her father's description of Elliott being in his employ. Updating the Hetheringtons' will every five years couldn't amount to much of Wyndham's revenues.

"No, my dear, it is your husband who has alerted me to your follies. It's a good thing your mother is otherwise occupied, because she would find it difficult to cope with her daughter being an adulteress. I've wondered for the past two days how you would explain yourself." Kenneth lifted the saucer, took his cup and sipped at his tea.

"What are you talking about, Dad? What's this adultery stuff?"

"I'm merely repeating what David tells me. He says you've been sleeping around, quite apart from throwing him out. He also tells me you're at risk of losing your children, which is a possibility you should take seriously."

"And what do you think happened, Dad? Really...what do you think?"

"My dear, what am I supposed to think? I've heard David level some specific accusations at you. And you, without even contesting them, are asking me what I think?"

"Well yes. What do you think?"

"Claudia, I would like to think that David is entirely in the wrong, but your actions indicate that there is merit to his accusations."

"What actions, Dad? What are you talking about, for Christ's sake?" Claudia jumped up.

"Calm down, my dear. Let's try to discuss this without getting emotional, shall we? The actions David refers to, of course: adultery, turning him out, trying to break up the family."

"I can't believe it. Those are David's accusations. You haven't even heard my side of the story...you're not even asking me where I stand on all this!"

"Well, are you suggesting none of this is true? Why would

David make up such a story?"

"Dad, David is the creep who's humiliated you for years. He calls you Ken when he knows you hate it. He's belittled your insurance career, slighted you whenever he could, insulted you to your face. And you're tempted to believe the bastard? Think about it and then decide who you want to trust. The guy has abused me and the kids for years…okay, not physically, he hasn't actually beaten us, but he's made up for it in psychological terms. We're scarred for life, for God's sake!" She looked out the window, wondering how she could get through to him. "How many times have you been to our place when David's gone over the edge? Have you forgotten the Christmases and Thanksgivings when he lost it and drove us all to tears? How can you even listen to this adultery bullshit? I've been the most faithful and loyal wife any abuser ever had. How can you doubt me?"

Kenneth sat in his wing chair, stiff and erect; mousy, crusty and grey. He'd contemplated Claudia during her outburst, the tips of his outstretched fingers drumming a slow but steady beat on his pant legs, but his facial expression never changing. It was that of a statue erected centuries ago, dispassionately taking in the goings on in a contemporary setting. Claudia was pacing the living room when her father finally responded.

"Well, I must say that it doesn't terribly matter who's done what. The fact is that we have two viewpoints on most issues of debate. No matter who's right, we must make sure the children's interests are observed. Whatever you did in terms of breaking up your family must be reversed at the earliest occasion."

"Are you telling me you won't believe me, Father?"

"It's not that simple, Claudia. You and David accuse each other of different things and since I wasn't present I cannot take sides. Surely, you do understand that?"

"No I don't. Haven't we just gone through the salient facts? That David has treated you and Mom badly for years…and that you've witnessed David mistreating the kids and me on countless occasions? How can you suggest that his word should be equal to mine? Tell me I'm missing something, Dad. Tell me I'm missing *something*!"

Kenneth poured himself more tea.

"My dear Claudia, no matter what has come between you and David, you made certain irreversible decisions when you got married. You committed yourself to David and you put in place an institution to protect your future children. You must be true to these commitments now. Invite him back and make your peace with him. If you don't, David will succeed in ruining you financially and taking the children away from you. And in that context you must realize that your mother and I are deeply attached to Jason and Karen as well."

"Is that what it's all about? You're worried about having to support me and lose your grandchildren? Look, I understand that both these issues are concerns, Dad, but what about the possibility that David's accusations are lies? And what fate do you think would await the kids and me if we got back together? What about that, huh?"

Kenneth reiterated she should swallow her pride and invite David back.

"And what if I don't? I suppose you do realize that I'm nearly forty and that you can't do a damned thing if I don't listen to you."

"It would pain me if you didn't abide by my advice, Claudia. I believe I can say that both your mother and myself would not be able to accept such a decision."

"Well, Dad, guess what? What you've said hurts, but it doesn't surprise me a lot. When mom phoned to say you wanted to come over, I asked myself what your likely position would be. And you know what? I've been right on target." Claudia sat down again. "Here's what I've decided. It's not what I want to happen, but what you're forcing on me. Alternative one: support my decision to leave David and fight for the kids. Alternative two: don't see me again. If you can't have faith in me and stand behind me there's absolutely no reason to pretend that we have any kind of relationship."

Kenneth got up, muttering something about Claudia being emotional and irrational.

"I'm not irrational. You have a good relationship with the kids and they love you. So whatever happens between us can't affect them, okay? Provided you don't talk about me or David, you can see Karen and Jason whenever you like and I'll tell them the same thing. But between us, it will be civility and nothing more. And you know what, Dad? I'm thrilled that Wyndham wouldn't give you any information. I have a lot of faith in him."

Kenneth was stunned. For the second time in three days, he encountered a situation for which his insurance career had not prepared him.

From what I can piece together, Claudia's dealings with her parents unfolded much along the lines she envisioned.

Claudia urged the children to visit their grandparents whenever they wanted. Kenneth stuck to his bargain, too. Claudia never once had the impression that her parents tried to make her look bad with the kids. After all, her father was a man of honor, or at least a man who kept his word.

Two or three times a year, on major occasions, Claudia went along with her children, trying to maintain a façade of normalcy. A few times, overcome by the desire to make amends, Claudia brought up the topic of their estrangement. But Kenneth was woefully inadequate at handling any form of unpleasantness and to him the topic of his daughter's stubbornness was unpleasant in the extreme.

Under different circumstances, Claudia might have viewed her mother as a go-between, but such a thought never crossed her mind. After all, she was Mrs. Kenneth Robert Hetherington.

Claudia was traumatized by her father's response. To be a good parent became a passion of hers.

"Just think about it, Jake," she told me one morning, as we stood on the dock at Christian's cottage. "I can't recall my parents ever once telling me they were proud of me. Did yours?"

"I don't think so," I had to admit.

"I've asked Christian, too…of course his father died early. But he thinks that's actually the norm."

"You mean parents not praising their kids?"

"Yeah, even if they do well. Even if they end up being big successes."

We were standing. The wooden planks and the red Muskoka chairs we usually sat on were covered in dew. It would take a while for the morning sun to burn it off. Both of us held on to brightly colored coffee mugs.

"I'm really determined to do that differently," Claudia vowed. "Even now, before I really know how well they'll do, I'll try to remember to give them praise."

"For small successes, too," I added.

"In your case, does it bother you, not having been told you're a good person?"

I laughed, but I felt like crying. "My parents were such fuck-ups, I'd be worried if I'd had their approval."

"What happened, Jake?"

"You don't want the details," I said. "My father was a womanizer. And knowing my mother, I probably would have been, too."

Somewhere in the distance, I heard Claudia say she was sorry.

When his father-in-law told him what happened, David slammed down the receiver. His plan to get some leverage through Claudia's parents had failed. Blood throbbed in his temples. *The bitch.* He had to find a way to get her to invite him back.

David knew he had behaved atrociously against his wife and even cheated on her a few times. But what was marriage about if you couldn't tolerate your partner's flaws? Besides, whenever he'd gone too far he'd more than made up for it by treating her very generously.

He couldn't forgive Claudia. He'd fight. David knew that Claudia had only two alternatives: to take him back or be piss-poor. And the latter she'd never accept. She was too used to her lifestyle and too protective of the kids. He'd get the best lawyer he could. Lawyers were mercenaries: as long as you paid, they did what you asked.

David chose William Trebillcock. If I'd been asked to name the two best-known family lawyers in Toronto at that time, I'd have said Bill Trebillcock and Elliott Wyndham without much thinking. Their establishments were strikingly different. Trebillcock was one of the stars at a huge firm downtown—the type Wyndham would call a "factory". Elliott Wyndham, in contrast, had helped build a niche business.

Most successful lawyers insist on an exploratory meeting, in which the client gets to state his situation and objective and the practitioner has the right to accept or deny the case. David Talbot's case was not one that William Trebillcock thought of referring. His client was a well known professional, who had come recommended. Moreover, as David related his story, Trebillcock couldn't help feeling sorry for him. If first impressions were to be believed, here was a calm, well-adjusted family man hurt by a wife of, at best, dubious character. He pictured David in court; any judge would feel sympathy for a victim so articulate and, especially given his harsh circumstances, so composed and even-tempered.

Even so, part of Trebillcock's job was to leave nothing to chance and so he made three things clear to David. The first concerned the kids. Just as Wyndham had told Claudia, he explained to David that it wasn't unusual for judges to determine custody according to the children's wishes. At 11, Karen was still a bit young for that to happen, but who could tell when the case would be heard and who the judge might be?

"Ergo, David, if you're going to get into a pissing contest over custody, you better be sure that the children, if left to choose, will actually choose you over your wife."

David looked confused. "I see...but who determines what the children want? How is that established?"

"Usually in counselling. And in the sessions that really matter, neither parent is allowed to attend. For the protection of the children, you understand?"

The second thing Trebillcock brought up was his insistence that David adhere to whatever they agreed to. "This may be difficult at times, David, but I want you to understand that I have a zero tolerance policy on this score. For instance, if you and I agree on a specific way to handle money or if we decide on a particular approach to custody, you'll have to stick to it. If you don't, I'll have to withdraw as your counsel. Do you think you can do that?" David agreed, even though he knew that it wasn't in his nature.

"And finally, David, a third thing. Don't call Claudia or go near the children or your house. I don't want you to be accused of harassing or stalking her. And, by the way, I'd prefer if you stayed in a hotel, ideally an expensive one…rack up some serious expenses on meals and stuff and keep the receipts. I'm sure you'll find that easy to comply with. Above all things, remember I'm on your side. Once I've talked to Wyndham, I'll have a better understanding of where he wants to take this. So, until you hear from me, stay put."

What followed were ten tumultuous days. After a week at the Four Seasons Hotel, where he now rented a suite, no one wanted to serve David any longer. And at his practice, one of his assistants quit. Yet none of this overly worried David. What really mattered was that he and Trebillcock could get Claudia to change her mind.

In his second meeting with his lawyer, David was fidgety. When Trebillcock asked him how he was, David answered he was determined to thwart his wife's ambitions and leave the meeting with a comprehensive plan.

"David, that's not what I meant when I asked how you're doing. What I want to know is how you're holding up."

"I'm sure you know how I'm doing," David said defiantly. "Two weeks ago I had a family, now I don't. Anyway, let's talk about your plan."

After talking to Wyndham two days earlier, Trebillcock had sensed that this would be a tense meeting, but he'd planned to start it on a cordial and relaxed note. He'd develop a feel for his client.

"David," he said, as though he was unaware of the tension in his client's demeanor. "Before we talk about any plan, I have to be fully conversant with your situation. I'm afraid that's not yet the case. Wyndham made me aware of a few twists you hadn't mentioned. Perhaps they don't exist at all, perhaps you think of them as peripheral, and perhaps you forgot to tell me. My job is to find out."

David grew irritable. "Last time you didn't give me much of a chance to omit anything. Come to think of it, I remember it more as an interrogation than a meeting."

"I'm sorry you think so, David. But, nevertheless, there are a number of key points we have to revisit before we can go off in any direction."

"Like what?" snapped David.

"One major issue Wyndham has brought up is what he calls a multi-year record of psychological abuse perpetrated against your wife and your children."

"That's a lie."

"Are you saying there's no substance to her claims?"

"No, there isn't. And it's irrelevant, anyway."

"Not if it gets to court, David. But let's leave it at that." Trebillcock could see that he needed to change his strategy. "Look, today I'd like to take you through the issues we didn't discuss last time. On each point, I'll give you the aspects that I know will matter. Maybe you want to take some notes. You can think them over and when we meet next we'll talk them through in detail." Trebillcock paused just long enough to assess David's reaction. "In reference to Wyndham's first major issue, that of…" and here he glanced at his pad as though he couldn't remember the exact words, "…psychological abuse perpetrated against your wife and your children over a matter of years, I'd like to say this. All of us let off steam every now and then, sometimes by having emotional outbursts. The difference between letting off steam and psychological abuse is that the latter concentrates on a specific person, with the purpose of diminishing that person's dignity. If you repeatedly put down your wife, belittled her, said things…"

"I didn't come here to get a lesson in psychology."

Trebillcock picked up a pencil and tapped it against the desk. "This is not about psychology, David. It's about law. You're paying me a fat honorarium to represent your interests and I think you should know how the courts define abuse. So let me try again. I repeat: If you repeatedly put down your wife, belittled her or said things to make her feel inadequate, you're at risk of being guilty of abuse. More so with the children. If you're merely guilty of cursing at the wall or the woodpile, then they have no case. Also ask yourself how, in mediation or in front of a judge, your testimony would differ from that of your wife or your children. Any questions on this one?"

"No."

"Good…excellent," Trebillcock felt back in command. "Let's move on then. Wyndham tells me his understanding regarding the coffee incident differs from mine…on a major point. They readily agree that she threw the scalding coffee in your face, so there's no contest there. But they claim that, shortly after, you jumped up screaming that you'd kill her. That's when she ran away, down the stairs into the basement. When she fell, you grabbed her, yanking her by the hair. You didn't mention any of this last time, David. I'm not particularly interested in the hair pulling. It doesn't look great, but after all she threw a pot of hot coffee in your face. But the 'I'll kill you' could be a problem, depending on context. Did you say, or scream, those words or anything that's similar?"

David looked at the ceiling. "I can't remember."

"All right. Try to remember. And let me know next time. And, as before, ask yourself how your wife and the children would testify on that count. I understand the children were right there."

"Bill, I don't like the way this meeting is going. I want to establish a plan and discuss how we can achieve results. As you said, I'm paying a fortune, while you're interrogating me."

Bill Trebillcock and David Talbot were now a study in contrast. Two figures sitting on opposite sides of a table. One confident and tranquil, his hands relaxed on the polished surface in front of him. The other squat, tense and unpredictable, both in mood and appearance.

"I'm sorry you're disappointed. I'm trying to do my job and experience has taught me a few things. For starters, that I can't successfully represent a client if I don't know the details of his case. And these are exceptionally important details, David. So far, we've dealt with abuse and with a threat of murder. If we end up on the wrong side of these accusations, we're toast. You'll lose your family and you'll pay a fortune in support payments." He let these words sink in. "I don't usually lose cases, David, but in order to win I need your help. And I haven't even finished with my list." Trebillcock tapped his pencil again. "Why don't we do this. Listen to the rest of what I have to say and then think about it for a couple of days. And here's how we'll deal with the fee. We're on again in three days' time. If you show up with the answers, you owe me my fees; if you don't show up, I'm off the case and you owe me nothing. What do you say?"

David looked no happier, but nodded.

"Back to my list. The other side alleges that you defamed your wife, telling her parents she'd had extramarital affairs. She, in contrast, claims to have been faithful to you since she took her vows."

"I doubt she'll be able to prove that," David said cockily.

"So do I. But you're the one who'll have to prove that she *did* have affairs. Unless you have names, dates, addresses and, ideally, photographs—all in addition to witnesses—I urge you not to make such statements to anyone. Let me have your response next time. And finally, David, the money thing. Your situation is not unusual; every case includes a money problem."

"What money problem are you talking about?"

"It's pretty universal. I'm sure you have strong feelings that your wife and children shouldn't have access to your money while you're not allowed in your own house…no need to go into details. But I would like to say this. Our position is much stronger if you don't make any threats or take any action concerning money. Specifically, no instructions to banks blocking accounts, cancelling credit cards…"

"Why not? It's my money."

"I don't yet fully understand your household's financial intricacies. But what you think of as your money may not be yours in law. Other than assets you and your wife brought into your marriage at its onset or under a specific agreement, the basic formula is that you are each entitled to half."

"That's ridiculous!" David jumped up. "I'm bringing all the money in and she's spending it. I'm not willing to accept that!"

Trebillcock decided to end the meeting on a calm note. "This is why I have to learn a lot more before we can determine a strategy. For now, it's best if you leave things the way they are. Wyndham is a superb family lawyer and I'm convinced he's told your wife not to plunder your joint accounts."

And with that, Bill Trebillcock held out his hand to David. "Come back to me with your answers and we'll start talking strategy. And remember: if I don't hear from you by week's end I'll declare myself dismissed."

David hadn't expected Claudia to move so quickly, especially in going to see a lawyer. And he could tell that Wyndham was out to destroy him. If Claudia were on her own, her train would never have left the station. But her talking to Wyndham had changed everything. The accusations against him were hogwash, but they proved Wyndham knew where to throw his barbs.

David thought of changing his legal counsel. He hated Trebillcock. The man didn't know anything about him, but was already trying to take control and set the agenda. On the other hand, David might end up trading in one of the city's best legal minds for an inferior one. He spent the whole weekend stuck at this point, trapped in an inescapable loop, his frustration at risk of exploding into uncontrolled rage.

When he woke up on Monday morning, everything seemed clear to him, as if the formula needed to bridge his impasse had been written in glaring chalk letters on a colossal blackboard. There was only one area in which he could squeeze Claudia: money. On all other fronts, he was in trouble.

On the adultery issue, how could he ever prove Claudia's infidelities? Not that he had any doubt that she'd had an affair. She simply didn't have the strength and cunning to pull things off the way she had. There had to be someone else!

The idea that he'd threatened to kill his wife was ridiculous. But David sensed he was destined to fail here, as well. He knew he'd prevail in a courtroom, where it would just be Claudia's word against his. If he managed to project his reassured, professional self, the odds favored him even with the sternest, most discriminating judge. But Trebillcock had said that a counsellor might interview the children and that worried him. Karen and Jason were no match for a psychologist, and who knew what else the kids would volunteer, once their resistance was broken. After all, he *had* screamed he'd kill Claudia and the children *had* been right there.

And the same could be said about Claudia's accusation of psychological abuse. Again, the children were the weak link. Eventually, Wyndham would get at the truth, possibly on all three fronts.

In the end, what had seemed so confusing boiled down to just a single reality: Wyndham needed the truth to keep David from getting his family back. Hence, he had to frustrate Wyndham's search for the truth wherever possible. That's why money was important: the longer it took, the more desperate Claudia would become.

Bill Trebillcock noticed that David's gloom was gone. He was calm, charming and reasonable After a few minutes, the lawyer concluded that his client must have been in an uncharacteristically bad mood the previous week.

David had the requested answers, repeatedly consulting a binder filled with pages of notes.

On the psychological abuse issue, he flatly denied that he'd ever wilfully diminished Claudia's or the children's dignity. He even remembered Trebillcock's definition. The odd loss of temper, perhaps…that he could admit to. After all, he was the owner of a large chiropractic clinic, from the rewards of which his family had benefited immensely, but which also exposed him to stress and left him overworked. Was it unreasonable for him to relieve pressure?

This was in stark contrast to Wyndham's allegations, who'd said that Claudia had numerous examples of severe abuse and that the children had almost always been present. Over a matter of years! Wyndham had said he'd subject the children to a series of interviews with a psychologist, if necessary.

Trebillcock found it harder to assess David's version of the adultery issue. He said that Claudia was a slut who'd slept around for years and, worse, had freely admitted it to him. That was why he didn't have names, dates and witnesses. The simplest explanations were usually closest to the truth and a few years earlier Trebillcock had come across a similar situation: a wife had boasted to her husband about her infidelities. But was David the type to be repeatedly cuckolded?

Other aspects suggested that David was telling the truth. He readily admitted that, yes, he'd screamed he would kill his wife, and apologized for not volunteering this information earlier. In court, it would be easy to explain his client's behavior: David could reasonably be expected to say or scream almost anything after having a pot of hot coffee thrown at him.

What also gave Trebillcock pause was David's apparent interest. While his client had appeared intransigent and disinterested last time, he busily scribbled into his binder throughout today's meeting. He even thanked the lawyer for his pointers regarding money, saying he could see that it wouldn't serve his cause if he sabotaged Claudia's access to their joint resources. That impressed Trebillcock.

When the meeting ended, he was tempted to revise his earlier judgement. Perhaps Talbot was simply going through a very difficult time, the victim of a deceptive and malicious woman. But then, Trebillcock mused, David might also be a highly gifted actor and a

. . . .

skilful liar. He rated the chances about equal.

Quite a bit of guessing on my part has gone into what came next. Some of the details were given to me by Claudia years ago, while others never came up.

Suffice it to say that David and his legal counsel finally decided on a strategy. Trebillcock convinced himself that they should vehemently deny the accusations of persistent psychological abuse. On the subject of David's threat to kill Claudia they admitted defeat, but maintained that David's scream had merely been a justified reaction to a brutal, preconceived assault.

Regarding Claudia's infidelities, Trebillcock was in a bind. He had little choice but to accept his client's position as it was related to him. David's views on custody were strong; his wish was to return to his family, but if that wasn't possible, he wanted Claudia denied access to the children.

Trebillcock argued the point with David, telling him his chances of getting full custody were minuscule. Sole custody could only be won if he could demonstrate the mother's utter inability to care for the children in a responsible way. Adultery was highly unlikely to be sufficient cause for such action, especially when there was no evidence. But nothing could dissuade David.

Weeks of meetings followed. Battle lines were drawn on each of the issues earlier discussed and some new ones, as Trebillcock and Wyndham, on behalf of their respective clients, rejected each other's interpretations of what had happened and what it meant. The whole case settled into a state of listlessness.

David was impatient, but he reminded himself that the more time passed the better it was. Claudia must be running out of money.

For Claudia, the weeks since the coffee incident had been difficult. Some of her challenges, like her parents' lack of support, were easier to deal with, because she was on familiar terrain and had low expectations. But David's actions greatly upset her. What infuriated her most was his charge of adultery. Had he come up with it merely to annoy her or did he really believe she'd had affairs? And how did he intend to prove such a thing? For fifteen years, she'd spent most of her days and nights in either the children's or David's company. Thank heavens, the bastard was gone! She'd never have to worry about his moods or be subjected to his abuses again.

Claudia had far more energy than she could remember—positive energy. Why had she waited so long before taking action?

Claudia's most difficult decisions lay with the children. They'd settled into being alone with her, but had started asking when David would come back. She'd told them their father would not return and she hoped they would decide to stay with her. Later, when she learned of David's intention to press for custody of the children, Claudia informed the kids of that, too.

"Mom, I'd never leave you—you know that," Karen had said and they'd cried together. Jason had watched them silently, then asked what it meant if both his mother and father demanded custody.

"First of all, Jason, I'd never do that unless you wanted me to. I'd let you decide whether you'd want to live with me, with your dad, or split your time between us. But if your dad didn't agree with that, then a judge would decide."

"Come on, Mom, I'd have to go to court?" Jason asked in disbelief. "There's no way I'd do that!"

Claudia clarified. They'd be asked to see a counsellor… a psychologist who'd be bound to keep their conversations confidential. And based on Jason's and Karen's input, he'd help them make a choice.

Now Karen spoke up. "I don't really want to talk to anyone about this stuff, Mom. Why should we have to talk to some stranger?"

Claudia explained that she had to be fair to herself after years of great unhappiness and told them how sorry she was that she had to hurt them in the process. She hoped they'd support her.

She also had to find work; she'd soon need money.

Wyndham had cautioned her not to try to transfer any funds from their joint account and not to make cash withdrawals from her credit card. She could write checks or use her card for school and household expenses, but not for discretionary, personal spending. Claudia could see that what was left in the account sufficed for two months of expenses, at most. That meant she'd soon have to tap her retirement plan. She had the bank fax the latest statement to her and found that it was worth just under sixty thousand dollars. Wyndham told her that no one could touch this money except her, but also reminded her that any money withdrawn from it would be fully taxable.

The bottom line seemed obvious: Claudia had to find work fast. But Wyndham argued that getting employed was a two-edged sword. If she demonstrated that she could earn a livelihood, that would almost certainly become an arrow in Trebillcock's quiver, once the financial battle began.

There were other irritants, such as David's demands to get to his belongings. The first time he simply showed up and rang the bell. When Claudia threatened to call the police, he cursed and kicked her car violently, before leaving.

Claudia called Elliott. Hadn't he told her that visits by David had to be arranged through his lawyer? Wyndham fired off a letter to Trebillcock, advising him of his client's offensive behavior and demanding that any future contact with Claudia be conducted through his office. From now on, one of his law clerks would be there to escort David while he retrieved a coat or a pair of cufflinks.

David entered the house twice under this new regime, each time accompanied by an employee from Atkinson & Wyndham, who walked with him wherever he went. Items David wanted to take were meticulously recorded; then, Claudia had to verify that she agreed to their removal. She could tell that David detested these encounters, which is probably why they soon ended.

Once, and only once, did David try to interfere with their *de facto* custody arrangement. If he'd tried the same thing with Jason, he might have succeeded, but he made the mistake of going to pick up Karen at the end of her school week, asking her if she'd like to come to a movie with him and visit him for the weekend. Karen refused.

"Don't you think, Dad, that you should talk this over with Mom first?" was her plain and irrefutable response. David mumbled something about having the same rights as her mother, but Karen stuck to her guns.

Soon after Karen's and Jason's winter break started, Claudia received their tuition bills for the winter trimester. Private school costs were substantial, especially at St. Michael's Boys School and Essex College, which were among Toronto's best. *Next time these payments are due, I may have to fight over them,* she thought as she stuck the two envelopes into the mailbox.

She wouldn't have to wait till next time. A few days later, an accountant from St. Michael's called her, saying the checks she'd written had been returned. The day after, Essex phoned with the same message, as did the gas company.

Claudia contacted her account manager at the Royal Bank, a Mrs. Pettigrew, who was helpful and, when she learned what had happened, sympathetic. That didn't mean she had any practical advice for Claudia. Both Claudia and David were empowered to individually operate the account and David had used that power to transfer the funds out.

"Don't we both have to agree to close the account?"

"That's an interesting question, Mrs. Talbot, but technically the account is still open. It's just that your husband transferred everything except twenty dollars."

"What about my credit card?" Claudia's voice choked.

"That's still fine up to your limit of ten thousand dollars, but remember we have instructions to debit your joint account for the minimum funds due."

Claudia barely had enough money for her immediate expenses, unless she plundered her retirement account or asked for a loan against it. She phoned Wyndham, who in turn phoned Trebillcock, who attempted to phone David and was told he had left for a three-week holiday.

David had not left any details of his whereabouts. Trebillcock was furious, but the terse note he fired off to Wyndham didn't betray that. It merely stated that his client had left for a much-deserved vacation and could not be reached until early January.

Claudia had another surprise waiting for her. She'd been invited to several holiday events and decided that she owed it to herself to attend. If she lost contact with the few people she knew, she'd be completely isolated. The first function she attended was Mary and John Drake's annual Christmas party, a neighborhood favorite.

She'd lived next door to Mary and John for about ten years, ever since she and David had moved from Kingston. She liked their casual and open ways. Occasionally, she and Mary swapped recipes and gardening tips and, back in summer, John had asked her to help him renovate his home office and library. She'd replied that she'd have to discuss it with David.

Claudia had seen John a few days earlier. They'd both been shovelling snow and she'd told him then that she and David had separated. She picked the moment deliberately, knowing that John, a semi-retired executive who worked mornings, would soon have to be on his way. John had put down his snow scoop and listened to her sympathetically, before giving her a hug and telling her he was sorry. Claudia could come over or call any time.

"That's really nice of you, John, but I'm fine for now.

Remember, I still have Karen and Jason," she'd said.

The party was in full swing when Claudia arrived. She couldn't see Mary or John, but ran into several of her neighbors, with whom she exchanged pleasantries and small talk. The early winter and the latest increase in property taxes were the topics *du jour*.

Almost everyone Claudia chatted up asked her where David was. At first, she thought they genuinely wanted to know in which of the Drakes' rooms he was right now, but then she realized they knew. A lady living three doors down from her clarified the issue. "I've heard about you and your husband…so sorry dear," she said, touching Claudia's arm lightly and walking off before Claudia could respond. She didn't even know the woman's name.

Finally, Claudia saw Mary Drake in the distance. She was standing near the kitchen, talking to a group of people. *Maybe family…or John's colleagues*, Claudia thought. Then Mary recognized her.

"We must talk, Claudia." Mary took her by her arm and guided her toward the stairs. On the third floor, she opened the door to John's office.

"Claudia, you know John and I love you. And when John told me a few days ago how sorry he was that you and David had split I told him he shouldn't be. I know David was a moody rat and I have a feeling you'll be better off without him." A smile crossed Mary's lips. "I'm taking a chance telling you this, because I'll look like an idiot if you decide to get together again, but that's what I think."

"That's nice of you." Claudia's eyes filled with tears. "He *was* a moody son of a bitch, you know." They hugged and Claudia thought how far more compassionate this elderly neighbor was than her own mother.

"David's been up to a lot of mischief. I'm not sure anyone here has told you, but they all know. You know the bastard called up Bob Demers and told him you'd had affairs with just about everyone on the street…and when he found out, you ditched him. And you know how Demers talks. I've already been told by two of our more gossipy friends…Laura Capstain and that dreadful Mackenzie woman up on Hillsdale. I wish I could do more than just tell you…*is* there anything I can help with, Claudia?"

Claudia was blushing. "No, no, thanks. It's very kind of you to tell me." Then the full impact of the mess she was in registered. "What the hell can I do, Mary? Yell out to the whole congregation that it was all lies, and draw even more attention to myself? Or hold my head high and ignore it all? Jesus, what a mess!" Her voice choked. A moment later, she was in Mary's arms, crying, telling her how she'd never once even thought of being unfaithful.

"Well I tell you one thing, my dear," Mary said. "We've been here a long time and I think people in this neighborhood listen to John. Tomorrow morning, I'll make sure he calls people. They'll get to know what really happened, I promise."

David felt elated when leaving for Nassau. Virtually overnight, he'd managed to wreck Claudia's financial prospects and spoil her reputation. Maybe he'd also succeeded in subverting her position with the children. He'd left his secretary two envelopes, one for Jason and one for Karen, to be hand-delivered to them on Christmas Eve. Each contained a letter, in which he expressed his love for them and assured them that his not seeing them was their mother's decision. A postscript said they should spend the enclosed five one-hundred-dollar bills on something they'd always wanted.

As his vacation got underway, his thoughts kept returning to Claudia. How he'd love to be present as she struggled through his consecutive surprises!

When he returned, two messages waited for him. In the first, Trebillcock said he'd just learned about David's instructions to the Royal Bank. His actions weren't in the spirit of what they'd agreed. The other message: there was evidence that David had defamed Claudia with several neighbors and the matter would be brought before court.

When David phoned Trebillcock's office, the lawyer's secretary wouldn't even let his call go through. David used his whole arsenal of intimidation tactics.

Shelly, Bill Trebillcock's assistant for eighteen years, had dealt with others like him. "If you're trying to intimidate me, you may as well hang up. Mr. Trebillcock said I'm not to let you talk to him. But you're free to book an appointment, Mr. Talbot." She pronounced his name deliberately slowly, causing David to slam down the receiver.

David got to see his lawyer a week later. After being shown into Trebillcock's spacious office by Shelly, whom he stared at icily, he tried to put on a relaxed air. "Happy New Year, Bill…how have the holidays been treating you?"

Trebillcock had thought that David knew what a jam he was in, but by all appearances this wasn't so. His client was even more out of touch with reality than he'd thought.

"Bill, before we review the strategic issues of my case, I'd like to launch a complaint against your secretary. You've got a real problem there…if she were on my team I suspect she'd have been fired long ago."

"It's me you want fired, not Shelly. Because I instructed her not to let you talk to me. The reason, as you might suspect, is that I'm quite pissed off. Do me a favor and don't ask me why."

"I suppose you're disappointed that I transferred funds out of the account. I really didn't have a choice…I needed the money."

"David, from my perspective you violated our contract. We agreed on a set of rules and you broke them." He grabbed an envelope and held it up. "I also have a letter here that alleges you went out of your way to defame your wife with various neighbors. Wyndham claims he has several witnesses willing to sign affidavits. Then there are the letters to your children, not a big deal really, but *de facto* accusing your wife of not giving you access to them. You know that's a lie…you've never even asked me to arrange for you to see the children. Meanwhile, all this was miraculously and, may I say strategically, put into action a day or two before you disappeared. For three damned weeks. Making sure there was no way to get in touch with you." Trebillcock let his words sink in. "Tell me, David, do I have a right to be pissed off?" All through his speech, Bill Trebillcock had looked right at his client, but David had never looked up from the carpet in front of him once.

"I can see why you're upset."

"That makes me feel a whole lot better." Trebillcock had long learned to keep his emotions under wraps and to save pathos and grandstanding for the courtroom.

David kept an equally calm surface, but inside him all was chaos. He found it difficult to think straight. His lawyer was treating him like an errant schoolboy, and there was nothing he could do about it.

"Look," he finally said, "This is a very difficult time for me. My wife had extra-marital affairs, she threw me out, she's trying to steal my family from me. I haven't had a good night's sleep for a couple of months now. I'm living in a hotel. Frankly, I'm amazed how well I'm holding up. So I've allowed my emotions to take over....Is that such a big deal?"

"David, let's get one thing straight. You retained me to come out of this separation a winner. We started on very shaky ground. There are accusations of psychological abuse against you, the details of which Wyndham assures me will be devastating. Despite this, you seek custody of the children, an idea I've supported only because of your adultery charges. But now you've destroyed those by telling your ex-neighbors your wife had an affair with almost everyone on the street. Wait till you're called upon to provide volunteers who admit to having slept with your wife. You've also complicated things by transferring funds out of your joint account. Just in time to make it impossible to have the kids' school fees paid. 'Custody-seeking-father cuts off children's tuition payments'...the judge will be impressed."

David sat, his head lowered and his eyes unfocused.

Trebillcock got up and moved behind his chair. "Where do we go from here? I find it difficult to trust you now and I no longer think I can successfully represent you. Quite candidly, I can probably negotiate a decent settlement for you, at least from a financial viewpoint. But if you insist on pressing the adultery charges as a means to seek sole custody, I'm afraid I'll resign from the case. I'd like you to think this over, David, and let me know what your decision is. Until I hear from you everything stays on hold."

He didn't give David a chance to respond. He walked to the door, opened it and called for Shelly to show Mr. Talbot out.

Four days later, William Trebillcock received a registered letter in which David dismissed him. It was what Trebillcock had expected.

One summer evening at Christian's cottage, we were sitting on the open porch, a breeze cooling us down. In our hands a sunset drink, a cottage ritual. In my case, that meant a whole series of drinks, but Claudia was more mellow than usual, as well. She'd been with Christian for more than two years; the time and the occasion were right for a personal question. I asked Claudia what had attracted her to David.

"I've thought about it many times, Jake." Her eyes scanned the water. Below her, it reflected the blue expanse of the fading sky, bordered a bit further out by the sun-steeped tops of the trees from the opposite shore.

Claudia stepped to the other side of the porch, to catch a glimpse of the sinking sun. The water here was wide open; the nearest shore a mile away. Where the breeze stirred it, thousands of blinding silver dots danced on the surface. They were hard to look at.

"David was not a great-looking guy, but he had some attractive features. Dark, expressive eyes, full of passion, but also capable of looking sad…like yours."

I've often been complimented on my sad, black eyes—the mark of the Sullivans, my grandfather had called it. I was pleased that Claudia liked them.

"Why did you marry him?"

"I guess the girls in our class all seemed headed for marriage and my parents never made me aware that there were alternatives. Only four of us girls graduated, you know."

"Interesting…the parent thing again. Remember we talked about this a few weeks ago."

"Yup, my parents. I've never been able to relate to them, but they relate to each other splendidly. Each has a different role, but they've always been a team. Maybe it's a generational thing."

"What do you mean?"

"Put yourself in my situation. My mother and father all harmony and bliss, so I think marriage is always like that. I marry the first guy who comes along because he's charming and pushes all the right buttons. Next, I have no idea how to handle him, because exposure to my parents never prepared me. Then the kids and the feeling of being trapped…" Claudia looked at the lake below. "Where do you think *they* are headed…the children?"

"They're fortunate you've ended their trauma. Plus, they have a great example in you and Christian. Stability, love, mutual respect. The whole package."

That's when Karen came up the stairs and joined us. I couldn't help thinking that she'd heard the last part of our discussion and I thought: *That's good, I hope she did.*

Where should I start with Christian? In the middle, I think.

What we did together in our childhood and adolescence bonded us, but it wasn't extraordinary in itself. Christian was quieter, more reflective than most. Not that he missed out on the fun or didn't participate. Quite to the contrary, Christian was always there and often the ringleader. But he never got carried away like most kids and when things went wrong he kept a cool head.

We both hated school, but we ended up with a great English teacher. Most of our classmates hated him, because he was as demanding of us as of himself. Original thinking was rewarded. Christian and I did well and we realized that we were different. We learned to respect each other.

At university, we shared a tiny apartment above a convenience store in the Annex. After classes, we usually went our separate ways: doing homework, reading, going to see a movie. Around ten we met in the kitchen to share a few beers and talk about girls, music, existentialist philosophy and avant-garde movies. Girls intrigued us more than they should have, because we'd both attended a boys' school. But thinking of ourselves as intellectuals mattered even more. Christian and I formed the core of a discussion group.

Others were enthralled with Marilyn Monroe and *Mad Magazine* and prepared for marriage; our discussion circle wanted to change society. We didn't yet have the understanding of those who followed a few years later, who recognized that political activism was needed to force change. We were more idealistic, believing that thought alone could bring a revolution.

Our circle grew and we became a force on campus. Before long, we had our own newspaper. Whenever a decision had to be made, everyone looked to Christian. A few times I asked myself why it was he who'd always accepted responsibility, even when we were children. Perhaps people are born that way.

One day, we were summoned by the dean. Our newspaper was running a series on student protests in Germany and France, which suggested that North American campuses should consider similar action. The dean wanted it discontinued.

We had an intense debate on how to deal with the challenge, when Christian told us to leave it to him. "I think I can change the dean's mind," he said and that's what he did.

Only years later did I find out how.

"Now that you're a lawyer in your own right," he asked, "will our conversations be subject to attorney-client privilege?"

I nodded. I was desperate to learn the truth.

"You remember Diane Farley?"

"Who could forget Diane? The petite blonde with the bedroom eyes and the big boobs, right? The subject of countless wet dreams."

"Some had more than just dreams…"

"You mean the dean?" I burst out. "How did you know?"

"Remember Roberta, the girl I went out with? She knew."

Christian had told the dean that we could withdraw the series, but it would mean that we'd substitute it with an investigative piece on the teaching staff's illicit affairs with students.

We completed our series on proposed campus reform and several professors cheered us on. I started thinking of myself as a journalist. One day, I'd work at a great newspaper and influence its editorial policy. Perhaps I could become Canada's future Sartre and present my ideas in the form of a novel. After all, what's the use of evolving your thoughts if you can't get through to the masses?

"Why even think of doing what's already been done?" Christian argued. "Sartre isn't that original. And remember, Marx, Kierkegaard and Nietzsche already exist. The importance is to get their ideas through to people. Become a teacher, Jake, or a lawyer or politician. Or if you must, a priest."

I resented Christian's interference and we argued for months. But in the end I had to admit he was right. If I became a journalist, I'd be side-tracked by daily events and I'd lose sight of what mattered. Besides, everything of any lasting importance had already been said. What mattered now was to take what had been written by my idols and help translate it into reality.

Being a lawyer would help me become a social activist. Independently, if I wanted to, or through politics. I had no idea then that labor law was what I'd choose, but that was how it began.

Others thought the same way: they hoped to become part of an organization opposing the current social order. Christian, however, wanted to join the mainstream. He was convinced that the only way to effect real change was from within. I viewed this as convoluted thinking or, worse, as betrayal. When he was accepted at business school, I was devastated.

The next few years we saw each other on weekends and holidays. I went to Windsor and Christian ended up at the University of Western Ontario in London. Toronto was our crash pad. It was where we were comfortable, where we'd always accepted each other and where we'd known common ground.

We were near the end of our first year of graduate school when Christian explained why he thought capitalism might not be such a bad thing after all. It wasn't corporations who were evil, but the systems they used. And, in some cases, the people who were running them. Christian talked a lot about social responsibility and corporate ethics—terms which are now the mainstay of any business program, but which at that time no one considered. Perhaps there was such a thing as being a capitalist and a good human being.

We had long discussions about where the world was headed if corporations continued to spread their power. I thought Christian was being swallowed whole by a devilishly clever, but undeniably corrupt system. I missed no chance to tell him so.

It wasn't long before Christian started to shoot holes into *my* new identity, too. Windsor, a city with an enormous constituency of factory workers, had exposed me to union activists. Some of them were closely connected with the labor movement in Detroit, a fifteen-minute ride across the border.

The activists were highly organized, divided into working cells. Everyone shared a sense of destiny. As undergraduates, we'd used the infrastructure of the university; here, we drew on the resources of the union. I soon was a regular contributor to a newsletter widely distributed among autoworkers. A few times, my comments even appeared under my name, which broadened my contacts.

Weekend after weekend Christian and I got together; I talked about my first steps as an activist and Christian encouraged me. In return I bashed his love affair with business, sometimes in banter over a beer, but increasingly often in debate, particularly when I'd drunk too much.

It was on one of those unbearably muggy August days Toronto is famous for when we had a serious argument at his parents' house. The air conditioner was droning and we sat on the couch straining to hear a tape one of my union friends had lent me. It fea-

. . . .

tu... he music of Bob Dylan, a name new to Christian. ...s excited about the lyrics, but Christian found them difficult t... ...derstand. The music didn't sound that original either, he said. W... y Guthrie with a twang. I told him about Dylan's appearances at the Purple Onion in St. Paul, which was where it was all taking place. I was going to go there, even though I was broke. Christian didn't show any enthusiasm; he seemed distant and uncaring. So I levelled a vicious attack against the big banks.

Christian agreed that much needed to be changed in big business, especially in industries where power was concentrated in too few hands. Then he used the unions as a prime example not only of concentrated power, but also of corruption. Imagine my reaction. I'd spent every spare hour helping my fellow labor activists. Christian had uttered the ultimate blasphemy! I walked out on him.

But Christian's words had got me thinking. I realized when some of my articles were pulled by the editor that our outspoken and provocative style was welcome at times when it was politically expedient and suppressed when it wasn't—evidence that our activist group was being used by organized labor. When mentioning these abuses to my activist friends, I was puzzled that they refused to consider them as problems.

I started to see other faults. Once I allowed for the possibility that Christian could be right, I noticed glaring improprieties in the financial practices of organized labor. Not to mention the union leadership's disregard for rank and file members.

Meanwhile, Christian had applied at several banks, hoping to get a junior management position. That way, he could study corporate attitudes and practices and later change them from within. I decided to become a labor lawyer. The class struggle had remained my priority, but I had seen enough to know that the big unions were as suspect as the big corporations. Wherever we looked, it was the song of the ages: a few at the top exploiting the masses beneath. Thanks to Christian, I'd become more objective.

And because of me, he now liked Bob Dylan. I never made the trip to St. Paul, but when Christian told me he'd landed a job, Dylan wailed in the background. "And the times they are a-changin.'"

I have tears in my eyes and a glass of Courvoisier in front of me as I write this. I fucking miss him. The man who urged me to fulfill my dream of becoming a labor lawyer, who opposed my decision to declare myself homosexual, but stood by me after I did it anyway—my childhood friend and, more importantly, my best friend, is gone. With Claudia, the love of his life.

I look at the sheaf of paper. The top sheet contains Christian's notes about the thug. 'Black, collarless shirt and black suit,' it says. 'Strange hairdo: sides shaved, crew cut on top, shoulder-length in the back.' Underneath something about the guy's nose and lips, partly obscured by my overflowing ashtray and a pack of cigarettes. Lucky Strikes, without filter.

The taste of raw tobacco touching the tip of my tongue is even more exquisite than drawing smoke into my lungs. It leaves an acidic taste, slightly tickling, that can only be improved with a sip of cognac.

Time for a refill.

God, Christian, how did it come to this?

I met David's second lawyer a few years later at a cocktail party. He offered me a ride home in his brand-new black Porsche, which he probably regretted, as we approached the run-down part of Queen Street West, on which I live.

Joseph Ferrer's ground rules for David Talbot looked much like Trebillcock's, except they included an understanding that David would immediately pay the outstanding tuition bills. With a case like Talbot's, nothing could be left to chance.

Yet Ferrer's relationship with David turned sour after a mere three weeks. That's when he received a letter from Elliott Wyndham, saying that the children's tuition was still unpaid.

When he confronted his client, he was stunned at his response.

"I'd love to pay my children's tuition, but I first want to be sure I'll still be their father," David said.

"What's that supposed to mean?"

"Very simply, I want to be sure I'm getting custody of Jason and Karen."

Ferrer sighed deeply. "David, this is frustrating me. Apart from the fact that you told me you'd pay, our chances at sole custody are piss-poor. To get the odds up we've got to be seen doing the right things and one of them is for you to show some concern about your kids."

David stared at his knees.

"Would you please tell me what your response is?"

"Joseph, I don't like the way you talk to me. I've lost my family and I'm upset. I want my children, and until I have them, I'm not paying."

"I'm reminding you that we agreed on a course of action. And now, three weeks later, you're changing your mind."

"It's me who pays the bills, isn't it?"

"David, money is not what this is about! I'm trying to win your case, but you're reneging on your commitments."

"Is that how you see it?"

"What other way is there, for God's sake?"

"Well, there's my perspective…as a father who can't see his kids, but is asked to pay their school bills."

"Look, here's how it is. Paying the school bills was one of my preconditions to act on your behalf. You accepted. I'll resign from the case if you don't pay within ten days."

David convinced himself that the legal process was responsible for his misery. The lawyers were an obstacle, not a help. He wanted what was best for the children; surely that was first on Claudia's mind, too. If she understood, maybe she would listen. And if she didn't, he'd have to show her how grim her alternatives were.

When David arrived at what he still thought of as his Forest Hill house, Claudia was leaving. She wore jeans and a black leather jacket, her chestnut hair cascading over her shoulders. Her face had a healthy glow.

"David, aren't you supposed to arrange visits through your lawyer?"

David stood there, glowering.

"Well, I'm off anyway."

"No, we have to talk." David blocked her. "What happened was unnecessary, but it's the past. You can't keep me out of my family. We have to get back together."

"Look, David. I know that's what you'd like. Elliott Wyndham keeps me informed. But it wouldn't work and it's just not what I want, I'm sorry."

She tried to get past, but David stepped in front of her again. He stared at the bits of snow covering the shrubs to the side of the staircase, glistening in the sunshine.

"Listen, even if you feel this way…we can't do this to Jason and Karen."

"I disagree. We didn't give them a very happy time last time around."

David's voice hardened. "You know I can take them from you."

Next door, John Drake quietly walked down his driveway, then across the snow-covered lawn toward the tall cedar hedge, which separated his property from the Talbots'. He couldn't see anything, but he could hear them.

"Don't come here to threaten me. Just tell your lawyer what you want to say."

David's voice rose. "*I'm* here to tell you what the fucking lawyers don't!"

Drake had trouble hearing Claudia, as she quietly pleaded. "David, I'm not interested. You know you're not supposed to be here and there is nothing you can do to change things. I made up my mind a long time ago."

David was certain she'd been coached by someone. *A long time ago,* she'd said. She must have been having an affair when they were still together and that had given her the strength to pull this off.

"Whether you like it or not, you bitch, you'll fucking listen to me!"

John Drake knew he had to intervene, but he wasn't sure this was the right time. He started walking along the hedge to where it met the sidewalk.

"Get out of my way or I'll call the police!"

John came around the hedge and saw David grab Claudia, holding her arms firmly. "You're not going anywhere until you've thought about this. If you don't take me back, I'll take the kids from you and ruin you…and if I can't do that I'll kill you!"

His hands dug into Claudia's shoulders and bits of spit hit her face. She rammed her knee into his groin. Then John Drake came running.

"Are you out of your bloody mind, David? Stop this nonsense…what the hell do you think you're doing?"

"Stay out of this, John…this is between my wife and me. Go back to your house and get lost, you old clown."

"If I go to my house it's to call the police, you crazy bastard. But Claudia, *you* should go in and call the cops. I'm afraid what he'll do to you if I leave."

Wyndham was delighted. Once he had the police report of David's out-of-control behavior, he supplemented it with affidavits signed by Claudia and John Drake, then submitted the package to court and obtained a restraining order. David now had to stay away from the house he jointly owned with Claudia. He was also barred from contacting his wife or his children, without first obtaining Claudia's consent. Wyndham then collected signed affidavits from two of the Talbots' neighbors. Both testified that they'd received an unsolicited phone call from David, in which he'd told them that Claudia had slept with several residents of their street. Wyndham challenged Ferrer to supply him with the name of a single person admitting to adultery with Claudia, in the absence of which he'd sue for defamation.

A few days later, he informed David's lawyer that he was initiating a court proceeding to permanently gain custody of the children. If contested, he was prepared to supply a chronicle of the worst recent incidents of abuse and ask the court to appoint a counsellor to determine what was best for the children. Next, he sent off a letter stating that he would file suit for David's removal of funds from the Talbot's joint bank account.

Then Wyndham called. "Joseph, I'm just following up on this silly thing your client did…you know, defaming his wife with her neighbors."

"*Alleged* defamation, Elliott…alleged. And, while we're at it, *their* neighbors, not hers."

"I think you'll have to agree that it was defamation of the most malicious kind. Unless you have the name of a confessed adulterer for me, that is. Otherwise you'll have to start talking…by end of the week."

"Talking about what?"

"About how to split the pie. Tell Talbot he'll face annihilation if we can't initiate talks about the only thing that still matters—money."

"And if he doesn't want to talk?"

"I'll advise my client to proceed on all fronts. On the other hand, if she gets the kids and we come to a financial settlement, we agree not to press ahead. What do you say, Joseph?"

Ferrer's case was in tatters. He expressed outrage, but he agreed to try.

When Joseph Ferrer saw his client, he insisted on an immediate change in strategy. Talbot had to accept the inevitable and give up on the custody front. He could still end up winning, if they negotiated a financial settlement.

David was disappointed, but realized that he'd already made most of the mental adjustment required. Even though he blamed

Claudia for driving him to do it, he knew he'd made some key mistakes. Ferrer was right. What mattered now was to destroy Claudia financially…rip the whole rug of upscale living and comfort from under her. Once she felt the pressure rise, the kids would feel it too. He was willing to bet that in another few months he'd show up at Karen's school and she'd treat him differently than last time. All he had to do was promise her a trip to Florida or a new stereo. Money was the key.

David's strategy, which he kept to himself but was fairly apparent to his lawyer, was to sign an agreement which would give Claudia the house and a minimal sum of money now, and oblige him to make support payments. That way, he could frustrate Claudia forever, forcing her to take him to court, if she wanted to be paid. He relished the thought.

Elliott Wyndham didn't want Claudia to agree. But when he told her that a better settlement was likely if she held out, she replied that she had to move on with her life. And when he argued that David was getting away with too much, she answered that she didn't care. Maybe, if she wasn't vindictive, David would finally go away.

In the end, Elliott Wyndham had to concede that months of intense legal wrangling had strained her emotions to the limit.

On a pretty afternoon in late June, Elliott took Claudia to lunch and, after returning to his office, presented her with a separation agreement signed by David.

Everything had gone her way except the financial arrangements, although she'd by no means be a pauper. David undertook to pay Claudia one half of what had been in their joint account, which meant she'd end up with enough money to pay off her bills. He also guaranteed to pay off the mortgage and deliver to her clear title to the house. And, finally, he agreed to pay her monthly support of $3,000 and pay Jason's and Karen's tuition until they were twenty-seven years of age or graduated from university with a master's degree, whichever occurred first.

Elliott Wyndham doubted that she could keep up her life style on such modest monthly support, but Claudia had shrugged off such concerns.

She fought back tears as she put her signature to the agreement. She'd taken a huge risk and prevailed. Even the months of legal jousting and David's attempts to discredit and manipulate her had been nothing when compared to the misery of living with him. What a joy her new life was!

She shared some of Elliott's concerns about money. But once she'd get back to interior design, she'd at least survive without drawing down her remaining assets.

Before leaving, she gave Elliott a hearty hug, saying she'd miss him. He'd been her one friend and supporter.

David felt betrayed when Ferrer told him Claudia had signed the separation agreement. He'd convinced himself she wouldn't agree until she got exactly what she wanted. Now, news of her signing was confirmation that she'd won. In retrospect, all the lawyers had accomplished was for him to make endless concessions, apart from lining their own pockets at his expense. His one success was to have kept Claudia dependent on him and whose idea had that been? His, of course.

It was the only thing that made him feel good about the future. He'd make her life miserable. She'd destroyed his family and she would pay.

A desperate disease requires a dangerous remedy.

GUY FAWKES

PART 2

Claudia got up early. After waking the kids and getting breakfast ready, she considered what she should wear.

She first picked one of her favorite pantsuits. But then she decided it was too formal and chose a simple black skirt and a bottle-green alpaca turtleneck instead. She looked at herself in the mirror. Her auburn hair fell loosely over her shoulders; the contrast with the color and texture of her sweater was striking. She blew a kiss at her image. *I haven't looked this good for years.*

"Look at you, Mom!" Karen quipped.

"What do you mean, sweetie?"

"Your hair all done up and your dressy coat…that's not how you usually go to work."

"Well, I do have a special day today."

At the office, Claudia impressed on Jackie Hunter, her assistant, that she'd have to leave by four.

"That's kind of early for a date," Jackie said non-chalantly.

"You know, when I left the house this morning Karen teased me. And now you. Why is it so damned obvious that I'm going out with a man?"

"Well, if you really want to know.…Even though it's been

quiet, you've been nervous. And the way you're dressed. Not the knock-'em-dead outfit you'd put on when it's time to take action, but less formal than what you'd wear to see the lawyer or account-ant. Plus, no one schedules a meeting this late on a Friday after-noon. I bet it's a first date."

Jackie did her best to keep the afternoon stress-free for Claudia, until a quarter to four, when two calls came in.

"Claudia, Karen's teacher is on the line. Sounds like an emergency. And Chuck Fernaux wants to talk to you, too. He says it's urgent."

Claudia cursed. "Let me talk to the teacher first…and tell Fernaux I'll call him back."

Karen had fallen off the diving board onto the edge of the pool, during swimming class. After the teacher's description, Karen herself came on, in tears: "Mom, I fell on the concrete, and now my shoulder's just killing me. They want to send me for x-rays, but they need your permission."

Claudia calmed her daughter down, then told her to lightly rub her shoulder. When Karen said that didn't hurt too badly, she asked her to squeeze it. "How is that, sweetie?"

"Not worse than rubbing…but it's really swollen."

Claudia decided x-rays weren't necessary. She suspected that all the school wanted was to relieve itself from liability.

Afterwards, Claudia phoned her mother, explaining what had happened. Since it was a Friday, Harriett suggested, why not pick up the kids and take them to her place? Claudia's relationship with her parents was difficult, but when it came to their grandchildren, Kenneth and Harriet were always there.

Finally, Claudia called back Chuck Fernaux. She was running late.

. . . .

On the phone, Christian had suggested they go to see a movie and have a bite to eat afterwards.

"I'd love to do that. But I've been cooped up with my children so much, I have no idea what restaurants…" *Oops…there it was, the children thing.* She hadn't wanted to bring that up.

Christian hadn't responded and she was thankful for that. Instead, he'd talked about the little-known restaurant he'd discovered on College Street, a place run by a man from the Cape Verde islands. "Fresh fish, good music, cozy decor…I think you'll like it." They were on the way there now.

Once inside the restaurant, Claudia said she had to make a phone call to see how her daughter was doing. When she came back, Christian was talking to a stocky man, who looked the way she would have imagined the owner of the place. Christian introduced her to him: Baltasar Tavares. His handshake was that of a peasant or fisherman and he had a simple, unstudied charm.

Claudia looked around while Christian and the owner talked about wines. The guests looked as though they were all part of Mr. Tavares' extended family. Christian seemed to read her mind. "This is the most authentic Portuguese place I've come across yet. I've been here numerous times and still haven't heard anyone speak English. Right, Baltasar?" The owner beamed and confirmed that almost all his customers were Portuguese.

Claudia had instantly felt comfortable with Christian; now she could tell that he'd be good company, too. *But he's so formal…or maybe just shy.* Then she reminded herself that they'd just seen a serious film together and hardly knew each other. *What's it supposed to be like, anyway, on a first date?* She realized that she hadn't been on a date in an eternity.

"What did you think about the movie?" she asked.

"Every film as good as the one we just saw deserves to be discussed."

"I'm glad you said that. On the way over, I wondered whether you liked talking about movies. You know, not just the story, but its meaning…the metaphors. Do you?"

"It's one of the things I like best." As they talked about Fellini, Bergman and Kurosawa, Claudia became aware that Christian had seen just about every good movie and loved talking about them. *What a beginning,* she thought.

They'd drunk half the bottle of wine when they finally looked at the menu. Christian explained that the most authentic selections were the fish and seafood dishes.

"What will *you* have?"

"As a main course I usually have pork and clams. That's what the regulars order."

"Come on. Pork and clams?"

"Pork and clams. Doesn't sound like a good match, does it? But it is."

Claudia decided to be adventurous and so they asked Tavares to put a seafood appetizer together and bring them pork and clams as the main course.

"For the lady, too?" Baltasar asked.

"My friend tells me it's a must. If he's wrong he'll have to eat mine too," she giggled.

They were quiet for a moment. Then Christian commented on the wine: how harsh Portuguese reds were when first opened and how they could open up. Claudia said she'd like to learn about wine. And then she came out with it.

"You know, Christian, there's something I'd like to get out of the way. The kids…I wasn't going to tell you about them until tonight and after I blurted it out on the phone I thought I'd blown it. But here we are anyway."

Christian looked at her pensively. *He's weighing his words,* she decided. *I bet the kids will be a problem!*

"When you came back from the phone I was going to ask you if your daughter was okay, but I thought you should be the one to bring up the topic. I've never had children…I just never got around to it."

"Well, I have two teenagers, Jason and Karen. I may as well tell you, they live with me…all the time."

"That's very honest of you, Claudia, and courageous. What's it like, being a mother?"

"It has its ups and downs. There are days when I could strangle the kids and there are rewards too, usually when I least expect them. Tell me about yourself. Have you ever been married?"

"No I haven't, and since I'm in my forties that's got my mother seriously worried. But let me tell you all my secrets in a minute…I think Baltasar is approaching."

The appetizer was served on an immense oval platter: grilled sardines circled an arrangement of greens and potato slices, interspersed with squid, scallops and mussels. As Baltasar served the food, an intensely colored, crude fish pattern emerged on the platter.

"So how does someone like you stay single, Christian?"

"You mean what's wrong with me? That's how my mother phrases it, anyway. Luckily, she's far away in California, so she can only ask me on the phone. And when she does she can't see me yawning."

They laughed and touched their glasses. *He does have a sense of humor, after all.*

"I owe you a better explanation than that, Claudia. There are really two reasons. One's this: just because I've never been married doesn't mean I've never been with anyone for an extended period."

"Have you?"

"I lived with someone in the U.K. a few years ago, but we just never took the legal steps."

"How long were you together?"

"About three years. It just wasn't meant to be. Two terrific people, but neither right for the other…"

"You said there were two reasons…"

"Well, the other is that I worked like a slave ever after. Until recently, that is. I just didn't have time to be in a relationship."

"Tell me again what you were doing. When we met at that reception, you told me you were in the investment business."

"I was a merchant banker, a restructuring specialist…but I'd better explain what that is."

"You'd better, although I once attended a lecture on the basics of restructuring."

"That must have been some school," Christian proclaimed, and as they talked they realized that they'd both graduated from the same MBA program at Western. Claudia had taken her degree four years later, but they realized they had several acquaintances in common. They were swapping stories when Baltasar brought the main course.

Claudia had expected it to be fairly crude—some kind of pork stew to which a few clams had been added. But the presentation was wonderful: juicy, bite-sized pieces of pork mingled with clams sheltered by their half-opened shells, neither competing with the other. Bits of basil added color and promised to complement the taste. Baltasar asked if he should bring more wine, adding that it was also available in half bottles.

"Great idea, Baltasar, that way we'll have room for port, later on." They tasted the food and loved it. "Simple, yet hearty, isn't it?" Christian declared, while chewing.

"That's what you said about their wine, too. It's wonderful."

"About my job…I worked hard because I loved it. Most people think banking is boring and unimaginative, but I found it very stimulating. Probably because I was more or less left alone…free to realize myself through my deals."

"You make it sound very creative."

"Actually, I always thought of my deals as creations. My job was to get involved in mismanaged or under-capitalized firms, work with management and turn them around."

The band started up and it was difficult to talk. Claudia turned around and noticed that the restaurant was packed. She'd never heard Cape Verdean music, but found the rhythm delightful in its simplicity. There were only three musicians: a bass guitarist, a pianist and a percussionist. Their ruddy complexions suggested they spent a lot of time outdoors, but it was clear that they were equally at home inside this restaurant.

Claudia sat back contentedly and Christian studied her. He remembered how attracted he'd been to her last time; tonight she looked even more stunning. And she had an energy that intrigued him!

Claudia noticed and broke into a warm smile. "I'm glad you brought me here. It's so authentic! I imagine if we had dinner in a Portuguese village it would be very close to this. Tell me, where are the Cape Verde Islands?" She raised her eyebrows playfully and added, "They might become a favorite place."

"Wouldn't it be fun to go there? I'd be the wrong guy to find them, though. All I know is that they're somewhere between Africa and South America."

"What about their history?"

"You'd have to ask Tavares. I suspect the Portuguese colonized them and mingled with the natives. That would explain their dark skin."

"Some history lesson!" Claudia blurted out. They laughed and drank more wine.

She wondered what the kids would think of him. *He's great when he loosens up a bit. Still, Karen and Jason have probably never met any-one this serious.* "You were talking about your job, Christian."

"I spent ten great years there. But the hours! I hardly ever took a weekend off…and as to holidays, maybe a week each year."

"But you liked it…"

"I could do what I wanted to and I felt good because I did

something useful that produced tangible results."

"Healthy companies, I guess."

"Yes, healthy, growing companies. The clients were happy, my boss was happy, and so on. There was lots of positive energy."

"No disappointments?"

"Oh yes, there were projects that didn't work out. The worst was when people lost their jobs. But most projects worked out better than expected, so that there was significant job creation."

"Sounds a like a lot of responsibility."

"You don't notice responsibility if you like what you're doing, you know."

"And what about stress? That's more difficult, isn't?"

"Ah…the way we handle stress. I think it's self-imposed." The waiter took away their dishes. "I was several years into my job when I noticed how rarely I was thinking of my successes and how the failures were always on my mind."

"You blamed yourself."

"On a conscious level I didn't. I could rationalize that it wasn't my fault. But my emotions were a different thing. When things went wrong I ended up feeling guilty."

"How did you get out of it?"

"One day a reporter wrote a grossly unfair story about a job I'd handled. I knew the story had no substance, but somehow it kept eating away at me."

"It sounds like a nightmare," Claudia said.

"It showed up in my work. One day, the chairman called me. He repeated the allegations the reporter had made and asked me to defend myself, point by point. When I finished, he told me he'd known the answers beforehand, but obviously I hadn't. Then he gave me a suggestion. I should ask myself once a day whether I was doing my personal best, and if the answer was yes, I'd have nothing to feel guilty about."

"And it worked?"

"Once I'd created that standard for myself, I could accept failure, as well as success. I suppose the ritual of assessing myself every day suited my way of thinking."

Claudia became aware that no one had ever talked to her like this. Everything Christian touched on seemed relevant and was delivered with an openness that overwhelmed her. "He sounds like a kind man…your boss."

"McAllister, yes. Kind may not be the word, but generous and very bright. He gave me an opportunity and let me run with it."

"What a break! It must be great when that happens…"

"I don't think it happens too often…which means I was extremely lucky." He raised his glass. "Well, here's to extraordinary things that come out of nowhere."

Claudia suspected that he was talking not about his career, but their meeting. They drank. For a few moments, it was only the two of them. The hustle-bustle of the restaurant seemed far away.

When Christian excused himself and walked toward the men's room, Claudia wondered why she felt so attracted to him. There were the obvious things. He was tall and trim, with a well balanced, angular face and wavy, light-brown hair. But the thing that set him apart was his eyes. Their color changed with light and expression, from a harsh grey to a soft, almost watery hue. They could be both probing and compassionate. Some would think of Christian's gaze as unsettling, while others would be captivated. Claudia found them positively enthralling.

Even though she'd been ready to label him as too formal, she now knew that she'd mistaken formality for seriousness and sincerity. Yes, there may be a touch of shyness to Christian, but not a lack of humor. And his humor was the type she liked best. He could laugh at himself! What attracted her most was that he seemed self-confident without being self-absorbed. A man who was accomplished, yet could still find interest in what others had to say. She'd never met anyone like him.

As Christian made his way back, he asked a diner to move his chair a bit, so that he could pass through, then smiled at a waiter coming the other way. *What a contrast to David!* Where David would have been abrasive and inconsiderate, Christian was kind and thoughtful.

There it was again! Why did she have to compare everyone to David? *All I do is upset myself.*

She closed her eyes and listened to the band. The tune they performed seemed endless, but not in an annoying way. More the type of song that resembled surf washing up against a beach: repetitive, but soothing. The vocalist sang in a high key. If she'd heard the song on the radio, she'd have thought the singer was a beautiful, exotic woman, not the stocky old man on stage.

"It's beautiful, isn't it?" she heard Christian say.

"Yes…seductive."

A waiter put fresh plates in front of them, then placed a bowl of fruit on the table. Behind him stood Baltasar with the port.

"Christian, why did you leave your job? Do you mind the question?"

"Not at all. I left because I'd worked at it for a long time. Doing the same thing."

"You couldn't stand it anymore?"

"No, not that at all. I liked it. It was seductive, just like this song. I knew what the next beat would be…was more familiar with the rhythm than anyone else in the firm. I was content and people respected and liked me. And I wasn't just part of the game, I was one of its architects."

"You were too secure and contented."

"Yes. It's good to move on when you've done something well for a period of time."

"I suppose. But it still must have taken courage."

"It's interesting you say this. When I left, my colleagues had three types of responses. Some thought I was just saying I was quitting the industry…in reality I had something else lined up. A few others said, 'You can't do this.' They had me labeled as a financial executive. I had no right to leave them behind and move on to something else."

"I guess people really do resent that. Like my parents when I left my husband…you can't do that." She made a face. "This is what you chose for yourself, so you better not change the script."

"Different circumstances, but probably the same reaction. And then there were the ones who said what you just said a moment ago. They thought it took a lot of courage."

"I can see that…it sounds like you took a huge risk. What if you couldn't find something that kept you equally happy? I'm not sure *I'd* have the courage to leave a position in which I was that content." Claudia wondered if she'd ever been content. *I guess during my school years.*

"I know what you mean, Claudia. But you have to understand that even though I was content, the spark was gone. Do you understand that?"

"I think so. I experienced something vaguely similar in my marriage."

"What happened?"

Claudia searched for the right words. "All was well for a year or so, but then it became impossible to please my husband. No matter what I did."

"I'm sorry." Christian could see it wasn't easy for her.

"For a little while I tried to put up with it and then the little while turned into many years. There were the children…"

Christian nodded, encouraging her to continue, before he realized that was all she'd tell him tonight.

"How long did it take you to find the courage to quit your job…once you knew it wasn't right for you?" she asked.

"Only a few months. I'm sure what you did required far more courage, Claudia. There was no adversity in my relationships at work. And there were no children. And I was financially independent, so there was no material risk whatsoever. So what if I didn't like life after resigning? If Global didn't take me back, someone else in the industry would have loved to have me. So you see: there was no risk."

"I suppose. And now you're completely free?"

"Free as a bird."

Claudia tasted the port. "I've done wonderfully following your advice so far. The wine, the appetizer, the pork and clams ...and now this."

"Here's to real courage!" Christian proposed, holding up his glass, and they clinked.

"How long have you been on your own, Claudia...I mean without your husband? Do you feel all right talking about it?"

"Yes, no problem. It's been three years. He was quite a monster, you know, and I guess that made it easier. Also, I left *him*..."

"How do the kids handle it?"

"It's tough on them, but we're coping. They trot off to school; Mom trots off to work. When we're all together in the evenings it can be a lot of fun."

"You said they're with you all the time."

"That's what the agreement says. Occasionally, my boy, Jason, gives me a hard time about it...usually when I try to enforce a rule."

"Well, if after three years he's still there, that's a good sign."

"He did leave once, telling me his dad treated him a lot better."

"What happened?"

"I was afraid to let him go, thinking I'd never forgive myself if he stayed with his father. But ten days later he was back".

"I'm starting to think that managing a family is harder than running a business."

Claudia noticed the port's dense, brick-red color. Then she cast a glance at her watch. She was shocked to see that it was nearly eleven.

"Last time we met you told me you were an interior designer. Are you working full-time?"

"Uhumh. It's tough, with the kids and all, but I manage. And after being cooped up as a *hausfrau*, it's good to be out in the real world."

"What type of work do you do?"

"At first, I took on whatever came my way…mostly remodelling homes. Then I lucked into a project for a hotel chain. They liked my work here in Toronto, on a fairly small project, and that got me a job with them in the U.S. And two months ago, I took on a resort project in Malaysia for the same people."

"In Malaysia? That's quite a leap. Do you get to go there?"

Claudia's mind turned to Chuck Fernaux. He'd told her that an environmental group was lobbying the Malaysian government to halt the project and that their contracts might be terminated.

"That will be the real fun. Getting to know Malaysia…picking materials and textures with which I haven't worked before." She wondered why she wasn't telling Christian about Fernaux's call. *Because I'm not ready to give up on it, that's why.*

"You must be very good at your job."

"I'm sure they like my work, but I suspect the main reason they want me is money. I don't mark up the cost of the furniture and accessories as my predecessors did. So flying me to Chicago, San Antonio or even Malaysia is cheap by comparison. The place in Malaysia is a resort with 600 rooms. You can imagine what they'll save."

"How did you get into the business?"

"I started after I got married, but my husband made such a fuss that I had to stop. It was the first thing I thought of after leaving him…"

"The bad husband again."

Claudia smiled and raised her glass. "To leaving bad things behind us!"

Stepping outside was a shock. The noisy diners, the luscious res-
onance of the band, and Baltasar, standing at the door and saying
goodbye, were still fresh on their minds, when the merciless snow-
storm enveloped them. Christian said he'd leave his car behind and
take Claudia home in a taxi. Given the quantity of wine and port
they'd both consumed, she was relieved.

The black and orange Diamond Taxi was overheated. The
driver, a black man, was bundled up in a puffy parka and wore a red
wool hat with a white maple leaf embroidered on each side.
Claudia gave her Forest Hill address.

They settled back, taking comfort in each others' presence.
Claudia thought she'd have to find a way to see more of Christian,
while Christian wondered if all their times together would be
so perfect.

The driver, confident in his ability to slot his passengers, concluded they were co-workers on their way home from a staff party.
Or relatives leaving a family gathering...cousins perhaps. There
was definitely not enough excitement in the air for them to be
lovers, and neither of them tried to impress the other.

When they got to the Forest Hill address, the driver felt his
judgment was confirmed. The lady had given the directions to the
driveway in front of a stately Tudor house; obviously, her companion hadn't even known where she lived! *Co-workers*, he decided,
definitely co-workers. He loved choosing two or three scenarios
when he picked up his fares and then pare them down to one, and
nothing was sweeter than when he was right. Today it had taken
him a bit longer to guess, but he was doing fine.

Then his hypothesis fell to pieces. Christian kissed Claudia on
the cheek, drawing her closely to him and said: "It was wonderful,
Claudia...I'll call you tomorrow." Claudia nodded, then looked at
him for a couple of long seconds, before opening the door and
stepping into the cold.

"Let's wait a few seconds, until she's inside," Christian told the driver. They both watched Claudia walk up the driveway, then start up the front steps toward her door. Halfway up she stopped, then paused for a moment and turned around.

Christian looked down at the seat and the floor, thinking she'd forgotten her purse or her gloves, but couldn't see anything. He opened the door and got out—maybe she needed help.

Claudia moved a few steps toward him, then deliberately stopped. He walked up to her and when he saw her eyes he knew why she'd come back.

"I forgot to say something, Christian." She held her hands out to him. "I had the best evening in many years with you. Why don't you come in and we can make it go on a little longer."

Claudia was in a huge domed train station, looking at the immense windows above: some round, some triangular, some straight and others curved. With all this glass, she wondered, why was the station so sombre? She kept looking for a reason, intent on putting down something tangible on her note pad. She had to get to the bottom of this before her meeting.

An instant later she was standing at the edge of a magnificent square, surrounded by dazzling palaces and a splendid cathedral. The brutal heat and the radiance of the light said she was in Spain.

One thing was perplexing, though. The hundreds of vehicles that passed through the square did not make the slightest noise, so that she could hear the announcements of arriving and departing trains coming from inside the station. The loudspeakers made the words sound tinny, but the reader spoke each syllable so clearly and slowly that it was beautiful and poetic in its distinctiveness. Then there was a marching tune. Claudia listened to it for a while, then found herself watching the station from one of the corners of the square, some two hundred yards away. She was curious how she'd got there.

The square on which Claudia stood was on top of a hill and

from it she could see down its side. A short distance below her was an enormous parking lot filled with hundreds of shiny Studebakers, all in tones of green, ochre and yellow. There were drivers, too, she now noticed. They all had the same thin mustache, were deeply tanned and had their curly grey hair slicked back. Most were sitting in their vehicles, but some stood beside them, smoking cigarettes and watching the perfect sky. *What an extraordinary feast for the eyes,* Claudia thought. *How fortunate I am to see this!*

She thought she should talk to the drivers, but as soon as she approached one of them, he got into his car and drove off. She noticed that each of the men looked utterly identical. The face was familiar, but she couldn't remember where she'd seen it before.

She gave up and walked down the hill. The lower she went, the more decrepit became the houses lining the street. Some were altogether unfinished, while others had been painted so long ago that only the faintest trace of color remained on the sun-bleached wood. Litter was blowing around and rats scurried away as Claudia approached. It bothered her that things could become so dilapidated.

The weather was deteriorating, too. Black thunderheads moved over her, then cold rain hit her. She ran back up the hill at a pace known to her only from dreams. She exhausted herself and her fear turned to panic. On top of everything else, the contents of her backpack kept being thrown around and made a big racket. She worried about her notes being damaged…she needed them for the presentation!

Somehow she made it back to the parking lot, where all the drivers were now standing outside their Studebakers, busily conversing over the gleaming car tops. The heat was as blistering and the sky as cloudless as it had been earlier, but she could still sense the darkness and cold behind her.

As she got close, she could tell that the drivers were agitated and occasionally she heard one of them speak her name. They were upset that she'd gone down. She knew it was hopeless trying to explain herself. They'd simply get into their cars and drive off, if she tried to get close.

Then she heard the phone ring inside the train station. The sound carried all the way down the hill and the drivers stopped talking and looked up toward the dome. In profile, she noticed the sameness of their faces again. As if a cookie cutter had turned out the whole army of them. Except there was something menacing that complemented the perfection of their features. Cookie cutters didn't turn out menacing things. She knew she'd seen that face countless times before, but she couldn't tell where…couldn't tell where.

She ran up the hill. The phone had been ringing for a long time.

Torn from her sleep, she lifted the receiver. There was a long silence.

"I hear you have a man in your life."

"Are you crazy to call me at this hour?"

"Of course I'm crazy. What else would I be, having had my family broken up by a deceiving slut? I knew you had something going on all along."

Claudia considered hanging up, but she knew that David would call right back.

"He's the guy you had the affair with, isn't he? And now you figure you've found a way around your financial problems, don't you? I know who he is, you know."

"David, you're sick! You're calling me in the middle of the night to tell me I had an affair while I was with you?"

"That's what I'm suggesting, you manipulative bitch. And you know what? It won't work. The guy will leave you before you know it. He'll learn what a slut you are."

Then there was silence…five, ten seconds of silence. Claudia looked at the alarm clock, taking deep breaths. Large, red characters said it was 2:11 AM.

"One more thing. He'll pay for this, too. No one steals my wife and children without paying for it."

"David, I met him just a few weeks ago. I can't believe we're having this conversation. It's been more than three years.…Can't you get yourself a life?"

"As I told you. He'll pay for it. You'll both pay for it." Then there was a dry click.

Thank God it's over, thought Claudia. But she couldn't get back to sleep.

The phone call had left Claudia tired. She hoped this wasn't the beginning of a whole new round of middle-of-the-night calls. The Malaysia project, which was back on, would consume all her energy.

While driving to work, she kept thinking about her strange dream. She wished she could have recorded the peculiar train station. Nothing like it had ever been built anywhere. *And the colors! Where could I use them?* But what she really wanted to know was whose face all the Studebaker drivers had worn. Surely, there was some meaning to it.

At the office, she was in the middle of leaving a message for Elliott, when he picked up.

"I was just walking by our reception desk when I heard your voice, Claudia. How are you?"

"Not well…David was on one of his rampages."

"I see."

"He called at two in the morning, Elliott. But it's not just that. I've been seeing this man…and I like him a lot. Well, David's found out."

"What did David have to say?"

"He's convinced himself I was having an affair with Christian…when we were together."

"Christian?"

"The man I met. I've only known him since December." Then she added: "By the way, he knows your partner…his name is Christian Unger."

"The investment banker?"

Claudia couldn't tell whether Elliott sounded amused or excited. "Well, he used to be in that business. Do you know him, Elliott?"

"I certainly know *of* him. He's got an excellent reputation, both as a businessman and an individual. And you're right, Hal Atkinson has done business with him."

"Anyway, David's threatened he'd make sure Christian would leave me."

"Leave you, why?"

Claudia found it hard to find the right words. She heard Elliott tell her to repeat what David had said.

"He said he'd make sure Christian would learn what a slut I am. And then he said that Christian would pay for destroying our family, too. We'd both pay."

"I'm sorry you still have to put up with this. I'll phone Ferrer and threaten to take action."

"Thanks, Elliott. I have a feeling he isn't just harassing me… this time he was very distraught."

"Let me ask you a very personal question—is Christian Unger living with you?"

"No, but we're spending quite a bit of time together."

Claudia could hear someone talk to Elliott. "Leave it with me…I'll call you back before the day is out," he said.

Jason and Karen loved the spontaneity and adventure their mom's boyfriend had brought to their lives. Apart from teaching them to skate, Christian had taken them to the planetarium. And the other night, he'd even shown them how to play poker. For money, too! They'd only been able to bet dimes, but at the end of the evening Karen had made more than eight dollars.

Now their mother had wanted to take them skating, at a time they should be home preparing for their exams. Their dad's idea of spending time with them was watching TV, but this was a lot more exciting.

On the way home, they stopped at McDonald's. Claudia was pleased that she'd refused to let David spoil her day. And the kids were happy, too.

Christian had shown her was that it was much better to spend her energy on doing things with the children than doing housework for them. Instead of cooking dinner at home, she'd gone skating with them. She could see that Karen and Jason were having a far better time than if she'd cooked at home.

When they got back, Claudia left the kids to their homework and went upstairs to check her answering machine. There was a message from Elliott Wyndham.

He sounded concerned: he wanted Claudia and Christian to meet with him immediately. He was aware that it was an unusual request to draw Christian Unger into this matter, but he felt it was in her interest. "Call me back later today or first thing in the morning." Wyndham was all business.

Claudia looked out at the cold evening sky. The face! She knew whose face it was! She'd seen it on hundreds of bits of paper when collecting stamps as a girl. Stamps of different colors, sizes and denominations, always with the same face in profile. The face of a dictator, her father had taught her, of a totalitarian ruler. She hadn't understood then, but later, at university, she'd read up on him: tyrant, tormentor and arch-manipulator. Generalísimo Francisco Franco.

Franco's face on hundreds of identical taxi drivers? She laughed out loud.

In winter, Christian's schedule was flexible. But in another two months, he'd spend as much time at the cottage as he could. Would Claudia's presence in his life change that?

He'd always associated his log cabin in Georgian Bay with freedom and made himself completely self-sufficient on his little island. He'd learned to repair docks and leaks in the roof, fell damaged or dead trees, and chop firewood.

On occasion, Christian had taken visitors from Europe or Asia along and shown them what he did there. Invariably, they'd asked why he didn't get some workmen to do these jobs. They'd always been eager to get back to civilization after a day or two.

Christian also did his best creative work at the cottage. When at Global Capital, he'd often escaped to his cabin when he was stuck with a problem. Seemingly insurmountable challenges had resolved themselves. And last year he'd started to sculpt. He'd found that in the city he could procrastinate for days, while up North his energy level and imagination soared.

Christian suspected that the simple and well-ordered life on the island had also given him the courage to leave Global Capital. When first considering it, he'd come up to his retreat for two weeks of soul-searching. Would he challenge himself in his "retirement" or would he go as flat as old champagne—like Fred McIntyre, who'd moved to the islands? When he'd run into him in New York a couple of years later, he'd been interested in little else but drugs and whores.

Everyone had told Christian he was too young. But after being at the cottage for only three days, he'd known they were wrong. Two years had passed and he'd never regretted his decision.

Christian had taken some trips abroad, read a lot and spent long periods of time on his island. In fall he'd visited Argentina and then, in December, he'd met Claudia. She'd changed his life, adding a dimension that had always been missing, but little had changed in how he spent his days. He got up at six, read for a couple of hours, then went to the gym around nine-thirty and finally ended up at his office, where he and Melanie, his part-time employee, reviewed what needed to be done. At three, Christian usually left. Some days he took in a movie or visited a gallery. On others, he explored parts of the city he'd never been to. Yesterday, he'd driven to High Park to cross-country ski. Today, he was to meet Claudia at her lawyer's office.

The offices of Atkinson & Wyndham were in a capricious Victorian house off St. George Street. Small, whimsically shaped windows broke up the red brick, giving the building a fairy-tale appearance. On the right, there was a turret and in it, Claudia said, was Elliott's office.

The receptionist greeted him. Christian noticed her pink hair, which seemed out of character with both her otherwise professional appearance and her age. He guessed she was in her sixties. She said Mrs. Talbot had already arrived and asked him to follow her to Mr. Wyndham's office.

"Christian Unger,…" the lawyer beamed and held out his hand, "I've followed your accomplishments for years, so what a surprise to learn that you've become part of Claudia's life!"

Christian immediately felt comfortable with Wyndham. "It's good to meet you, Elliott…you're quite a legend yourself. I owe you my thanks for what you've done for Claudia."

Elliott brushed the compliment aside.

"I would have asked my partner, Hal Atkinson, to look in, but he's in Ottawa this week."

"Too bad. It would have been fun running into him." Christian kissed Claudia on the cheek, then sat down next to her.

"Look, Claudia and Christian, I've had a talk with Joseph Ferrer, David's lawyer. He's as upset with David's behavior as we are."

"What does he suggest?" Claudia asked.

"That's the problem. He's no longer on the case."

"What? David fired him?"

"Apparently…"

"God, I can't believe it. Each time I think he's gone away, he comes back with new energy," Claudia burst out.

"I'm afraid you're right. That's why I'm having both of you here. Ferrer asked me to pass on his concerns—a warning, so to speak. Look, it appears that David has convinced himself that you, Claudia, have been involved with Christian for some time…and that it was Christian who coached you on how to get rid of him. Or, as David thinks of it, how to break up his family."

"The bastard can't even give me credit for leaving him!" Christian gently took her hand.

"Ferrer is worried. He says David is livid, arguing he has every right to destroy the two of you." Elliott let his words sink in, then turned to Christian. "When Ferrer advised him to lay off, David fired him, saying that this time it wouldn't end with threats, so why did he need a family lawyer anyway?"

Christian shook his head. "His lawyer must be really concerned to pass this on to you. It's not normal, is it?"

"That's precisely it, Christian. Joseph Ferrer is discreet. I think he's convinced that David is serious."

Claudia and Christian looked at each other.

"He's losing it, I can tell," Claudia said, almost inaudibly. She raised her hands up to her face and Christian noticed they were trembling. "What can we do?"

"I'm not sure, really." Wyndham answered. "Maybe I should ask you two how often you see each other and what plans you have. I don't mean to be intrusive, but we have to consider all the facts."

Christian nodded at Claudia. She answered. "Look Elliott, maybe it's good we have this conversation. I met Christian just before Christmas. But we're spending a lot of time together. Some nights Christian stays over. I have no idea how David found out...probably the same private investigator who keeps getting hold of my unlisted phone numbers."

"Could be," the lawyer agreed.

"Christian and I have talked about moving in together. The kids like him and I'm crazy about him."

"I see." Elliott nodded pensively. "I'm not sure what advice I can give you other than to be aware that David is dangerous."

"You're not suggesting it would be better if Christian didn't move in?"

"What I'm saying is that there is no right way. On the one hand, it might be safer for you and the children if Christian does move in, or at least stays over as often as possible. On the other hand, that may further provoke David. You should consider what *you* think is right."

"Can we get the police to pay him another visit?" Christian wanted to know. "Or can he just phone Claudia and make threats forever?"

Elliott considered. "I know this is difficult to accept, but the police can't do much. If they go to pay David a visit, he'll probably be nice to them and then carry on with his plans anyway. Of course,

I can file a complaint with the court that he violated his restraining order and harassed you...threatened your life again. By now you know what that implies, Claudia. Would you like me to do it?"

"Yeah, just to get him to know we're on the case. I know I'll have to take time off for the affidavits and maybe to testify."

"I'm sorry but that's how it is. I wish I could produce better results for you."

"Don't be silly, Elliott...I know you can't do more. I'm just so frustrated!"

Christian couldn't think of anything they hadn't covered. "I guess the rest is up to Claudia and me, isn't it?"

"That's right, Christian. There's no concrete advice I can give you."

"It looks like Claudia and I have to think how we can protect ourselves. I'll do some homework. One advantage I have is that I'm retired. I have lots of time on my hands."

When Christian came to see me after he got roughed up in the bathroom at Paiazzo, I told him he was out of his fucking mind. Did he need this kind of a relationship? No!

People have told me my black eyes gleam when I'm furious. It's as if I see the world through a pool of blood. Everything darkens when I lose it.

Christian sat in the chair and held his hands behind his head, waiting for the storm to blow over.

Still, it was more than just unbridled anger. I was deeply concerned. "And she's got kids, for Christ's sake! You, who've lived on your own into your forties, with kids? Then there's her wacko husband. He threatens your lives, so you buy yourself a shotgun. Next, a real live gangster hits you up while you're taking a piss. Where's your shotgun now? Can you fucking see it, Christian?"

Christian didn't say anything.

"Where did you get the shotgun, anyway?"

"On King Street, in a hunting store."

"Great. So what will you do when your fancy-haired mobster shows up at night to pay you a visit? Show him your certificate? Or blast him out of the doorframe and go to jail for murder?

Christian, this is all so fucking bizarre." I gulped down more cognac. "You probably think if you shoot one of them you claim self-defense and it's over. But no one gets into a pissing contest with the mob and survives it!"

Christian had bought the gun so he could feel they were doing *something* proactive. Was that really so unusual, given what had happened?

It told him he could simply leave her and all his problems would instantly go away. As opposed to staying with her and fighting it out with the mob.

Christian started pacing the room. "You've always given me the advice you thought was best for me and I've done the same for you. But there were times when we didn't listen to each other. Like when you decided to declare yourself gay. With all your union clients, I was convinced it was professional suicide. But I was wrong. Your clients recognized you were the best, no matter which cubby-hole you belong in. And you've been wrong, too, Jake. You did everything to dissuade me from quitting my job, didn't you? And yet my instinct was right."

"So what's your point?"

"This time, no matter what the consequences, everything inside me tells me to stay the course with Claudia."

How could I keep fighting him? He had this way of getting through to me. Not a shred of manipulation, no agenda. I was melting into my fucking chair.

"I love her and I'll stick with her. So if you have any opinions you'll have to include Claudia in your equation. I want your advice, Jake, but on the basis that Claudia and I are an item."

I opened another bottle of Courvoisier, poured each of us a generous shot and we clinked.

"To our friendship," I said. "And may you still be fucking alive a month from now."

He held his nose to the crystal rim, drawing the condensed

fumes deeply into his lungs. Then he savoured the cognac and looked up at me, realizing I'd already emptied my glass. He was embarrassed. I laughed and felt close to him.

"Where do we go from here?"

"I've done a lot of thinking, Jake. Let me bounce a few things off you."

"Okay, shoot."

"Is David just bluffing or will he keep raising the ante?"

"He must already have decided that you can't be intimidated. Otherwise, why would he have hired the goons?"

"If we follow through on this escalation thing…when Claudia and I move together, he'll go ballistic."

"Right. But what will he do about it?"

"I think he'll send in the thugs again. The only question is how far he'll go."

"Fuck." As I listened on, I became increasingly cynical. I felt resentment rise again. Christian could get out of this, if only he wanted to.

"Each time I think this through I get to this same point. Since I don't want my legs broken or to get killed, I'll have to think of a way to defend myself."

"You can either go to the police…we've already been through that…it's useless. Or, wait for the mysterious midnight visitors and shoot them dead, with the already mentioned consequences. You in jail and Claudia and the children still subjected to David's whims. And all of you at war with the mob."

"What if I pay a visit to Talbot? Maybe I can convince him that Claudia and I only met in December."

"Come on…"

"Okay…if that doesn't work, I'll remind him of the consequences of hurting us."

"What consequences?"

Christian threw up his hands. "It's a long shot, but can I afford not to try?"

"And what will you do if it doesn't work?"

"Then I'll have to do it David's way…hire a thug of my own and send *him* a message. Maybe if he thinks he'll get his bones broken, he'll back off."

"I don't like it. You're being drawn in more deeply with each turn." I poured myself another shot.

"I'm surprised, Jake. You don't like me waiting around for the midnight visitor, as you call him. But you ridicule my alternatives, as well."

"Okay, I'm being negative. I have to say your idea of going to see this David guy is constructive. You're right…you can't afford not to try it. As to your other scheme, I think you're raving mad. How the hell would you go about hiring your own team of mobsters anyway?"

"*You* might be able to help me."

"Why me? And how?"

"We've sometimes discussed the links between organized labor and crime…me accusingly and you defensively. I thought you might know how to contact some of the players."

"Christ, that's like me asking you to arrange some insider trading deal for me. Once you fuck with these guys there is no going back. They'd own me! They'd ruin my career…my whole life, for Christ's sake. I can't believe you're asking me to do this!"

For a while, neither of us said anything. I got up and, glass in hand, disappeared down the hall toward the bathroom. I felt like an idiot. I thought about the three decades we'd known each other. About how much trouble I'd always had controlling my temper. How Christian had always overlooked my volatility. I took a piss and splashed water on my face.

I flushed, then sat down on the toilet, my pants done up as if I was on a park bench, thinking. Hadn't Christian looked around this dump? Framed posters commemorating labor struggles in the hallways. Legal titles on every shelf: Marx, Lord Keynes, Clarence Darrow's biography. And it wasn't just a professional thing. Labor law had determined my ideology, become my passion. Christian had to know that my profession was everything!

I thought of the evening when Christian decided to end his financial career. I'd been against it. How could anyone leave his chosen field without losing direction? Especially Christian, who was as passionate about the free market as I was about socialism!

My head was spinning. How did tonight fit into all this? Hadn't Christian just forced me to consider doing something that could ruin my career? Or had he merely articulated his alternatives in an impossible situation?

That's when Christian called to me, asking if I was all right.

When I opened the door he was standing there, then gave me one of those I-know-how-complicated-life-is-and-I'm-here-for-you hugs. "I'm sorry. I know how much you love your job and I should never have said what I did."

I laughed, but felt my eyes moisten. "Come on. There's no need for this, Christian. You've got enough pressure right now, so don't worry about me. And you know what? I've been thinking, sitting on the can and sipping my cognac. You really are stuck in a pile of shit. If the meeting with David fails and he keeps putting on more pressure, you'll have no alternative. If you get to that point, I'll do it."

I watched Christian struggle for words, then give up.

"I hope it won't be necessary," I said. "But if it is, I'll do it."

Claudia watched him get out of his car and open his arms. Karen ran down the driveway to him and he lifted her slightly off the ground. Jason looked on awkwardly.

When Christian came up the stairs, she opened the door to an icy blast.

"So early?" As she kissed him, she thought he felt tense.

"I was up half the night anyway..." Christian said.

"Why? God, you feel cold."

"I've been in the park since six, walking."

"All the more reason for a hot cup of tea."

He took off his coat and boots and then they walked to the kitchen.

"I'll make you some breakfast, too. That'll warm you up."

"No, thanks, I'm fine."

Claudia turned toward him. "Christian, what's wrong?"

"I feel terrible."

He seemed agitated. Then she remembered his smile as he'd seen Karen and lifted her off her feet. She gave him a hug. His body felt rigid and cold, like a suit of armor.

"Are you okay?"

"Claudia, we need to talk…"

"Let's do that over tea." She filled the kettle, then turned back to Christian. He was still standing. Maybe he was hung over. *That must be it—he had seen Jake.*

"Would you like an Alka-Seltzer? Was it one of those nights with Jake?"

"No, I didn't drink much."

"Then what's wrong? You look like you've been hit by a truck."

"We need to talk, Claudia."

"About what?"

"About David…"

She felt alarmed, but then she'd wanted to talk about David for some time. "I'm glad you're bringing it up. We can't just let David jerk us around like this. We should have some kind of a plan. At least we'll feel like we're doing something."

"It's not that." He rasped his front teeth against his lower lip. "I've been thinking."

"Thinking about what?"

"I'm really not helping things with David. The guy is deranged and anything could happen."

"I understand there isn't much you can do. David's a nut case. You being here is what matters! You make us all feel better…you know that, don't you?"

"Yes I know."

"Without you, life for me and the children would be unthinkable!" She tried to hug him again, but he stepped back.

"God, Christian, what is it?"

"Claudia, I know it's good for you and Karen and Jason to have me." He reached for her hands. "And I'd love nothing better than to be in your life…"

"What…?" Claudia couldn't think.

"I've been thinking…Shit, this is difficult."

"You're not suggesting…" Tears filled her eyes.

Christian wanted to embrace and kiss her, but he knew if he surrendered to his emotions now, he wouldn't be able to express himself. "It's my fault. I am the reason David is after us. I love you, I really do, but as long as we're together, you and the children are in danger. I've thought this through from every angle. While I'm around you might get hurt…maybe killed."

"I can't believe this, Christian. I've trusted you so completely…"

"I couldn't live with myself if something happened to you or the kids," he pleaded.

"We've always known that was a risk. Why the hell didn't you think of that earlier?"

He tried to hold her.

"Don't touch me." She started to tremble. "I've been here before…I can handle this. Just leave me."

"The last thing I want to do is to hurt you…" Tears now formed in Christian's eyes.

"You should have thought of that earlier, for God's sake!"

"Look, we can work on this together…I mean I want to keep helping you, but we've got to eliminate the danger you're in."

"If you loved me you'd say it would be better to both get killed than be apart!"

"Claudia, what if you got killed and I still had to live? I couldn't go on…." He held her arms firmly.

"Leave me alone. I don't want to be touched right now. Just go away!"

He tried to hold her.

"Don't touch me! You're making it even worse…" She pulled herself away and ran toward the stairs. Between her sobs, Christian could hear her repeat she could handle it, she'd been there before.

He didn't know what to do. He felt an overwhelming need to hold her and help her, but what about her pleas to be left alone?

The front door opened and Karen stormed in. "Mom, Christian! I missed the stupid bus. Could you give me…" She saw Christian.

"Your Mom and I had an argument." He tried to be strong and serious, but he still had tears in his eyes.

Karen looked distraught. "Where's Mom?" she said, instinctively turning toward the stairs.

"It's better you leave her alone," Christian said. "I'll take you to school."

"I want to see Mom."

Christian walked up to her and held her tightly and rocked her. "Don't worry, my sweetheart. No one's ever going to hurt you again. Everything's fine with your mom and I."

Karen cried softly as they stood hugging each other.

When Christian entered the bedroom, Claudia was lying on her side. He sat down next to her and started stroking her hair.

"I'm back."

"What for?" Claudia started crying again. "I asked you to leave me alone, you jerk."

"I know…and I couldn't. Can we at least lie and just hold each other?"

"You're making it worse, Christian."

He lay down anyway and for an hour they didn't say anything. Christian tried to comfort Claudia, and every now and then she cried.

When Claudia finally turned toward him, Christian told her what an idiot he'd been and that he'd always be with her and look after her. And the children.

He told her about Karen and the hurt he'd seen in her eyes when he told her they'd been fighting. "I couldn't bear seeing her like that."

Claudia looked up at him and noticed his lip.

"Now you're bleeding," she said.

A small traffic jam prevented Christian from backing out of his parking spot. Intermittently looking at his rear view mirror and turning his head, he watched the line-up of vehicles wanting to pass. A red truck and a cube van painted with yellow Ryder graphics eased by slowly. Then, a small black car came into view. It stopped almost directly behind him.

He wouldn't have given the car another thought had its driver not honked, then lowered his window and gestured at the Ryder truck. Christian recognized the driver: it was the man who'd followed him into the washroom at Paiazzo. He was wearing a purple polo shirt and a beige jacket today, but his fleshy nose and the exaggerated lower lip were unmistakable. And no two people could have that haircut in common. Next to him was a second man. Christian could only see a small part of his silhouette. Had they followed him here?

The Ryder truck moved aside and the black car drove on, continuing to honk. Christian followed its movements. It swung into a parking space, where the driver and passenger got out almost at the same time. For a moment, they both stood outside the car, pulling their shoulders back, as though it was choreographed. Christian felt certain now that they didn't know he was here.

When they walked toward the building, he could see them more clearly. The one who'd assaulted him, his haircut very notice-able even from a distance. And his much taller companion, dressed almost identically, with blond, short-cropped hair. Maybe he was the guy who'd watched the door.

Christian tried to slow his breathing, then opened the glove compartment to look for a pen. He'd wait three minutes, then slow-ly drive by the black car and memorize its make and license plate. He reached for the newspaper on the backseat…something to write on.

Christian's mind raced back and forth between the experience he'd had with the two thugs at Paiazzo and what they were doing here. Obviously, they were visiting David. And they couldn't be here to report on the restaurant event. Too much time had passed.

David probably knew about their visit to his building, too. Bernie, the concierge, had later related how the two had asked for him and how he'd sent them away, telling them Christian was at the cottage. And then, last week, the phone call in the middle of the night. When he heard the thick accent and the guy called him "buddy," he felt the same sensation of helplessness as when stand-ing over the urinal at the restaurant. He could almost smell the thug's aftershave. The message was simple: if Christian didn't make his move soon, he and his nice new family would pay.

And now they're here. No doubt to get new instructions, perhaps final ones! Christian felt blood thumping through his temples. When he gripped the steering wheel to back out of his spot, he noticed how wet his hands were. At this rate, he'd have trouble remembering the plate number!

As he approached the parked black car, he got lucky. A pickup truck pulled out of the spot next to it, forcing Christian to stop. He had the perfect chance to do his homework.

The car was a Mustang. Christian noticed its strange ordinariness: no mag wheels, no special trim or graphics. It wasn't what he'd have expected; in all other respects the thugs seemed eager to show off.

When the pickup truck started to move, Christian followed. Further down the lane, he pulled up on the curb and wrote:

AWS 222 (Ont.)
BLACK MUSTANG
JUNE 02 – 09:25

Claudia had always portrayed David as a manipulator, who routinely hurt and degraded others, then charmed them, before throwing the next tantrum. Christian had thought of him as a coward, too—someone who felt most comfortable operating behind the scenes.

Today he'd seen the real David. It was clear that he was a master manipulator; the fact that his paid thugs had been on their way to his office, while he'd met with Christian, confirmed that. But Christian was equally shocked by his deliberate transparency. David hadn't denied that he'd ordered Christian roughed up. He'd just answered Christian's pleas for restraint and sanity with the same words, spoken almost dispassionately: "I've set my course and I'll stick with it."

The bastard hadn't even come out of his shell when openly challenged. Responding to Christian's warning that no move against him or Claudia or the children would go unanswered, David's face had filled with loathing, but all he'd said was: "If you fight back, you'll lose everything. Just like I did."

The traffic flowed fast as Christian approached Toronto. His thoughts turned to Claudia—the unnecessary pain he'd caused her when suggesting they should go their own ways. How he could have thought of that as a solution was now beyond him. *I did what*

David would have done…I raised her hopes and then smashed them to bits!

Only one good thing had come out of his senseless behavior: he was absolutely determined to protect Claudia and the kids. They were his family now, and no one would hurt them.

David had declared war. But Christian would find a way to come out on top, no matter what the odds. Winning had been a constant in his life and, from what he knew about David, losing had been a constant in his. He vowed to remind himself of that at least once a day.

The pile of paper in front of me is growing by the day. How many typewritten pages will my scribbled notes fill? And why do I need to write down what I know? If I don't, I'll go crazy, that's why.

Christian was the best thing that ever happened to me and I owe him. By recording what I know, I'm bound to come across something that will put sense into what happened. Or maybe invisible threads will link up and, even though I won't be able to see the connections, I might arrive at some kind of truth.

Christian and Claudia disappeared several months ago, probably on the weekend of November 16–17, 1996. The police report says they might have drowned, but insinuates that foul play could have been at work, too. In other words, the cops don't know a fucking thing!

That's why I sit here every night, writing. If I haven't solved the riddle by the time I'm done, I'll revert to this resource as often as I need to, because that's what the purpose of this narrative is: a resource. Until I know what happened.

Our Wednesday meetings always started out at my apartment
on Queen Street. We usually had a beer, then went to a nearby pub
where we drank more and ate lots of junk food. Around ten, we
ended up back at my place and turned to cognac. By then, small
talk had usually turned to protracted ideological debate. And when
that ended, Christian either took a taxi back to his place or settled
down on my couch. That was in winter.

In summer, the focus shifted to Christian's island retreat. I
went up for four or five long weekends.

When Claudia came into his life, I told Christian I would
understand if I was no longer invited.

"I've never *invited* you up, Jake, and I'm not starting that now.
You've always told me when you'd come and I want you to keep
doing that."

I was skeptical. "How will Claudia deal with it? Vehement discussions until daybreak, accompanied by lots of drinking—not the
kind of stuff that turns on future wives."

"Let's see how it turns out. Claudia and I have talked about it.
She doesn't think it's good for me if I give up this part of my life.
She says that maybe she'll enjoy all the yelling, or maybe she'll just
put in her earplugs and go to bed. Pragmatic, isn't she?"

"And wise. I'm impressed. But I'm still not crazy about sharing
our ideological contests."

Christian, forever rational, proposed that I try to arrive at the
cottage a day before Claudia had to return to the city and then stay
on a couple of days. That way, Claudia and I could get to know each
other and the two of us could still have time to ourselves.

I left Toronto mid-day and Christian picked me up at the Parry
Sound docks. Once at the island, we took a swim and watched the
sunset, while Claudia prepared a spectacular meal.

Christian fussed over her a bit too much, probably a telltale sign of their recent upheaval. Someone else might not have noticed.

Most of the evening was taken up by polite, but stimulating conversation. I liked Claudia and, by the time we went to bed, I'd convinced myself that she liked me too.

The next day, we were off to a late start. We swam, lay in the sun, read and talked. Later, Claudia and Christian went for a long ride in the canoe and around five Christian took her back to town.

Sitting on the dock and dangling my feet in the water, I tried to imagine the two of them on the boat. It was a game I often played with myself, picturing what judges, witnesses or clients were saying to themselves or each other when I wasn't there. It was probably nothing more than a diversion that people who spend a lot of time alone indulge in. But I never fought it, convinced that it sharpened my intuitive skills.

"Jake's quite a sweet guy," I imagined Claudia saying. "Where's that temper you always talk about?"

"Oh, it exists. You just have to push the right buttons and he'll explode, but he'll recover just as fast."

"I'd like to see that. I bet he looks great when he's angry...those expressive eyes. If Jake ever looks for a woman, he'll have no trouble finding one."

"I think he knows that. Jake was quite a ladies' man when we were in our twenties. I always envied him. He'd have dates and I'd be left figuring out how he did it. Jake was a natural. But I don't think he's interested in changing."

I was having fun. I could tell by the way she'd looked at me that Claudia found me attractive. Not in a flirtatious or seductive way— just open, interested and accepting. I felt relieved. If we hadn't liked each other, it would have complicated things.

Christian had been pleased, too. I'd noticed him watching us, keeping out of the conversation as though he was thinking that it was good for us to get to know each other. Part of me regretted that my friendship with Christian would be redefined, but another part looked forward to seeing more of Claudia and Christian as a couple.

I tried to visualize Christian gliding across the water; by now he had to be on his way back. The sky was taking on its evening softness. A few strips of cloud gathered low on the horizon. It was still hot, but the air was fresh and without humidity. The water was of that luminescent intensity at which tourists to Canada marvel and locals take for granted.

I moved to the porch, where I gathered my pile of books and papers. I'd work on my case until dinner was ready.

Claudia had asked about my upcoming battle the night before. I was representing a partially disabled worker who'd been discriminated against by her employer and was now being denied her social benefits. In an interview, the civil servant handling her application had determined that *she* was at fault for losing her job and would therefore not receive any government assistance. My firm had already launched an action against the employer, which I knew we could win. On the strength of that, I'd challenge the government's decision. That meant I'd be stepping outside the labor laws, maybe into a constitutional battle. Taking the government to court when they broke the law, which they did with frightening frequency, gave me the most satisfaction.

I heard the boat come in and a few minutes later Christian walked up the path toward the cottage.

"Working on your case, huh?" he asked as he entered the porch.

"Is it okay if I keep going while you cook?"

"Sure. You can reciprocate by cleaning up the huge mess I'll make in the kitchen."

I grunted and returned to my papers, positioning myself so that my back was to the shore. Notepad, files, ashtray, Lucky Strikes and drink in front of me, then the length of the rough wooden table, and behind that the open kitchen door. I could see right into the kitchen.

Christian took the first of the two bottles of Barolo and slowly poured its contents into a decanter—a simple glass jug. He was opening a long package of pasta, when he noticed I was watching.

"I'll make us a deliciously simple pasta. Capellini and bits of tomato, slightly fried in olive oil and garlic." He spoke with an Italian accent, theatrically extending the vowels and rolling the rrr's. "At the end, I'll put a slice of ahi tuna on the grill, searing it just enough to cook the edges and leaving the centre raw. I'll cut it into bits and, with a few basil leaves, mix it into the pasta. *Eccola!* Having been a bachelor for so long has its rewards, *si?*"

My concentration was shot. I was thinking of what tonight's conversation would be.

We hadn't talked since the day he'd visited David. He'd come straight to my office and asked if I could spend some time. Not much came from our conversation, except that it made him feel better. We discussed whether he should tell Claudia the part about the thugs being there. Christian argued that he shouldn't burden her with it. David alone was enough to handle.

We ate pasta and drank Barolo. Christian was busy decanting the second bottle when I told him I was worried about him.

"The bastard's pretty well confirmed that he'll have you maimed or killed, right? If it was in my nature, I'd shoot the fucker through the head myself, but as you probably suspect, it isn't."

Christian raised his glass and bowed. "That's nice, Jake. It's the thought that counts."

"No one will find you on a remote island, but you can't stay here forever."

"There's something else, Jake…they were in my apartment."

"What?"

"I was with Karen, who'd had a doctor's appointment near my

place. I'd take her to her home, cook dinner for the whole gang and stay over. In the morning, I figured, I'd drive straight up here."

"That was Friday."

"No, Thursday afternoon. I got here Friday. Anyway, Karen and I were halfway to her house, when I realized I'd forgotten the damned cottage keys, so we turned around and went back to my building. When I opened the door I could smell his cologne."

"What cologne?"

"The guy in the restaurant bathroom…he reeked of this sweet stuff. Then I saw the note taped to my fridge. The only thing I could think of was to get Karen out of there, so I reached to the peg-board behind the door and grabbed a set of keys. In the elevator back down, I noticed they weren't even the cottage keys."

"Did Karen notice?"

"She must have noticed that something wasn't right. I was completely rattled. But she didn't ask."

"What a fucking mess. Have you been back?"

"Yeah, Friday morning. I told Claudia I was off to the cottage, then went back. I was terrified."

"No wonder…"

"Once I opened the door and that smell hit me, I had to run to the toilet and relieve myself. Can you imagine if I'd come there with Karen and run into them? I don't know what they'd have done."

"That's a terrifying idea."

"Think about it. Karen coming in behind me and scream-ing…Karen being slapped around, or knocked out or tied up and gagged.…It makes me sick."

"How badly is the place ransacked?"

"That's the amazing thing, Jake. It isn't. They moved the TV set to the kitchen counter. Not sloppily, either—it looked like it had always been there, plugged in and all. And my night table was in the bathroom and the phone I keep in the living room was on my bedroom floor. They left a bullet next to each item that had been moved…"

"A bullet?"

"Yeah, a shiny new bullet. Like the ones I use with my rifle here at the cottage. That's what really got me, once I was over the terror. The manner in which they'd violated my space. It was done in such a sterile way. I almost wish they had vandalized the place. It would have frightened me less."

"What about the note?"

"It was typed and said that time was short and that our next encounter wouldn't be so neat." Christian finished off his wine in one gulp, something I had never seen him do. "All of which confirms your point, Jake. I do need a firm plan."

We sat silently for a while, looking at the water below us. The evening breeze was stirring things up, sending a thousand ripples our way. Christian and I took turns cursing or sighing or sipping at our wine.

Then I got up and helped myself to more food. I urged Christian to do the same and he followed me, but I could tell he wasn't hungry.

"They're professionals," I said after a while. "Top of the fucking line."

"I know. I'm really worried about Claudia now."

"I guess you haven't told her."

"No, I couldn't, Jake. I've got to protect her against the scum, not let him hurt her even more. Anyway, don't you think they'll take out their frustrations on Claudia, if I stay here much longer?"

"I think they're fucking unpredictable. Although I'd say you're their first target. Anyway, let's be practical about this. Last time we went through this, we ended up with two options."

"There aren't any left now." Christian's voice was strained.

I took a last stab at my food, poured more wine for both of us and got up. Christian joined me at the edge of the porch.

"It's glorious here, isn't it?" Christian had great sadness in his voice. He made a sweeping gesture, then drank deeply.

"Christian, listen to me. I never would have thought that I'd ever give anyone advice like this. A few weeks ago I questioned your sanity. Yet the truth is I've changed my mind. There's only one thing left."

"What, to have him shaken up or killed?"

"You'll be surprised that I think you should consider the latter."

"I agree. Why give him a warning?"

Christian suggested that we take a break from our discussion. After being on the water for a few minutes, we came across a beaver pulling a tangle of lush green leaves across the surface of the water. And later, two loons accompanied us, close enough that we could study their splendid markings.

Our paddles entered and left the water without a sound and with hardly a ripple. Only behind the graceful shape of our green canoe was there evidence of our presence. A wedge formed on the water, not much different from the ones the loons left behind them.

When we returned, it was almost dark. I once again filled our glasses; by now, the Barolo had opened up to its full potential.

"Maybe next year at this time, David won't be spoiling your life."

"Don't get emotional on me."

"I'll be all business…promise!" I lit the kerosene lamps, then gazed at the unsteady flames. "If you went through with it, do you think you could live with yourself?"

"Maybe I'm less of a human being than I thought. I can't imagine feeling anything but relief. Except for the fear that I'd complicate Claudia's and the kids' lives. The police inquiries, you know…"

"You'd inconvenience them a lot more if David had you killed, don't you think?"

"I know…the consequences of not doing him in. That's why I don't think I would feel any guilt."

"What about the code?" I got up and started pacing around, regretting the question.

I thought of the campsite in Quetico Park, our canoes turned upside down on a sandy beach, one red and one green. The tent fifty feet further up. And in between a fire…he and I crouching there with our mugs. One of the few occasions when I was forced to drink tea.

We were in our early thirties then, old enough to have learned that not all of our society's conventions and laws were for us. We'd establish our own morality code.

"Remember the row we got into, drafting it?" I said.

"*Drafting* it? Once a lawyer, always a lawyer."

"That's *why* we got into an argument…"

I remembered showing off my newly gained legal skills, trying to make our code immensely complicated, and Christian insisting that it could only work if it was kept simple—otherwise we'd be forced to keep changing it to suit the occasion.

"I'm sorry, Christian, I shouldn't have brought it up," I said.

"It's okay. It's been on *my* mind a lot."

Christian's eyes were on the kerosene lamp. A large moth was climbing up the side of its glass chimney, then for a second perched itself on the edge, before falling. The flame turned white for an instant, as the wings ignited.

"Remember why the code had to be simple?" I asked.

The kerosene light didn't reach me. He was seeing me against the fading sky, a silhouette who was his closest friend.

"So that it could be an absolute. Something we'd never have

to change."

"That night you explained to me why Christianity had survived. Because there are only ten very simple laws to be followed. As opposed to the thousands of labor laws…"

"Or tax or securities or banking laws. When I left Global Capital, there were so many, you couldn't go through a week without breaking one."

"That's why they're written today and forgotten tomorrow."

"Maybe even ten laws are too many, Jake. Everyone on earth agrees on 'Thou shalt not kill,' but when it comes to lying or what we eat or how many wives we should have, there are already disagreements. And now I'm confronted with the one that's accepted as the most necessary."

"Something we couldn't have imagined when we built our morality code."

"We vowed not to wilfully and unnecessarily hurt anyone, or interfere in anyone's potential as a human being." Christian stood up. "What never occurred to me was the possibility that someone would threaten to kill me. Even after David's thug cornered me in the bathroom, it took me a while to accept the idea. But after seeing David, I knew I was in new territory."

I went to get a sweater. When I came back, Christian stood at the shore, staring at the night-sky.

The moon had been hidden behind the foliage, but down at the beach we could see a sharp-edged sickle trying to distinguish itself against a sky which was still more blue than black. The stars would be spectacular.

"So, what do you think?" I asked, lighting a cigarette. "Am I bending our code if I physically hurt someone in order to prevent him from hurting me and others?"

"That's the question."

"A question, but not a dilemma. I might have felt guilt if I hurt David without taking the effort to reason with him. But I did do that, and not only did he tell me he'd proceed, but when I came out of the building I nearly collided with his hired thugs."

"I'm glad you're coming to a decision."

"Still, I'm concerned. Not because I wonder what it will do to me, but because I don't think I'll feel guilty."

Christian's words hung in the night air. Then two loons called to each other, breaking the silence.

Torontonians were returning from their cottages. As Claudia approached the city, it was bumper-to-bumper, stop-and-go driving.

Thinking of Christian made her feel better. *They're probably still eating.* She knew that Christian had planned one of his splendid pasta creations.

Claudia had hardly believed her luck when discovering that Christian was an enthusiastic and highly skilled cook. In the few months they'd known each other, he'd been in charge of the kitchen almost every weekend. And a few times, he'd even surprised her with dinner in the middle of the week.

She wondered how Christian's cottage season would affect their lives, then questioned whether she should allow herself to think ahead. Instinct told her yes: Christian would not disappoint her again. He'd always be with her and he'd always be there for her children. But the knowledge that he'd thought of leaving her still hurt, even if his sole intention had been to protect her. It had taken a lot of determination to treat him as if nothing had happened.

Her thoughts turned to the children; Claudia hoped her parents had already dropped them off. Another few weeks and Jason would be seventeen; Karen had already passed her fourteenth birthday. She'd soon have to think of a better solution.

Maybe Christian was part of the answer. He handled them well…better than she managed, especially Jason. Claudia was curious how Christian would handle the kids at the cottage. She was a bit intimidated by his set-up there; the children might feel the same way. The cottage was where Christian ruled.

She'd first visited the island six weeks ago. She'd expected sandy beaches and flat, coniferous shorelines. Instead, they'd navigated along shorelines marked by imposing rock faces, often rising almost vertically from the water, with birches and pines growing high above.

Then the cottage itself. The place where he'd created a degree of self-sufficiency he'd never dreamed was possible, Christian had explained. And what that had led to. The feeling of being completely sovereign, untouched and unseen by the forces that ran other people's world. It was only him and nature here—or, rather, nature and him.

It was a world Claudia had never considered. In less than two weeks she'd find out how her children would fit into it. She'd learn a lot about them.

The rolling hills north of Toronto gradually gave way to industrialized areas. She saw emergency lights flashing in the distance. She'd be home at nine, unless there was an accident ahead.

Her thoughts returned to Christian and Jake. She suspected they were talking about David.

"Do you think I'm in denial about this whole thing?" she'd asked Christian a few days ago. "I find myself thinking about the most banal things, like Karen's grades at school or my design projects. But what David is up to is floating somewhere far below."

"Maybe that's good," Christian had suggested.

"But something's wrong with my response, don't you think? Our safety is at stake, and probably the kids'. So what kind of a moth-

. . . .

er am I, if I can simply suppress everything?" She'd become teary-eyed and Christian had held her and kissed her on her forehead.

"You keep telling me that you're spending more quality time with Karen and Jason than you've ever spent. Taking the kids places is good, Claudia. Hiding at home and worrying about David would be bad."

"But we've got to do something…we can't just let things happen to us."

"I know it's frustrating, but let me deal with it for now. Like you say, you've got a job and the kids. I've got lots of time on my hands, so give me a couple of weeks to think."

She'd taken comfort in Christian's words then and they still calmed her now, as she pulled up between the sheltering maples which flanked her driveway. If anyone could get control of the situation it was Christian.

Jason was standing at the stove, cooking something. Claudia chuckled to herself. *Jason the cook…another one of Christian's accomplishments!*

"How was your weekend?" she asked, hugging him from behind.

"The usual…we watched a lot of TV and Karen was obnoxious." Then he turned around. "Mom, a really weird thing happened after Grandpa dropped us off. This guy rang the bell…you should have seen him. Some strange crew cut and then hair way down his back. Like some Indian chief in a business suit!"

Claudia managed to ask: "Well, what did the man want?"

"He left an envelope for you. I put in on your cabinet. I'm telling you, you really missed something."

On her way to Oakville next morning, Claudia was distraught. Maybe she should have talked to Elliott first…but what could he have done? Hadn't he pointed out shortcomings of the legal process and the futility of contacting the police in the first place?

That's why it was time she talked to the bastard in person! Things had gone far enough.

She felt badly about not telling Christian, though. Last night, she'd put it off and this morning, there'd been no answer. He had probably gone into Parry Sound, or was doing something outside where he couldn't hear.

She walked into David's office at 9:30. No one sat at the reception desk, nor were there any patients waiting. She sat down and collected her thoughts. Absentmindedly, she picked up a magazine and started to flip the pages.

How could she get through to David? She was afraid that he'd do or say something to derail her from her thoughts. How effective he'd always been that way!

Logically, there was nothing he could say to deflect her message. He'd gone too far and involved the children and that's where things would stop. How could he even think of it?

A pleasant voice asked Claudia if she had an appointment. The girl was tall, with long blond hair piled up into a bun and conspicuously long, orange fingernails. Claudia got up and walked over to the reception desk. She noticed the girl's low-cut blouse and the tight skirt.

"Actually, I'd like to see David Talbot privately. I don't have an appointment, but I'm his former wife. I need to see him about our children."

The receptionist's charm gave way to hostility. "Let me see if we can make the time for you," she said acidly, before strutting down the hallway. *She must be fucking him,* Claudia concluded.

She heard a whispered conversation, then the woman came back and started typing, ignoring her.

Claudia let a few minutes go by, trying not to feel humiliated. When she thought the time was right, she asked the receptionist when David would see her. She was told that she couldn't just walk in and expect to be seen—not without an appointment. Claudia said she couldn't see what the problem was. Obviously there were no patients, so could the receptionist please impress on Mr. Talbot to see her now.

As the blonde left her station again, Claudia speculated on how long her hair was, when she let it fall. *Down to her ass, I bet.* She was convinced that David and she were an item—why else would he allow his employee to dress like this? He had no choice, that was why.

This time the receptionist returned with David. "I hear you're in a hurry, Claudia. I'm kind of busy, but why don't you come in anyway?" David led the way to his office, where he asked her to sit down. "You're looking great, Claudia. What brings you here?"

"Oh, cut the shit, you bastard. I want you to look at this and explain yourself." She threw the envelope at him. "This was delivered to your son Jason last night, by your hired imbeciles."

David pulled the sheet out of the envelope and unfolded it. It was a photocopy of a newspaper article reporting the disappearance of a young girl. On the margin, the words THINK WHAT COULD HAPPEN TO YOUR CHILDREN were typed.

"How can you draw the children into this?" she said, her outrage threatening to upset any bit of control.

"I don't know what you're talking about, Claudia," David replied, with a smirk.

"You don't, huh? Well, let me enlighten you. The same thug who assaulted Christian and threatened to kill him, delivered this to Jason last night."

"I can't comment on that, Claudia. But just so we understand each other, you should know that I always carry everything through to the end. I made that clear to your friend Christian when he visited. He told you about that visit, didn't he?" David looked straight into her eyes, not something she was used to from him. "By the way, isn't Christian the fellow you had an affair with when you and the children left me? When exactly did that thing start?"

Claudia knew this would happen. He always did this to her.

Turned things around…made her the target. She no longer cared about keeping control. All she wanted to do now was to get her point across.

"Don't jerk me around, David. I'll tell you something. You fuck around with me and Christian and we'll pay you back in kind." She heard her own voice rise. "But you go near the children again and I'll kill you."

"And how exactly would you do that?"

"God, you haven't changed a bit, have you? Who cares how…I'll find a way, trust me. All I know is I'll fucking kill you!"

David didn't need to respond and probably wouldn't have done so, anyway. The blonde was standing in the doorframe behind Claudia and David said to her: "I think it's time you showed my former wife the door, Samantha."

And that's what Samantha did.

Three or four days after my return from the cottage, Christian was back in the city, too. He phoned me about the letter and Claudia's visit to David.

"Maybe we should go to the police, after all," I said. "A letter like that is something they'd take very seriously."

"Well, guess what? The letter's gone."

"How do you mean, it's gone?"

"Claudia took it along to demonstrate to him what his hired thugs were actually doing. But she was so rattled by his response that she blew up and left without it."

"She forgot the bloody letter? Christ, so much for calling in the cops....How is she, by the way?"

"Fine. She blames herself for not telling me first, but thinks she did the right thing. Except for leaving the letter, of course."

"Do you think her visit was a good idea?"

"That's what Claudia keeps asking me. I guess it confirmed once more that David's really out to hurt us. Despite the letter, it was probably worth it."

. . . .

A few days later, I received a hand-delivered envelope. The address and the word CONFIDENTIAL were in Christian's handwriting. My curiosity turned to apprehension after I opened it and found a smaller envelope inside, prominently marked TO BE OPENED BY JAKE SULLIVAN ONLY.

I got up and asked Agnes not to disturb me, then closed my office door, sat down and lit a cigarette. The paper was expensive, but coarse; the daringly executed letters followed even lines. While I made use of cheap ballpoints and, being left- handed, often smeared my wispy scribbles, Christian used a broad-nibbed fountain pen and he was a master at it. This time, he'd used black ink. The effect was so formal that it added to my discomfort.

Christian started out by saying how moved he was by my offer and that I had given him something that went beyond the call of even the closest and most giving of friendships. He recognized the risk I would be taking by contacting someone who might help him. Any glitch could ruin my life. And that was why he wanted me to think it all through again…to reconsider whether I really wanted to play a part in a murder.

As to myself, my dear Jake, I have thought it all through and come to an irreversible decision and I want to tell you again how it all came about.

You'll remember how, after our Italian dinner at the cottage, I told you that I'd give myself another week to make a final decision. You said time was short, but felt I shouldn't impose a deadline. Then you predicted that, given how long I'd been thinking of this, I'd just wake up one morning and know.

The next night we talked about your pending court battle. Did I tell you how relieved I was to change topics? Talking about your crippled client and the faceless bureaucrats to whom she'd been exposed was like balm to my soul—it focused my mind on what I should be thinking about all the time.

Around two, we went to bed and fell asleep.

A while later, I found myself walking through the cottage, deftly maneuvering through the narrow passages between the living room chairs and the fireplace, past the carved wood box and around the corner into the kitchen. The remarkable thing was that I was just dreaming this. I turned around again, eyes shut tightly, and walked the narrow passage again. There, I thought, I can actually do this without bumping into anything!

Then I turned back toward the kitchen again, and walked up to the counter, below me the sink and in front of me the window, which looks out onto the porch and the lake below. I could see the outline of the magnificent trees in front of the cottage, the dock reaching out into the water and the water itself, calmly reflecting the half-moon I'd observed earlier that night. And looking straight ahead, through the foliage, I saw small patches of sky with flickering stars. What a perfect night, I thought. Yet something was strange about it: I saw everything in monochrome.

I couldn't recall ever looking out that window at night, but it seemed there should be some color to things—even if it was muted, dark color. Yet the trees, the leaves and the dock were in the darkest imaginable shades of grey; the night sky a bit lighter; the water and a few clouds lighter yet. And the stars and the moon in the sky and the moon in the water were a milky white grey.

Then I remembered: my eyes were closed. I pressed my lids together even more firmly, but everything was still there outside the kitchen window. The trees, the dock, the patches of sky, the water and the moon. The same as a moment ago, but this time I was sure my eyes were tightly shut.

I thought about that, taking in the scene for what seemed like a long time, then I heard a sharp crack. It was the bathroom door; you had to be up.

I was resentful that I'd been awakened, but I decided to open my eyes. What I then saw took me completely aback. Before me was exactly the same monochrome nightscape I'd seen in my dream.

. . . .

I was frightened, because I'd never sleepwalked before and this was obviously what I'd just done. My navigating between pieces of furniture, turning back and doing it again, then going to check out the view through the kitchen window, I'd done it all in my sleep! How long had I been up? How could what I'd seen through my closed eyes be identical to the real view out the window?

Christian then related how, deeply disturbed, he'd been retracing his steps when I came out of the bathroom. I'd asked him what he was doing up at this hour—my voice groggy, but concerned.

I remember well. I'd gone to the can, my head pounding and my bladder bursting, seeing someone standing at the kitchen window and wondering what the fuck was going on. Only to realize that it was Christian.

After that I went back to bed, but not to sleep. Again and again, I thought about this peculiar experience. What struck me as the most unusual part was that I'd rarely looked through the kitchen window, at least at any length. And never, in my recollection, had I done so at night. Of all the windows in my cabin, this was the one I used the least. How could my mind have designed a scene which was identical to the real thing, in outline and in color, from a perspective with which I wasn't familiar? I couldn't make sense of it.

I lay in bed for more than an hour, dwelling on these thoughts. Outside, the night sky had started to brighten. I thought I'd witness the sunrise in the canoe. Despite our drinking, my head was clear and my mind alert.

The bay was covered in a seemingly impenetrable mist. I decided to head to the waterfall on the other side, as I'd done a thousand times, confident when I pushed off that I'd get there in a straight line.

At first, all went well. Compared to the frosty morning air, the water felt soothingly warm. I let it caress my hand, as I pulled the paddle along the side of my canoe. But the further out I got, the denser was the fog. After paddling for a minute or two, I couldn't see the prow of the canoe any longer! And when I was still going after what seemed like five or six minutes, I wondered where I was. I changed direction, subtly at first, looking for a hole in the dense, wet mist. Then anxiety took over. For a few long minutes, frenzied impulses bombarded my brain. I paddled desperately, then, after a few strokes I stopped again, realizing I might crash into the rocky shore. I must have changed direction a dozen times. ... I have no idea how long I was out there. Then I decided to stand up, thinking I might be able to reach above the mist and see. But each time I tried, I lost my balance, barely able to get back down without tipping the canoe.

Finally, I gave up, exhausted. As I slid to the bottom of the canoe and let go of my tension, I wondered why I'd bothered struggling. Any moment now, the sun would come up over the trees at the end of the bay and burn off the mist. I'd paddle back and make myself some coffee.

And that's what happened, but not the way I expected it. Only you know how much nature means to me, Jake; how nothing in nature is ever ordinary. Yet what I was about to witness was far beyond the miracle of even the most spectacular sunrise.

When the sun touched the water in front of me it changed everything. The first tentative rays turned the static, grey layer of mist in which I lay into a luminous dream. I could see individual droplets dancing in the air, as they reflected light and took on color. It was as if I lived inside a rainbow, Jake, but a rainbow that sat flat and stretched across the lake. Then, as the sun grew bolder and started to eat away at the moisture, I sat amidst a radiant, swirling mass of energy. Suddenly, I was witness to something much larger than the little bay I know so well!

And you know what? When I pulled my canoe alongside the dock and climbed up onto the glistening cedar boards, I knew I no longer had to think about my course of action. You'd been right—the decision had come all by itself.

It was still before seven. I went up to the cottage and made myself a cup of strong coffee. Then I went to the bookshelf—it was the first time in weeks that I felt the urge to read. Remember how we built the pine shelves together and argued which novels should grace them? I picked

The Razor's Edge. *The title seemed appropriate and, besides, I remembered it as an exquisite piece of writing. I recalled one of the characters in the book, the pompous mega-snob Elliott Templeton, who lived on the Riviera and had little on his mind but his own social advancement. What a contrast to the Elliott in my life, I thought—the polished but introverted Elliott Wyndham.*

I took the book and my coffee outside to the porch and settled into one of the deck chairs. I'd have a good long read and later, when you got up, I'd tell you about my decision. I felt better than I had for weeks.

When you finally rose, it was nearly noon. Even though you'd had a long shower, your eyes looked as moist as if you'd just made an impassioned argument, which you were in the process of losing. I couldn't help chuckle; I'd drunk a huge amount of cognac myself and I knew you'd had twice as much.

"My head feels like a fucking beehive," you announced.

"I guess it does," I said, "but look at all the fun we had." Then, thinking I should be more compassionate, I added: "You know there's Alka Seltzer in the bathroom cabinet." Remember?

I did remember. I'd been terribly hung over, but not enough to miss the change in Christian. Apart from looking far too energetic, he also looked tranquil, even serene, the first time he'd seemed so in weeks.

I remember how nasal my voice sounded when I asked him why he looked so chipper. He answered that it was probably because he didn't join in with the last four or five glasses of cognac. The rest, he said, was that he'd had a very good morning.

After you got your bearings, I considered telling you more about my sleepwalking experience. How disturbed it had left me and how it defied any logical explanation. And about my dawn ride in the canoe and finding myself sitting in the midst of this swirling mass of energy, as though the universe joined in my happiness and confirmed the decision I'd made.

But you were in no shape to listen. For a while you stood near the sink, downing glass after glass of water, smoking and looking confused. All I told you was that I'd made my decision. You suggested we cook something while I'd tell you what it was, although you said you had an inkling.

I might have had trouble standing up that morning, but I could perfectly recall this part.

"What's your guess?" Christian had asked.

I'd looked at him, feeling unsteady like a raft set loose in an irate sea. "You've got to kill the bastard, old pal," I heard my grating morning voice say. I'd gulped down more water, then told him how worried I'd be if he'd made a different decision…worried about his life and Claudia's and the kids'.

I'm not sure you were in any state to notice, Jake, but when you told me I had to kill David—and why—I loved you. More than ever before. I tried to understand your thoughts, but then gave up, sensing that what was going on inside you wasn't of the mind.

You made it very easy for me, saying you understood I couldn't go and kill him myself. I needed help for several reasons, you explained, and in doing so you sounded as logical as I usually do. First, I wasn't experienced in the art of killing…I might fuck up and get caught. Second, there was the need for an alibi—Claudia and I should be far away from the scene. And third, I didn't want to walk around the rest of my life recalling the guy's corpse and his defunct eyes staring up at me…something like that.

Then you said you knew I was too loyal to bring up the subject again—so, yes, you'd find out who did this kind of thing well and you'd make the phone call. I didn't know what to say then, but I'm sure you remember what I did. I lifted my arms, pulled you toward me and enveloped you in a long, loving hug. Your cigarette fell on the floor. We stood like that for a while.

I never got to tell you what my decision was. It was to let things go until David escalated the battle by one more notch. If he didn't, I wasn't going to do anything. If he did, I'd put the next task, getting me in touch with the mob, into your hands. I was looking for a sign. I was surprised that it hadn't taken more to make me feel better. I guess just moving the agenda ahead had restored my old self.

When I got back to the city I had my sign. As I mentioned to you on the phone, the bastard had raised the ante to include the kids, and Claudia had tried to reason with David, much the way I had. So now there's no turning back.

I have no idea how you plan to go about the task of finding a killer and I'm not entirely sure whether you know yourself. And that is why I'd like you to reconsider. Yes, part of me feels I have a better chance with you at my side, but there is another part, which would rejoice if you changed your mind.

Remember, Jake, this is my battle. A battle I took upon myself by linking myself to Claudia. There is nothing shameful in withdrawing your offer. On the contrary, staying the course and being part of this hapless enterprise may endanger your life and ruin your profession and challenge everything you believe in.

You may think me foolish putting this in writing, but that is this letter's purpose. I'm not risking more than you've already risked by listening to my musings about doing away with David. This letter, then, shall be proof positive that killing David Talbot was my idea and mine alone. It shall be something that will always force me to be true to the spirit of our friendship—no matter what lies ahead.

You have been my friend forever and a better friend no one could wish for. Hence, Jake, true to our friendship, keep this letter locked away. But despite our friendship, keep it!

I read the last few sentences again and again. My eyes strained against the light of the setting sun, but I knew that wasn't why they filled with tears. Christian's friendship had been a constant in my life and now its boundaries had been transcended once again.

Whether 'tis nobler in the mind to suffer
The slings and arrows of outrageous fortune,
Or to take arms against a sea of troubles,
And by opposing end them?

SHAKESPEARE

PART 3

Christian wanted to lift David's listless body over the side of the boat, but in the dark he had a hard time finding the ropes that held the heavy tarp together. His hands kept slipping on the wet vinyl. Everything was soaking.

At least the bastard is still out cold, he thought. He hoped to get David up to the cottage before he regained consciousness. He wanted him nicely tied up before he came to. The less struggle, the better.

The rain came down in thick sheets and there was lightning in the distance. Christian had noticed that the storm was coming toward his island. The sporadic cracks of thunder were getting louder.

Finally, he could feel one of the ropes. He pulled and managed to get David's legs over the side of the boat onto the dock. He was out of breath.

Streaks of lightning lit up the boat and, for an instant, the glistening black tarp turned silver. Christian had cursed the weather but now he saw the advantage. Maybe he wouldn't need a light. He thought about the next step and decided he didn't have the strength to lift up the rest of David's body, which was still slumped inside the boat.

He opened the hatch where he had a few spare mooring lines. He'd tie one around David's knees and another around the top somewhere near David's shoulders, and then get onto the dock and pull from above.

When he stepped onto the slippery planks, he almost fell. He cursed. His first tug was a good one. He was surprised at how much leverage he had. He waited for a few seconds, breathing hard, then tugged again. This time, the rope slipped to where David's neck must be. For a second, Christian wondered whether the pressure would interfere with David's breathing. Then he dismissed the thought: if he hadn't suffocated already, he'd survive this too.

When the tarp was sprawled across the dock, Christian knelt down to fix the ropes. A burst of lighting lit up David's face under him. Christian jumped back at his adversary's sickeningly white face. The night was pitch-dark again when his panic subsided, but etched into his mind were David's eyes: focused and following his every move, sizzling with black hatred.

Streaks of mud and water marked the path to the spot where Christian had placed the chair. David was alive and relatively unscathed, although he must have found it difficult to breathe. The shrink-wrap may have been stretched too tightly. David's cheeks formed a hollow, as if he was sucking them in. The eye sockets above and the jaw line below were bulging out prominently.

The mooring lines had helped a lot in getting the bastard up the hill and the cottage stairs. And now he could use them to tie him to the chair.

David's hands were already tied behind his back. For that Christian had chosen shrink wrap, too. It was tough as rope and would leave fewer marks. He'd also taken a length of wrap and tied it over the fingers of each hand. That would constrain him even further. Only one thing was left before he could get to the real job:

to tie David to the captain's chair, into which he'd sat him.

Outside, ear-splitting thunderclaps followed each series of flashes. Rain pounding the roof reverberated through the small cabin.

Christian used one line to fasten David's waist to the seat and looped the other around David's neck, down the back of the chair and around his tied wrists.

He carefully cut through the shrink-wrap that covered David's mouth. He used his crude kitchen scissors and selected the spot where the skin was least likely to break, right behind the jaw-line, under David's right ear. The wrap came off easily.

"What the fuck did you do to me?" was the first thing David said. His words sounded surprisingly flat, but his eyes were like frantic embers.

"I drugged you with chloroform. I'm surprised that you don't know that, given you're a medical professional. Now we're on an island somewhere in Georgian Bay, which, as you might know, is part of Lake Huron. That means you can scream and rant all you want. No one will hear you. You can escape and run along the shore in a circle until you collapse, but I don't think you want to do that tonight. Too wet out there…the bugs would eat you alive."

"You fucking bastard!" David snapped.

"Ah, I almost forgot—the ground rules! Your captivity here will be a test of your manners. Every now and then I'll stop talking and you'll be able to say something, but if it's a profanity or if it's not factual—based on what *I* know—I'll use this." Christian held out what looked like a spray can with a funnel on top. "It's an air-powered foghorn, available in marine stores the world over and kept on sailing boats in case of emergency. Push the button at the top and that funnel lets loose a blast that'll keep your ear ringing for hours. Come to think of it, you might lose your hearing alto-gether, because I'll make sure I'll hold it really close to the side of your head. So, as you can see, it may be better if you just listen. But

. . . .

if you feel like talking, please do—just think about what you want to say before you open your mouth."

This time, David stayed silent, but he had to hold himself back.

Christian left the room and came back with a couple of folded newspapers. He kneeled down in front of the fireplace and started tearing out pages, then crunched them up and stuffed them into the cast iron enclosure. Next, he took pieces of kindling and arranged them in a criss-cross pattern over the paper.

"In case you're wondering what I'm doing…I've decided to make a fire to warm us up. It's a cool night out there…perfect for it. Oh, wait a minute, *you* may not be chilled. I almost forgot, you've been stewing inside a tarp for the past several hours, haven't you? Still, it wouldn't be fair if I deprived myself of a warm fire. I usually sit back and watch the flames when I come inside and, after an hour or so, I feel nice and cozy."

Christian placed four thin logs over the top of his creation. He arranged them in the form of a pyramid, their tops touching. Then he lit a match and the paper caught.

"Of course, where *you're* sitting, it will be toasty right from the beginning. You see, your chair's position is calculated for maximum effect. Within fifteen minutes, you'll be unbearably hot, but you're just far enough from the flames that your clothes won't catch fire."

"You dirty fucker!" David shouted.

"Apart from being repetitive, you're testing me, David. And you shouldn't." Christian got the foghorn from the table and gave it a deafening blast. It was far louder than he expected. "The next time you say the wrong thing it'll go in your ear," he said. "Last warning."

They looked at each other. Christian with an air of distant amusement; David's face distorted by rage. At that moment, everything turned white and thunder rocked the cottage. David's face stayed illuminated for several seconds, as if a long series of flash strobes had been activated.

"David, you have sinned—to say the least. You've hurt others, unnecessarily and repeatedly. Your wife, your children, me. And after Claudia decided to leave you, you tried to interfere with her potential. First through intimidation and when that didn't work, you resorted to violence. That, David, contradicts my morality code." Christian was crouching in front of David, looking up at him from below.

"Who gave you the idea that I'd hurt Claudia?" David asked.

"That's a legitimate, but utterly stupid question. Your hired mobsters did and when I confronted you at your clinic you had every chance to disassociate yourself…remember? Then you blew it a second time when Claudia came by. Tonight you will face the consequences of your actions. You will suffer, David, as you've never suffered. Like the old testament tells it, you'll be bound with chains and imprisoned. All your deeds shall vanish from before the face of the earth and thenceforth nothing that is corruptible shall be found. Don't think that I'm religious, David, but at moments like this I think I understand the Bible well. What it says is that vermin like you will always be wiped out. Not because there is a God, but because there is justice. Push the envelope too far, as you just have, and someone like me will come along and do what's necessary."

Christian's voice had become louder and his speech more solemn during these last sentences, as if he were reading to a congregation from a sacred text.

"Now, one of the first things I want to do is to tell you a few things about purgatory and hell. Hot places, both. Places with unquenchable flames. And while I talk about them, let me move behind you, so that you can experience the full thermal effect of a fire in July."

Christian got up, studied the pile of firewood stacked against the wall and took two large pine logs, which he added to the now lively flames. He pulled a chair from the dining room table and placed it directly behind David's. A few small embers shot out from the fire and one settled on David's legs, slowly burning their way through the fabric of his mud-stained chinos.

David screamed. "You're sick…you're fucking insane!"

Christian picked up the foghorn and placed the funnel almost directly over David's right ear. "I beg your pardon?" he said, as if hoping that David might apologize.

"I'm just stating a fact, you sick fuck! You push that thing and Claudia will be in a wheelchair!"

Christian pushed the button. The intensity of the noise hurt his own ears and he could see David's face contort.

"I don't think your hearing will ever return to normal, David, but you had fair warning. It's a free world and you've made your first decision. You'll find all your actions here have immediate consequences."

Tears ran down David's cheeks, but the fire in his eyes held its intensity. He attempted to spit at Christian, but all that came out was a dry retching sound.

"You want another blast?" Christian picked up the foghorn again, then hesitated. There was too much he still wanted to say and David had to be able to hear him. He placed the horn against David's already damaged ear and gave it another short blast.

David's body tensed and a gagging sound came from his throat. Then, heavy sobs started shaking his body and the chair to which he was tied.

Christian placed himself behind David. "If we could return to the subject of purgatory, please. As you notice, I'm talking into your good ear, so that you can hear me. And I'm speaking more loudly, so that I can get through the ringing that will now be with you permanently."

David heaved and a trickle of green vomit dribbled down his chin. The stink of bile hit Christian's nostrils. David looked exhausted, his forehead covered with sweat.

I can't let the bastard pass out, Christian thought. *I still need his attention!* He walked over to the kitchen, where he soaked a dishrag.

Then he washed David's forehead and wiped the greenish trickle off his chin. "By now, you haven't had any liquid for well over six hours and if you drink water, the effect of what I've planned will be lost. I first want to see you shrivel up like one of those sun-dried tomatoes, David. And by the time you'll ask me to kill you, your tongue will feel like it's the size of a mango."

Christian was back on his chair, behind David's, and his voice was steady, without emotion. He was an instrument of fate, an agent of justice, here to mete out punishment.

"Let me tell you about purgatory, David, a place where you go if you've committed grave sins, but from which you can rise again after suffering. The concept was first introduced by Plato." He stepped in front of David, taking his chin firmly into his hand. His voice was wrathful now. "Now look at me, David, and tell me: Would you be sent to purgatory to rise again? Or would you roast in hell forever? Plato thought you'd get out if you did evil in moments of passion, but then spent the remainder of your life in repentance. I don't think that's you, David, is it?"

Christian wondered where his recollection of Plato had come from. It had been ages since his university days. But his words were not ones to be argued with.

"So there you are. According to Plato, you're out of luck...destined to burn forever. Now, luckily for you, the relativity of time doesn't make it necessary for your torments to be eternal. Your next few hours will be filled with such anguish that they'll feel like millennia to you. You'll pray for death and eventually you'll communicate it to me and that's when I'll oblige you."

David had closed his eyes and his jaw hung slackly. The ferocious heat from the fireplace had completely dried his brow. When Christian lightly slapped David's face, he realized that his victim was unconscious.

Dammit, he's slipping away from me! Christian was supposed to be in control of David's destiny, and yet David kept setting the agenda. *How the fuck can I continue with the guy half-dead?*

He went to the tool shed to pick up his Makita contractor's drill in its pretty turquoise metal case. He loved that case.

Back in the cottage, he opened it and took out the first of eight ultra-thin drill bits. He held it and watched a flash of lightning bring it to life. For a fraction of a second, the gleaming white bit turned into something much larger, a symbol of force and dominance. Christian inserted it into the drill's shaft.

He crouched down in front of David, his back now very close to the roaring fire. The heat was almost unbearable. Still, he had to finish the job.

Christian gripped David's right foot firmly and held the tip of the drill bit over the hollow between the big toe and the one next to it. Then he squeezed the trigger. It cut through the flesh in less than a second, but then hit the floorboard underneath; there was a noticeable change in the drill's whine. He drove the bit about half an inch into the pine floor and then took the chuck key and separated the bit sticking out of David's foot from the drill.

Blood welled up around the drill bit, but much less than Christian had anticipated. It was dark and ran in a tiny trickle down the pale hollow between the two toes. He took hold of David's left foot and repeated the procedure. A few times, he looked up at David's face.

In the kitchen, he ran the tap until the spring water felt ice cold and half filled a large mug. Then he walked back to David's chair and threw the contents at his face. David opened his eyes, looking exhausted and confused. And then he let out a deafening roar. Obviously he'd moved his feet.

"Look, David, I suggest you sit very still. I've taken the liberty of driving a drill bit through your feet. Any movement will cause you a lot of pain. Now, I know you're totally dehydrated and so I'll go and fill another mug. I'll let you drink a couple of sips. Not enough to reverse your condition, but enough to keep you awake for a while."

Christian came back with water and held it to David's lips. David pushed his chin against the rim of the mug. Then he stared at Christian, his face a mask of loathing. He spat the liquid left in his mouth at Christian. "You're insane".

Christian considered getting the foghorn, but instead returned to his tools. He grabbed another drill bit, holding it up so David could see it.

"You have a bit like this in each of your feet. In the hollow right next to your big toe. But I bought eight such bits…four for each foot. The hollows are ideal spots for drilling, because I don't have to perforate any bones. That's if you're nice and quiet, of course. If you aren't, chances are I'll hit one of those fine bones and then you'll be in much greater pain. Do you understand that?"

He looked up at David but what he saw was not what he'd expected. This was where David's brain was supposed to register that he was going to die here. Instead, David's face expressed contempt and determination. Christian's unease turned into anxiety. He had to get back to the script and the best way to do that was to continue his speech.

"Now, I want you to think about the people you've hurt, you swine. Think about Claudia. About turning on your charm, gradually diminishing the caution in her, to the point where she thinks maybe it's all her fault and opens herself up a bit. Then, and no sooner, you take a few jabs at her, making her feel a bit stupid, in front of others. Afterwards, the charm again, always keeping her off balance and then, unexpectedly, your tirades over nothing. No stopping before she's shrinking away, utterly devastated…before she's smashed to a mere shadow of herself. And then you feel badly. You have to prove to the kids and yourself that you're really quite a generous guy, so now you roll out the presents. Roses, jewelry…whatever trinkets you think might do the trick and confuse your victims all over again."

Christian was bathed in sweat. The fire behind him had died down a bit, but the room was extremely hot. Outside, the rain had stopped and silence fell whenever Christian stopped talking.

Then David's voice, completely parched: "You'll regret this... I'll cripple her..."

Christian ignored him and grabbed David's right foot.

"I'll now place another two bits, David, one in each foot. This time I'll drill on the outside, next to your little toes. It's going to be a bit trickier. A lot less flesh there and the bone structure much tighter. Think about what you did to Claudia, David...think about your cowardly, manipulative ways with Claudia."

David managed to keep still as the first bit pushed through to the floorboard. When the drill penetrated the left foot, however, David uttered a rasping cry.

"Oops, we've nicked the bone, haven't we," Christian said. "Don't want to do that too often, do we?"

Christian drilled two more sets. Before the first, he reminded David of what a lousy father he'd been to Karen and Jason. And before the second, he talked about what a poor idea it had been for David to want to kill him.

David stayed awake, his face ashen, his eyes possessed by fervent energy. Christian turned to get four sturdy logs and placed them on the fire.

He was frustrated. He'd expected his victim to repent and then beg for his death. Or at least for his life. Instead, David had stayed triumphantly obstinate. He'd thought through David's torture in every detail, yet nothing had so far worked out as planned.

"You're dead..." he heard David say, his words barely audible.

Then the room turned white again, but no thunder followed this time. *The storm must be moving away.* Christian started to count to see how far; he figured there would be a five, six second delay. But he kept on counting and nothing happened. And as he counted, he woke up.

. . . .

*Shit, this whole thing's been nothing but a dream....*He tossed restlessly, noticing that his sheets were clammy. He was hot and wondered why. It had rained for hours and he could feel the cool air coming through the window. *The damned fire...that's why I'm hot.* In the twilight zone between imagination and actuality, he reasoned that he wanted the dream to continue. *I've got to get the bastard where I want him...I'll have to get back into it.* He wanted to be there when David died.

He was fast asleep again. But now the dream moved away from him. Christian persuaded himself that David had escaped and when he checked, his fears were confirmed. Only the empty, turned over captain's chair and a tangle of ropes and crumpled shrink-wrap were left.

God, what a fucking mess! By now David would have swum across to a nearby island and, soaked and bloodied, woken up a neighbor. The police would arrive soon, to pick him up. There was no point in even removing the evidence. David was the bloody evidence and he was gone! He could imagine how Claudia, Karen and Jason would feel about what he'd done. He'd betrayed them!

Christian felt drained. For once, he decided to skip his morning canoe ride and instead made himself a pot of strong coffee.

While he watched the boiling water percolate through the grinds, he tried to make sense of his dream. *What kind of a mind comes up with a dream like this?* The violence he'd experienced—and his enjoyment of it—bothered him.

He marveled how he could have pictured David, whom he had met only once, in such vivid detail. And where had the idea of drilling through the guy's feet come from? He tried to remember whether he'd actually enjoyed torturing David. He remembered waking up and wanting the dream to continue. To David's repentance and pleas for his death. And when David had escaped, he'd been upset.

Maybe this was how a healthy mind dealt with his kind of dilemma. After all, there was every chance that David had ordered him maimed or killed. He and Claudia had feared David's actions for weeks now, so wasn't some kind of retribution sensible? Not only sensible, Christian reasoned—just!

Jake had phoned last night to say he'd arranged a meeting for him. Perhaps that had brought it on. *In four days, I'll place my destiny in some stranger's hands. In the hands of a criminal, no less!* On top of it all, Jake had suggested that he, Christian, think of an appropriate meeting place.

Fragments of his new reality drifted through his mind. The need to make sure that the actual events would differ from his night-time fantasy. David would die, to be sure, but swiftly, without fuss and torture. He'd have to arrange to be far away somewhere, just as David would be distant from the scene of his and perhaps Claudia's death.

Christian poured the first bit of coffee into a cold cup and swirled it around; he hated it when his tongue got scalded. He held his nose above the steaming brew and took a deep breath. He felt better. The specter of his dream started to recede and the world seemed a bit less troubling.

But the problem with David hadn't been solved yet. Claudia and he were still very much in danger.

It was Tuesday night and Christian sat on the porch of his cabin. His day had followed no particular pattern; he liked his summer that way.

After his morning canoe ride and swim, he'd cooked himself a hearty breakfast. Then he'd attended to some paper work, before spending the afternoon browsing through the books he'd brought from the city. They dealt with sculpting techniques—a topic which had fascinated him for years and which he now had the time to pursue.

Days on his island were a combination of the creative and the mundane, of mental pursuits and physical exertion. And dominating everything was nature, which embodied these elements. Relentless in its purpose, it encroached on his space—gradually and stealthily at first, but eventually building up to a finale so dramatic as to discourage even the most determined dweller. Like the time the beavers had singled out his property and two trees had crashed on the roof. Or when termites had eaten away the inside of the beams holding up his porch.

Nature had to be kept at bay; no matter how much time he devoted to it, it was never enough. Its march continued without pause, each species driven on by its instinct to survive.

The first few years he'd owned the cottage, Christian had struggled with the conflict between coexisting with nature and fighting it. In the end, there was no conflict. All that mattered was how much space he needed. Was it an envelope of thirty, fifty or a hundred feet around the cottage that he wanted to declare as his territory and defend? He'd decided on fifty. Everything within that perimeter, he battled.

The sun was descending into Georgian Bay and nature preparing for night. Small fish were jumping to snatch their evening meal of insects. Another half hour and the tree frogs would start their soothing chorus and, soon after that, Christian would see the first fireflies.

Some nights he watched them for hours. By turning their flares on and off and following complicated flight patterns, they could pop up several feet away from where you would have expected them. Only five or six of them were needed to create the illusion that there were dozens. Christian's field guide referred to them as *Photinus Pyralis* and explained that they blinked their yellow light organs to attract mates. It also said that fireflies didn't eat during their entire adult life. They lived for one purpose only: to procreate. Each day was spent waiting for the night, when they turned on their splendid beacons to signal their intentions.

The half-hour boat ride to Parry Sound took Christian past an array of familiar red and green buoys marking the many rocks and shoals along the way. His eyes swept the hazy horizon, where dozens of islands were blending into a deceptive, mushy-green shoreline. The water was choppy. Its color, an hour ago a rich summer-blue, was now a portentous grey. All morning, the temperature had been rising and moisture building up. These weren't good signs. Within another two hours Georgian Bay would turn into a vicious cauldron.

Christian's mind didn't dwell on any of this, but it registered all. He felt relieved that he'd miss the storm, but he was restless and preoccupied with his upcoming meeting.

The highway, as always on Wednesday mornings, was virtually deserted. It would be different past Barrie, but this far north there were only few vehicles, most of them trucks carrying loads of wood and building materials from Sudbury or even Thunder Bay to Toronto. Christian set his cruise control.

Tonight he would see Jake and tomorrow the hit-man. Christian doubted whether Jake's contact would deal with David himself, but he couldn't think of a better label.

He would not tell Claudia about the meeting. She knew that he'd be at Jake's tonight and that it would get too late to come to her place. Tomorrow, he had explained, he'd have to go to Global Capital and on Friday, they'd get ready to go to the cottage, this time with Jason and Karen.

The past days had been extraordinary. His dream, the night of sleepwalking, his dawn canoe ride, and finally his decision…a decision he would never have believed possible and which he felt was out of step with everything he'd ever stood for.

If, a year ago, he'd heard about anyone planning to take a life, he would have been appalled. And if someone had told him that he would one day contemplate murder, he would have thought the idea outlandish. Yet here he was, planning to kill, without a shred of hesitation. It had occurred to him that guilt rarely preceded the act, but usually followed it. But, even so, he could simply not imagine that this would be the case with him.

How should he communicate his plan to Claudia? If he waited, she'd feel betrayed. Yet if she knew before they left for the cottage, she'd be worried out of her mind.

As to doing away with David, he felt that he was on the right track. Not acting was as perilous a course as the one he'd chosen.

And this way, at least, it was Christian who'd be sitting at the controls and not David.

Perversely, like David, he was resolved to carry to its conclusion what he had begun. He could only hope that David didn't realize this.

Christian was now approaching Barrie. Toronto was less than an hour away and Christian hoped to be home around one. He could catch up with his mail and read a bit before heading out to meet with Jake.

Jake and Tila, he reflected. *If it weren't for them, this would be even more difficult. How generous of Tila not to ask a single question!*

A̲t Global Capital, Christian had been Tila von Hasse's champion and she his star. He'd first met her on a business trip to Montreal, where she'd worked for a German bank since leaving university.

Tila was prim, carrying her German ancestry like a shield, but she worked harder than anyone in the firm. Convinced that she had enormous potential, Christian started teaching her the art of restructuring companies. They soon worked as equals.

After three years, he shifted her training to another area. He'd started toying with the idea of leaving the financial industry and decided that Tila should be his successor. He'd quietly groom her to become a senior executive.

Not that Tila was in need of improving her manners or her appearance. If anything, she was in a class above that of most of the firm's executives, which gave her the image of being haughty and arrogant. Christian wasn't worried; as the others got to know her better, they'd revise their judgment.

Tila's greatest challenge was cultural. Where she'd come from, inquiring into others' affairs, calling them by their first names or openly discussing their compensation or even their failures had been unthinkable.

Christian began to critique Tila once a week. At first, she did-n't like it, but after a while they had fun together. Gradually, Tila's personality changed. Those who'd viewed her as inhibited or cold noticed that she went out of her way to be friendly and accessible. Some of the male executives took her new style the wrong way and saw it as a sexual overture, and more than once Tila had to ask Christian for advice.

Christian also pressed her to rely more fully on her intuition. He knew how women could judge situations far more accurately. In creative areas, like the one in which they operated, they had a huge advantage. But Tila had been brought up in a logical world.

Christian taught her that the best solutions in corporate reor-ganizations resulted when there was a confluence of reason and intuition. You could prepare yourself for a meeting only to a point. Once you sat opposite others, whose objectives were different from yours, you had to let your intuition take over.

In time, Tila became a person to watch. Few of her colleagues knew her well, but they all knew that she was among the firm's highest paid specialists and they sensed Christian's support. Five years after joining the firm, Tila was made a member of its Executive Committee. This had never happened to someone 32 years old, let alone to a woman.

Christian eased his car into the midday traffic of Yonge Street. Bicycles darted between cars. Drivers honked nervously. Pedes-trians crossed the road, weaving their way between the slowly mov-ing traffic. He started to feel anxious. Tomorrow he'd meet with the hit-man.

Good afternoon. You must be Mr. Unger."

The receptionist exuded the quiet confidence that had become the hallmark of Global Capital's front-line staff. Christian thought of Tila, who had brought this image to the company and had made Global Capital's operation so seductively professional.

"I don't believe we've met."

"We all know who you are…I'm Janice Broadbent. Anything you need, please let me know."

Christian hadn't expected this and wasn't sure he liked it. It meant that Tila had put everyone on high alert.

"Thank you, Janice. As you know, I'm here to use a meeting room."

"Ms. von Hasse thought you'd like the Blue Room. It's all ready for you. I've arranged for beverages and snacks; please tell me if you need anything else."

Others might have had the distinct feeling that they could ask Janice for anything their heart desired, during office hours or after. But Christian was fully conversant with the ways of the corporate world. Employees like Janice were paid well, precisely because they had the ability to make everyone feel as though the world was theirs and, at the same time, were skilled at extricating themselves if someone misunderstood.

The Blue Room had obviously been named after its art. There were two oils by Christopher Pratt, most of the tones cold as gun metal, one abstract piece that Christian couldn't identify, and a collage by Stephanie Rayner, in blues and greens so vibrant they bordered on iridescence.

Christian reflected on how much of his career had been shaped here. Before Global Capital had taken over the building's top floor, this room had been used for meetings of the board of directors and its various committees. This was where, time after time, he'd presented his latest corporate conquests, first as a one-man team, then, as his department grew into a major profit center, with Tila. Gordon McAllister, the firm's imperious and much-feared chairman, had anointed him his heir-apparent here, and, later, this was where Tila had made her breakthrough presentation.

He contemplated the faces around the table and recalled the voices: the chairman's booming with confidence and Tila's factual and composed.

Her discourse was hesitant, at first, but then she found her stride. Tila did what Christian had practiced with her: she let her intuition take over. Doing so allowed her to calm down, something none of her colleagues had yet achieved when challenged by their chairman. McAllister didn't like it; he interrupted her discourse with lines like "Are you wasting our time, Miss von Hasse?" or "Are you sure you know what you're talking about?"

Each time he did so, Tila calmly returned to the precise point where she'd left off. "As I was saying, Gordon..."

This was the part that had always been hardest for Tila, yet she was passing the most rigorous test with apparent ease. While McAllister called her Miss von Hasse, she called him Gordon and looked him straight in the eye. Christian knew how uncomfortable she felt calling others by their first name, even after several years at the firm. He remembered their coaching sessions together. *Whenever you can, use their first name and look straight at them. It puts you in charge of the conversation and, at the same time, it makes them feel good. Everyone likes being called by their name.*

As the meeting took its course, the expressions changed. The smirks on the faces of Tila's colleagues gave way to surprise, then respect.

The meeting ended when McAllister, his theatrical style now completely gone and his bearing pensive, told Tila that she obviously had a better handle on things than her colleagues did.

And then, the following week, the ultimate gesture: McAllister's gallant bow in Tila's direction and his generous remark to the assembled executives. "Let us never again doubt that young Tila von Hasse is one of those rare individuals to whom the less gifted among us refer as geniuses." Christian smiled, recalling the deep blush on Tila's face.

Gordon McAllister wasn't a man who frequently changed his views. From here on she'd command his respect and admiration, unless she made a huge blunder. And she'd be feared by everyone else.

There was little doubt: Tila would eventually take over McAllister's job.

Christian watched two small planes coming in, heading for the island airport. He was fascinated at how far below him they circled and how tiny they appeared. A ferry, jam-packed with tourists and people who'd taken the day off, shuttled across the water. Then he remembered the door behind him, through which the thug would come, and turned. *Shit! What if he records our conversation?*

Your guest is here, Mr. Unger."

Christian noticed two things about the tall man in the navy suit. What immediately put him at ease was that he looked so much like a banker that no one in the building would have noticed him. The other thing was that Jake had been right: he'd met this man before, although he couldn't remember where.

"Martin O'Shea." His eyes locked onto Christian's. "It's good to see you again after so many years." He held out his hand. "You can't remember where we met."

"So we did meet…," Christian said sheepishly.

"You were a manager at that Exchange Bank, remember?" There was an unmistakable Irish lilt.

"That *is* a long time ago…." Christian recalled Jake asking if he could see one of his firm's clients. Jake had emphasized his contact would need to remain unidentified, not an unusual request in Christian's business.

Jake's acquaintance had been on a learning mission. He'd asked Christian how to open an account with the bank's Geneva office, how to deposit funds there without causing a paper trail and how, if the need ever arose, funds could be repatriated. Christian remembered being impressed by his visitor; because Jake had sent him, he'd pegged him as a union boss or a high-ranking government official. Now he knew better.

"You helped me quite a bit in those days," O'Shea said jovially. "I hope I can be of help today."

Thank God the ice is broken! But how on earth am I going to bring up David?

"Using this place is an excellent decision," O'Shea said unhurriedly.

Christian was grateful for the opening. "Look, this was not easy for me. I was worried what you'd look like, whether you'd be followed, or whether you'd blackmail me a month from now." His words made him realize just how well he was adapting to the situation, and he felt appalled and relieved at the same time. "Thank God it's you, Martin."

"Not all of us wear black shirts and loud ties and have a finger missing," O'Shea chuckled, his perfect teeth showing. He had the easy good looks of the movie stars of the fifties and sixties. Not the mob types, but the good guys.

"And you're not even Italian…"

O'Shea laughed. "The Italians are the fastest shrinking part. Anyway, Christian, this is a good place to meet. You have influence here and that's a guarantee that our conversation will not go anywhere. Even if I was followed to this building, no one could know which floor I went to. Office buildings are such a convenience."

"How do you mean?"

"It's easy to shake people in these towers. All you need to do is change elevators a few times…"

"That's a relief. Martin, what has Jake Sullivan told you about my situation?"

"He didn't say much. He told me you had family problems. Someone was harassing you and you were worried about getting hurt. And did I know someone who could meet with you."

"I suppose I'm lucky to have you on my case. I don't mean this cynically…" Christian wondered what organization O'Shea belonged to and what Jake's dealings with it were. "I'm sure you don't generally meet with people who feel threatened and want professional help."

"Once I knew it was you, curiosity overcame me. But, no, I don't usually get involved in this type of thing. Where family is involved, we try to stay away. Too dicey."

"I'm sorry I don't understand the reference to family."

"You see, with all the different tribes who come together in our business there are a lot of cultural differences. But on some things we agree and family is one of them. No one will hurt a family." He held out a pack of *Players*. Christian declined. Then O'Shea produced an expensive lighter, lit up and inhaled.

"I still don't quite understand, Martin."

"Right." O'Shea's voice sounded harder. "You see, we don't generally get involved in family disputes. Someone might have been badly cheated by a business associate, that's another thing. But we won't help a husband do away with his wife, or the other way around. Especially if there are children."

Why on earth are you here then? Christian had pulled a pen from his pocket and his thumb clicked while he talked, making the tip extend and recede. All he could think of saying was: "I'm sure there's a reason for it."

"You have no idea how many wives would like their straying husbands shaken up. And before you know it, they're more in love than ever."

"Look, the lady I hope to marry and I are not the ones trying to break up the family. Her ex-husband is." Christian told his story.

O'Shea pulled a small black leather diary from his jacket and started taking notes. Christian noticed his visitor's fine hands: long fingers, perfectly kept nails.

When Christian finished, O'Shea kept scribbling for a while.

Then he said, "The guy who roughed you up sounds professional."

"Yeah, I think you're right. He acted as though he did this kind of thing two or three times a day."

"He's in it for the love of it."

"Do you know who he might be working for?"

"There are dozens of outfits. If we had a picture I could show it around."

"I guess my descriptions are useless. What about the accents, though?"

"If they're Southern European they probably work for the Italians. But at the lower level everything goes. You get Portuguese guys doing protection for the Italians, or Serbs handling a shake-up job for an Israeli loan shark. It's not like the old days."

"Is the car information valuable?"

"We'll find out whose it is…probably within a day. Tell me the license number."

"Let's see…Ontario AWS 222," Christian read from a piece of paper. "A black Mustang. There wasn't anything special about it. You know, no spoilers or special wheels and stuff. Although I only saw the car from the back." Christian looked up at O'Shea. "One thing I want to stress, Martin, is that I'm not trying to uproot a family…I'm trying to keep one together and alive!"

"I can see that. But that other guy, David, probably thinks of himself as the victim." O'Shea lit another cigarette, his eyes squinting through the haze. "I'm just making sure you've thought about the other side."

"Jesus, I've done more than that. I asked the guy to lay off and all he said was that he'd carry it through to the end. And Claudia got the same response!"

O'Shea threw up his hands.

Christian bit his lower lip. "Is this a polite way of telling me you won't even consider the job?"

"Let me try to find out who these guys are and then we'll

understand the situation better." O'Shea leaned forward on his elbows and looked straight at Christian. Smoke wafted in Christian's face. "Look, in banking you don't get a loan commitment until it's been discussed by some committee, right? It's the same in our industry. I'll argue your cause, but I can't make promises. We can cover you until we've done our homework. It'll take three or four days, maximum. And there won't be any charge, unless we go to the next level." The merest hint of a smile crossed O'Shea's face.

Christian felt better. He decided to pursue his agenda. "Martin, let's assume there are no problems from your side in taking this on. Where do we go from there?"

"That would depend on your mandate."

"Well, I'm sure you know what I'd like done, don't you?"

"You'd like him iced. But surely there are things you'd like us to consider. Timing, for example. Or whether you want an accident or a simple hit?" O'Shea sounded like an investment officer explaining different retirement plans.

"I must admit, Martin, I've never thought about that. But I guess it does matter."

"Right. You should give it some thought."

"Two things I do know. One is my new family and I won't be around if it isn't done soon. And two, there can't be any evidence that he was killed. It should be as if he's just gone missing."

"That helps."

"Can it be done, though?"

"Certainly, but planning is essential. It will take several weeks. And I should tell you that it's costly, although I think you're accustomed to thinking in big amounts." O'Shea looked completely at ease, sitting back in his chair as though he regularly spent the afternoon in this room.

"What are we talking about, Martin? Can you give me an indication?"

"I can, but I'll have to fine-tune when we next meet. The ballpark is a hundred and fifty."

Christian had expected more. "I had no idea it was all so structured."

"You should be glad it is. Improvisation doesn't work well in our trade." O'Shea smiled. "You're in good hands. And you once helped me, so I'll be doing what I can to help you now."

"Where do we go from here?"

"I need a few days. If you want to, we can meet here again. Otherwise I can come up with a place."

"Why don't I book a room for next week? Would Tuesday work for you?"

"Done. If we need to change it, I'll phone Jake and tell him to let you know. Before I leave, Christian…I need some details. Where you live, where the children go to school, where you plan to be, what cars you drive, and so on."

Christian explained their living arrangements. He also told him about their plans to be away at the cottage.

"Don't you worry about your family, Christian," O'Shea said as he stood up. "We'll have you covered until we meet again, at least at your city places. If you notice someone you're not used to, it's us. We'll be using some official looking vehicle. You'll think it's the police."

Karen gave Christian a big hug. "Mom's gone food shopping."

"And what are you up to, Karen?"

"There's this big project on Africa we have to do for summer school. Come and take a look." Karen showed him a map. "Everyone's got a different country to cover and I got Kenya.

Christian glanced at it. "Lucky you! There's lots to say about Kenya."

"I was hoping you'd know something. Do you think you could help me with it if I took it along to the cottage?"

"I'll be happy to, but do you think that's what your teacher has in mind?"

Karen smiled mischievously and said that all parents helped their children.

Christian didn't know whether she'd said "parents" to make him feel good, but he thought of it as a good sign. He looked forward to having the kids at the cottage. Maybe their week together would lessen the shock of him moving in, which he and Claudia had agreed would happen this summer.

The basement door opened and Christian could hear the TV in the background. Jason emerged. "Now she's got you doing her school projects for her, huh?"

"Hey, how about a hello first? And what's wrong with helping Karen?"

Jason poured himself some milk. "I know what's going on. She usually gets Mom to do her stuff, too."

"You liar," protested Karen. "And anyway, it's better than not doing anything at all—TV addict!"

"Okay, so I watch TV. But at least I don't get others to do my homework." He left before Karen could respond.

"That stupid idiot. He always has to be mean. I hate him!"

Christian could see that it would be difficult to stay impartial. Jason had mellowed, but he could still be difficult with his mother and downright monstrous toward his sister.

When Claudia came home, Karen and Christian were still sitting at the table, now engaged in a game of cards.

"All these school things on the table and the two of you playing cards?"

"That's for my summer course, Mom. Christian's helping me with my Africa project." Then she put down four kings and placed a card on the pile between them. Claudia kissed Karen on her head.

"Karen's turning into a real card shark. Take a look at the scores. If Rummy were a school subject she'd land straight A's…"

Karen giggled.

Christian waited until Jason placed the first piece of toast in the sizzling pan. They were cooking an enormous breakfast of French toast with sliced strawberries, scrambled eggs and sausage. The toast and berries were for Claudia and Karen; the eggs and meat for the men.

"Jason, I want to talk about last night…about your reaction to my helping Karen. You know I'm always willing to help *you* when you need something, right? Like passing on my most secret recipes, or teaching you the finer parts of skating? So from here on, no more of this jealousy crap, okay?"

Jason reddened, but took it well. "It's just that she annoys me so much, sucking up to everyone."

"Brothers and sisters always annoy each other. Try to make the best out of it."

"Do you have a sister?"

"No, but I grew up with a brother and we used to get into awful scrapes, just like you and Karen."

"Where's your brother now?"

"He died. His name was Jamie."

Jason looked uncomfortable. "He died, huh?"

"Along with my dad, in a brand new convertible." Christian poured himself some coffee. Jason's eyes were on the frying pan, but he wasn't missing a word.

"My dad was between jobs, so he suggested to my mom and Jamie that they should go on an extended holiday…take the railway across the Rockies to Vancouver, then fly to Los Angeles to visit my uncle Hannes. My dad would buy a Thunderbird there, then drive it back home. He had the whole route mapped out. Along the California coast to San Francisco, then inland to Nevada and across the desert to the Grand Canyon. From there they'd go through Colorado and back home through the Midwest. Do you know where all these places are?"

"I know about California and Death Valley and the Grand Canyon. We've had that in school. But I've never heard of the Midwest."

"That's that huge expanse between the Rocky Mountains and the East. Kansas, Missouri, Illinois—those states. Anyway, my brother Jamie loved the idea of going, but my mom didn't. So they left without her. Jamie wrote me a postcard from Flagstaff—that's where the Grand Canyon is. It was the first time he'd written to me. Two days later a truck slammed into them. I lived in London then and had left for a week's holiday in Scotland the same day it happened. When the news caught up with me, my dad and my brother were already buried."

Jason looked mortified. He held up a piece of French toast with a fork. "What do you think, is this okay?"

"It's perfect. Anyway, the point I was making wasn't just about brothers and sisters. Wherever people live and work close together, they annoy each other." Christian put his hand on Jason's shoulder. "You can try to tolerate it, or you can let it aggravate you. Think about how each of these responses makes you feel. If you tolerate, you feel that you've overcome a challenge and that makes you feel good about yourself. And if you let yourself be aggravated it ruins your day." Christian heard one of the upstairs doors open. "This is between us, okay?" He ribbed Jason with his elbow, which prompted a nod.

Karen appeared, inhaling the kitchen smells and declaring how famished she was.

"That's a good thing…there'll be nothing to eat till we're at the cottage. And I promise you, after tasting your brother's French toast, you'll be addicted."

Karen and Jason were city kids and there were things on Christian's island that they found difficult to accept. Both of them screamed when they first walked into the lake water and felt the sand under their feet turn into silty mush. The water's earthy smell and the presence of dragonflies skimming along its surface were other reasons for complaints.

By the middle of the week they relished being in nature. Karen spent hours in the canoe and quickly caught on to even the most difficult paddle strokes.

Jason loved being on the boat. Christian had realized he had to find something at which Jason could outshine Karen, and took him on the open water a few times. Jason learned what a protractor was, how to look at a map and plot a course and, with the help of the on-board compass, to scan the horizon for the next lighthouse, channel marker or island. Harmony was restored, at least between the two of them.

Christian and the kids were sitting at the table, the soft yellow light from the kerosene lamps reflecting off their sunburned faces.

"When did you bake that cake, Mom!" Jason asked.

"Your favorite, too…chocolate-raspberry," Claudia beamed. "I've been planning for your birthday dinner all day. I thought that after cake we could play poker, since you love it so much."

"Maybe I can show you some of those card tricks from the Hoyle book, too."

"Okay. The card tricks will warm us up for the cake and for poker."

Jason performed two card tricks. They were of the kind that didn't require dexterity but were merely mathematical riddles. He'd studied his book well and must have practiced at great length. Claudia praised him profusely and Karen asked whether he would teach her.

As they indulged in dessert, Christian made an announcement. "I think on the occasion of Jason's seventeenth, we should make him into a real gambler. I'll give everyone ten dollars' worth of chips. So someone will end up with forty bucks!" The kids hollered with delight, then speculated what they'd buy with the winnings.

Karen and Claudia were off to a roaring start. For well over an hour, they took turns producing full houses and flushes. Then Jason won a major bet, in which he took all of Christian's remaining chips. He kept on playing skillfully, gradually gaining back money from his mother and sister. At eleven, the three remaining players were more or less even.

Then Jason started taking unnecessary chances, until finally, in one reckless bet, he raised the ante until the last of his money was staked. He did all that on the strength of three kings. When Karen put down her hand, two tens and three aces, he lost his temper.

"How can you win? You can't even play properly, you half-wit."

Christian intervened. "Listen, Jason, you played and you lost. The reason you lost is because you took a huge chance and it didn't work out. Don't put down your sister now."

"You know she can't play…"

"If you'd played your last hand as skilfully as she, you'd be way ahead now. Don't be a sore loser now."

Tears were welling up in Jason's eyes. "Do you always have to take her side?"

"I'm not taking anyone's side. I'm interfering because you're taking out your frustration on your sister. What did she do to you? I tell you what: she won the game you wanted to play." Then he added in a more conciliatory tone: "You're not the only one who lost tonight, you know. I lost and your mom lost too."

"Mom? Not willingly, she didn't." Then he turned on Claudia. "All you ever wanted is to take my money away from me!"

Jason looked back at Christian as though he wanted to say something else. Instead, he jumped up and ran inside the cottage. Christian, Claudia and Karen sat for a while, listening to the sobs coming from his bedroom.

Claudia took a flashlight and they walked down to the edge of the water—Christian surefooted, Claudia probing the ground with each step. Once on the beach, Claudia switched the light off and they stood together, letting their eyes get accustomed to the night.

It was nearly moonless. The Milky Way seemed close enough to touch, arcing across the horizon like the edge of a colossal saucer.

Once in the canoe, they settled into an easy rhythm.

"I don't know how I'd cope without you," Claudia said. "You're so good for the kids…I think even Jason is coming along."

"Yeah, kicking and screaming. What do you think his problem is?"

"I know it's not Karen. His spats with her have gone on for years. What's new is that he's very resentful of me. At first, I thought it was some teenage thing…wanting to test the limits. But there's more to it. It's grown out of hand since David left. It's like he's resentful of me…"

"Because he misses his father?"

"I think. On the other hand, he wouldn't have you in his life if I hadn't done that. Obviously he likes you."

"Look Claudia, I don't think this is meant to be logical." Christian asked her to stop paddling and they gently drifted through the dark. "Perhaps you're just a lighting rod for all the upheaval in his life. His teen problems, your break-up, who knows what else. I doubt he even knows himself."

"How does that make things better?"

"It does, when you consider that you're the focus of his frustration, not the cause. He has no clue what the cause is, because teens simply aren't self-analytical. When things go wrong for them, they just resent."

She hit her paddle at the surface of the water, splashing him. "And what's to be done in a case like this, Professor Unger?"

"For starters, we mustn't tolerate his behavior. We have to make him understand that it's his duty to find out why he's upset. And if it has to do with us, he should talk about it. We have to impress on him that we're accessible."

"Wow…I can see things improving real fast," she teased.

"Let's try to talk to him. We can pretend that we don't know whether it's at Karen or you or me that his anger is directed."

"And you think I should be part of this? He'll clam up totally."

"I'm glad you're offering your non-involvement. I agree it's better if he and I are alone."

Christian steered them through the night, toward the uninhabited island. In the daytime, the crudely painted word BLISS could be seen on the rock face that rose behind the sandy lagoon cutting into its center. Now, there wasn't enough light to distinguish the tree tops of the island from the sky. Only when Claudia's paddle struck the sandy bottom did she realize that water was about to meet land.

"Is this the place where we made love that time?"

"Bliss Island," Christian confirmed.

They got out and settled down on the sand. For a while, they watched the stars, resting on their elbows and their heads tilted back. Then they shifted toward each other, their heads only inches apart and their lips touching every now and then.

Christian wanted to tell her about his meeting with O'Shea, but the setting was too perfect. Why ruin it now? This week was for holidays.

Claudia seemed to have read his mind. "What have you and Jake been up to, my love?"

"How do you mean?"

"I'm sure that the two of you have talked about what should be done…as far as David's concerned." She moved closer; let her head fall on his shoulder. "It must be on your mind twenty-four hours a day."

Christian struggled to keep his calm. Was this the time to tell her, after all? Or would he just burden her unnecessarily? At the very least, he should wait until he knew that O'Shea's organization was willing to proceed. He rolled onto his knees, facing her. "You know, I'm a bit afraid of this conversation."

"It doesn't need to be right now, my love." Claudia sensed his struggle. "It's just that I feel something's about to break."

"I'd never forgive myself if something happened to you or the kids." He was troubled by where this conversation might be going. While Claudia talked, his hands kept picking up sand and let trickles of it sift back onto the beach.

"Something has to be done. And yet, I'm not sure I could look the kids in the eyes if their father was hurt. Imagine the trauma."

Did she know something, or had she merely come to the same logical conclusion that he and Jake had arrived at? Christian got on his feet and Claudia followed. They walked a few steps until their feet were immersed in the shallow, warm water.

"There's got to be another way…some damned solution we haven't thought of," she continued. "You'll tell me Christian, won't you…before doing anything?"

His anxiety grew. He could not disappoint her again. He had to tell her soon.

Claudia put her arms around him and held him tightly. "I'm sorry. I know how unfair this is to you…all this shit because you got involved with me." He could feel her tears on his cheek. "If we could just stay up here, in this paradise. David would never find us." She sighed deeply and drew his mouth to hers and their tongues touched. "What will happen to us all, Christian? How will it end?" Claudia whispered, as she let herself slide down along his body.

"It'll be fine…all will be bliss, like it says on the rock over there…" Christian whispered back, as Claudia's mouth moved gently, first exploring the rigid muscles of his neck, then tasting the salt on his chest, caressing his stomach and probing his navel.

Christian went down on his knees and gently pushed Claudia onto her back. She moaned as the shallow water enveloped her and pulled him down. He felt her hand take him into her and thought he could see her lips part and her eyes lose focus. But that couldn't be. It was pitch-black night.

There can be no generalizations,
only one safe rule for the historian:
that he should recognize
in the development of human destinies
the play of the contingent and the unforeseen.

H. A.L. FISHER

PART 4

Her head nestled between his arm and his chest, Claudia listened to the pattern of his breathing. Deep, as if he'd been asked by the doctor to draw in air and exhale it again with exaggerated care. And very regular, although invariably slower than she anticipated.

In the distance, she could hear the surf crash into the sandy shore and she noticed that it held the same surprise. No matter how long she listened to it and tried to time its pattern, she was always a beat too early.

It started to fascinate her and, for a while, she intermittently listened to the cresting waves, then Christian's breathing. She felt enormously satisfied, as she always did after making love with him. Waves of contentment coursed through her body.

They'd spent their first day in Malaysia getting from Kuala Lumpur, the capital, to Mersing, a small port servicing Malysia's Pacific islands. Finally, after a two-hour boat ride, they'd arrived at Kobang Beach, a stretch of paradise on the far side of Tioman Island.

It hadn't taken long for them to understand the environmental concerns with developing Kobang and they found it even more puzzling that someone wanted to build a resort here. Doing so constituted a huge business risk.

Cyril Wolfson, the bald, wiry British expatriate who was in charge of the project, surprised them by voicing the same sentiment. "The only people willing to fly around the world, take a day's worth of bus rides and then jump on a boat to get here are philosophers and hippies...the world's penniless," he dryly commented. Then, seeing that Claudia and Christian looked embarrassed, he quickly added: "But rest assured, I'll do my utmost to make it superb."

Then he showed them their quarters, a newly constructed beach bungalow. Claudia's eyes scanned the room, taking in the abundant detailing. In the corners, massive teak beams rose from the floor, parts of them adorned with mythical carvings. The ceilings were open and the roof boards were covered with the same weave of palm leaves as they were on the outside, giving the solid structure a primitive, makeshift impression.

Afterwards, Wolfson took them to what he called "the compound," where they'd meet for meals, meetings and socializing. Behind it was a small cooking area, where two men crouched on the earthen floor, chopping up greens on a dark piece of wood.

The older of the cooks got up and grinned shyly, revealing his few remaining teeth, stained nearly black with betel juice. Then he ran out of the shed. Wolfson introduced the younger man as Rashid.

On their second day, they explored. The resort's location was breathtaking. The white sand beach followed a lazy arc, perhaps two miles long and was speckled with massive, black boulders, left over from some long-ago volcanic eruption. Behind the beach, palm trees rose out of a strip of bright green bushes. This was where the guest bungalows would be situated.

When Claudia and Christian walked further into the jungle, they discovered a magnificent waterfall. Armies of lizards made their home here: most as small as the digit of a finger, some more than a foot long. They sat down at a pool that belonged in a fairy

186 PETER C. CAVELTI

tale, a fine, cool mist descending on them. Claudia decided that she'd bring the children here, one day.

At their second meeting, Christian had complimented O'Shea on the job he'd done having Claudia's house shadowed. "The day we came back from the cottage, a neighbor told us the police were finally doing something about the traffic. They'd been there a few times in an unmarked vehicle...I guess that was your car, wasn't it?"

"We made a few appearances, wanting to find out who Talbot had hired. We also kept an eye on his place, but it was on your street that we lucked out."

"They showed up?"

"The day you left. The same license plates...the same Mustang you described. They passed Claudia's house without stopping. Our man stayed put and watched. The second time they came by, they slowed down and looked around." O'Shea pulled his cigarettes from his pocket. "This time, our man followed them. They went to Yorkville, where they pulled into a parking lot and walked into a nightclub. Everyone seemed to know them there...the bouncers, the dancers, even the bartenders. After they left, our man made inquiries. Apparently, the club is owned by Angelo Fiorentino. And guess what? Fiorentino lives in Oakville."

"Oakville? That's where David lives!"

"And has his practice. You told me. Maybe Fiorentino is Talbot's patient, maybe they're members of the same country club. Anyway, the guy owns a large bakery, lots of real estate, five or six restaurants and a couple of nightclubs. He's involved in construction, too. Typical mafia capo." Martin O'Shea was clearly in his element.

"And you think David's thugs work for him?"

"We know the guy behind the bar and he confirmed it. We even learned their names."

"I'm impressed."

"We still couldn't make sense of the vehicle registration. The first time around, we came up with a blank…the car was registered to a Giselle Ouelette, whose credit records say she's an accountant with Ernst & Young. We've since found out that her sister is the hostess at a certain Oakville restaurant…and the moll of your friend with the funny hair."

"The guy who shook me up?"

"Whose name is Freddie. Alfredo Falco."

"So they're dangerous?"

"As dangerous as they come. I can't tell you what their marching orders are, but judging by how many times they kept coming back to Claudia's house, they must be frustrated. Frankly, Christian, I think you're doing the right thing. If I didn't, I wouldn't be here."

Christian felt tremendous relief. "Where do we go from here?"

O'Shea's response surprised him. "Let's talk about money. I imagine your funds will originate from an offshore account. Instead of wiring it, why don't you ask your bankers to issue a draft payable to "Credit Suisse" and deliver it to the gentleman whose address I've written down here."

"Very clever. Your people will never know which account the draft came from and I'll never know where the money went, other than that it was sent to Credit Suisse's head office at Zurich's Paradeplatz, where a few hundred thousand offshore accounts reside."

"I see you're familiar with the address." O'Shea smiled. "Now, given that we settled on early August, do you think you could initiate the payment this week?"

"I'll tell them to have the draft delivered by Friday."

Christian felt fortunate that he'd hidden away money during his years in the financial business. He thought of how hard it would be for most people to pay a hundred and fifty thousand dollars without leaving a trace.

O'Shea brought up the topic of an alibi and Christian suggested he and Claudia could go away to the cottage. The kids were at summer school, but if absolutely necessary, they could pull them out and take them along.

Martin didn't like it. "I'd prefer you left for a place where you need hotel bookings and airline tickets. I know you're retired, but do you ever have to leave the country on any kind of business?"

"No I don't," Christian said, but then he remembered that Claudia soon needed to go to Malaysia.

"That's better…Asia's good. No one goes there for less than two weeks. That gives us the flexibility we need." He stared at the painting behind Christian. "Tell me, if you did go to Malaysia …what would you do with the children?"

"Probably leave them with Claudia's parents. That's where they usually go if no one's in the house."

"Excellent," O'Shea resolutely sat up. "It's the perfect alibi. Claudia is asked to visit Malaysia in the course of her work. You, retired and in love, tag along. And the children, as always when their mother is away, move in with the grandparents."

Christian said he'd double-check Claudia's dates and get her to book. He'd let O'Shea know…as usual, through Jake. They looked at their diaries, comparing dates like executives preparing for an annual meeting. Subject to Claudia's exact itinerary, they'd book to leave on Saturday, July 31, and return two and a half weeks later.

For his part, Martin O'Shea projected David would be hit on Friday, August 6, or that weekend. He'd be seen at work long after Christian and Claudia left and would go missing several days before they returned. O'Shea said he'd have someone call David's reception to make sure the days before and after his disappearance were days on which Talbot was scheduled to work. Neither of the two men wrote anything down.

When O'Shea was gone, Christian opened a can of pop and looked out the window. Straight down, on the roofs of the shorter buildings below him, flags snapped in the unyielding breeze.

Only a few more weeks, and his new family would be safe from David. What a dramatic turn his life had taken. He was a family man now and he liked it. Feeling responsible for Claudia and the kids appealed to some deeply seated emotions he'd never known he possessed: he wanted to look after them and protect them, and he knew he would.

Yet just a little while ago, his life and happiness had been here, in this and the other boardrooms of Global Capital.

He thought of the weekend just over a year ago, when he'd asked Tila to the cottage. He'd been tempted to invite her many times before, but he'd resisted. Workplace affairs were something he didn't approve of.

After leaving Global Capital, he allowed himself to think of Tila as more than a colleague. He finally had the time to devote himself to a relationship and he already knew his perfect mate. He was more attracted to Tila than ever and had shared countless intellectual and emotional successes with her.

The only problem was that he wasn't sure whether Tila felt the same about him, which is why he thought it safest to invite Fred Mulholland and his wife along. Mulholland was the Canadian representative of a British investment bank and both Christian and Tila knew Fred and Lillian from many professional and social occasions.

But fate intervened: Fred Mulholland phoned to say his wife had fallen ill and they couldn't come. Christian was terrified.

When he picked Tila up at her downtown condominium and awkwardly told her that the Mulhollands had cancelled, she embraced him warmly and said, "We'll simply have to have a good time by ourselves, Christian." Before they left her place, they made passionate love, and when they finally arrived at Christian's island the next day, they spent most of the time in bed there, too.

The next six weeks they saw each other daily, making up for the years they'd worked together side by side, deeply attracted to each other but unable to breach their self-imposed code of behavior. Christian spent his weekdays in the city and Tila her weekends on his island. They made love on the boat, the waves lapping up its sides and the sun beating down on them. They lay together on the sun-baked planks of the dock, and when the first leaves fell, on the moist ground of the forest.

By then, Christian realized that their relationship centered on sex alone. Their lovemaking was the best he'd ever experienced, but their compatibility in other areas was deficient. He was eager to leave the corporate world behind him, but Tila was still enthralled by its excitement; he was a creature of nature and she was a city girl; he read DeLillo to her, but she couldn't relate. Most of all, he longed for her to be independent, while she wanted him to be her mentor.

Tila was intelligent and mature enough to see it too. There were tears when it ended, but they could both see why it was the right decision. And, besides, they'd had the best summer of their lives. They promised each other eternal friendship and went their own ways.

Later, Christian had taken Tila to a couple of movies and once, on her birthday, to dinner. Then Claudia had come into his life.

He'd felt guilty when calling Tila about the boardroom, not having phoned for months, but she talked to him as though they'd been together just last week. How wonderful that their friendship could have survived that most difficult challenge, a relationship!

Christian's thoughts turned to Claudia. How could he be sure that his love for Claudia would be permanent? Claudia's integrity and character came to mind first...he admired and respected her for her strength. But that had been the case with Tila, too.

He was passionately attracted to Claudia, even though her beauty couldn't easily be pinned down. Her shoulder-length, chestnut hair was extraordinary, but neither her facial features nor any other part of her physique was particularly exceptional when taken on its own. But there was an energy in Claudia which tied it all together, which lent her a beauty at once so captivating and mysterious that it promised to endure forever. When Claudia walked, she walked with purpose, and when she looked out at the world, her eyes radiated the life force itself.

Perhaps that was the key to it all, Christian thought. Where Tila had wanted to be guided by him, Claudia was her own person. Her inner strength had pulled her through crises far greater than the corporate world could ever have sprung on anyone. She'd liberated herself and her children from the trap of an abusive, yet materially comfortable, marriage. She'd summoned the energy not only to go to work, but to make a success out of it. And all along, she'd managed to be a devoted mother and keep her household running. That she'd done all of it without any help or support from her parents and in the face of constant harassment from David was even more remarkable.

Christian's loved Claudia's strength and independence. Now he had to earn her respect, by filling her in on everything. O'Shea had accepted; this was the right time. If he waited any longer, he'd not only betray Claudia, but also jeopardize their relationship.

As Claudia walked along the beach she thought of how she could incorporate the natural beauty of Tioman into the resort's design. In many ways, this Malaysian island was similar to the volcanic islands of the Caribbean; what distinguished it was its culture. She'd try to get back to the mainland and spend two or three days there.

Then there was the challenge of making the guestrooms and common areas functional. Much had already been decided by Chuck Fernaux, the architect, and by Wolfson's building crew, whose choice of materials already gave the place a distinct feel. She hadn't expected to be so impressed. Fernaux had visited Tioman only once and had since worked from photographs and surveys. And what Wolfson had done so far was brilliant. He'd made extensive use of local woods and kept wall and floor surfaces simple and practical, yet created interesting textures imitating nature. Where had they picked him up and what was his story?

She heard a voice behind her, drowned out partially by the crashing of the surf. It was Christian, sitting in the sand, not too far from where she'd passed. She ran up to him, laughing and shaking her head. "Sorry, I was all business," she grinned, kissing him lightly on his cheek.

"What were you plotting while you marched by me?"

"I was thinking about the logistics Chuck Fernaux must have encountered, doing all this from afar. But we should talk about something else."

They walked back toward the compound where they had planned to meet for lunch.

"So, tell me what you were doing on the beach?" Claudia asked.

"Let's see…I found myself a good viewing spot and waited for pretty girls to walk by."

"I bet you've had a few of those in your life…"

"Is this an inquiry into the nature of bachelorhood?"

"A voluntary one…" She put her arm behind his back and gave him a squeeze. "There are times when I wonder if you really haven't had any great loves in your life. I mean after your early days in London…"

"You really want to know?" Christian said, wondering how he'd phrase his words. And started telling her about Tila.

"You've mentioned her a couple of times. Your protégé, wasn't she?"

Christian was taken aback by how distant she sounded. What was it about women? They wanted to know, but if you told them they resented it. "She was my protégé, while I worked at Global Capital. And afterwards, a while after I left, she was more than that. We were lovers for a few weeks."

"What happened?" Claudia was compassionate again, as if she regretted having asked, and Christian loved her for that.

"Well, it didn't work out. I think she wanted a mentor in the relationship, as well…and I was more interested in someone who could be my equal."

Claudia put her arms around his neck and placed her forehead against his. "Tell me, do you think I'm your equal?"

"Of course you are. I've thought about why I'm so drawn

to you…"

"Apart from the chemical storm I unleash in you?"

Christian felt the tension lift. "Apart from that, yes. I respect you immensely, you know. You've made some unbelievably difficult choices for yourself, harder choices than I've ever had to make. So, yes, I do think you're my equal, Claudia. The question is whether I'm yours."

Lunch was superb. Rashid called it Ayam Masak. In Toronto, it would simply have been called a chicken curry, except that the spicing was far better than Christian and Claudia had ever tasted back home. They detected traces of lemongrass, ginger and coconut and marveled at the way such subtle tastes could coexist with a flavor as powerful as curry.

After the meal, they excused themselves and withdrew to their spot by the "magic pool."

"If this is the way my working life is going to be, I can't get enough," Claudia gushed, as they settled down in the shade. "Just think of it. I'm sitting in the midst of a tropical island, in a jungle clearing, with water cascading down jagged cliffs, surrounded by orchids and in the company of my favorite person on earth!"

"Can life get better?"

"I don't think so. I think we need to etch this scene deeply into our souls." She leaned back and closed her eyes. "You know, Christian, it's a miracle that we're here. I mean, quite apart from the fact that I got this job. But how did I even luck into the design business?"

"I suppose you're good at it."

"Okay, I *am* becoming quite decent at it, but how did I ever manage to get work? How do things like this happen?"

"Tell me…"

Claudia lay back, her face speckled with bits of shade from the abundant foliage above them. "Amazingly, I'd never have become a designer if it weren't for David."

"David? I thought he wanted you out of the design…"

"He did, yes—after getting me in. The house we had in Kingston…I remodeled it and people started asking me if I could do the same for them. I was more surprised than anyone when that happened. But it did and for a while I was in high demand."

"What was Kingston like?"

Claudia and David had moved soon after she completed her MBA and he graduated from Chiropractic College. David had got a job at the prestigious Bessemer Clinic.

Claudia never looked for employment and never much thought about it. She was busy setting up their fledgling household and preparing for motherhood. Also, they'd agreed that she'd be in charge of all financial aspects of their lives, a task she happily accepted.

Situated halfway between Toronto and Montreal, Kingston is a sleepy, mid-sized city that serves as the administrative seat to a number of government departments and corporations. Among other things, it's the seat of a proud military academy, a notoriously brutal penitentiary, and one of Canada's best newspapers. Kingston was also Canada's first capital.

But none of that is why Dale Bessemer had come here two decades earlier from New England. Already an established professional in Boston, he immediately recognized that this was the ideal venue to attract up-scale American clients from across the border. Kingston's superb location, where Lake Ontario feeds into the St. Lawrence river, its outstanding sailing facilities and the breathtakingly beautiful countryside, all make it an ideal weekend and holiday destination.

Bessemer had recognized an even more important thing: those living in the rich nearby towns of upstate New York were in awe of

Canada's heritage. There was room for an illusion here.

He purchased an enormous, run-down mansion on one of Kingston's most dignified streets and completely recreated it as the Bessemer Clinic. Nothing in the clinic was remotely related to Canadian history, but his clients didn't know that. They saw culture! Isfahan rugs, French chests of the Empire style, German baroque armoirs, Victorian wing chairs and oils of naval battles effortlessly joined together. The only tenet was that everything had to look expensive in the extreme.

In time, the clinic's fame spread all the way to New York City. New clients were accepted only on the recommendation of existing ones and the length of the waiting list became a source of envy to other professionals. When David was accepted as a junior practitioner, he joined one of Canada's most admired private clinics.

A few months later, David made an offer on a house far larger than they could afford. Claudia strongly objected, but she was determined that nothing should affect her pregnancy. One unbearably muggy summer afternoon, sitting in her new garden, she thought she was going into labor. Jason was born at nightfall.

Once Claudia was over the most demanding period of nursing a baby, a host of new chores took over. They lived in a magnificent Tudor house with a large hall and generous rooms. A bit darker than Claudia would have liked, but the sprawling lawns and flowerbeds outside more than made up for it. That first summer at their new house, Claudia became an avid gardener and whenever she went outdoors to plant, crop, weed or water, baby Jason went with her.

Meanwhile, David made himself indispensable at work and ingratiated himself to the clinics' socially connected clients. By the time Jason was a year old, the Talbots were solidly introduced into Kingston's society. The Bessemer connection was what got them in; their educational credentials and their good looks were what kept them in. And, as David instinctively knew, their fine house served as a reminder to Kingston's elite that they belonged.

One day, David took Claudia's file boxes to the clinic and instructed banks and brokers to send all statements there. Claudia didn't mind. The huge mortgage on the house still irked her, but now that there was hardly any money left, what was there to keep track of, anyway? Besides, the demands of motherhood, house and garden, and the social events that David expected her to attend, kept her busy enough.

After Karen was born, David became progressively more unstable. One day he was charming, the next sullen and distant. When Claudia tried to talk to him, he withdrew further. With ever greater frequency, he threw insults at her. On occasion, he lost control of himself completely.

One day, on a trip to Toronto, Claudia shared her dismay with David's sister Judith. She was surprised to learn that David had always been like this. Apparently, the whole Talbot family had been in disbelief at David's change, after he first went out with Claudia. Evidently, what progress had been made was now becoming unraveled again.

Perhaps it was good that Claudia didn't have much time to think. Her children needed her and, despite their apparent affluence, David insisted that she do all house and garden work herself.

Little changed until Jason and Karen went to school. Now Claudia finally had some quiet time, which she filled with a new interest: decorating. For years, she'd wanted to remodel her home. Now was the time to read up on the subject. She went through stacks of books and magazines and took interior design classes at a community college. David didn't support her new interest, but he could see that the house needed work and that they'd save a lot of money if Claudia could do the job without an architect or general contractor.

When the project was finished, Claudia could tell that David was pleased, both with the outcome and the cost. He wasn't the type that would praise her, but his mood visibly improved. He insisted that they return to their intense frequency of entertaining, and each time they had guests over, the renovation became the focus of the evening.

It wasn't long before the Maturins, the owners of a substantial house down the street, asked Claudia if she'd consider managing their renovation. They met to discuss the parameters, and within a week Claudia landed her first project.

"I couldn't believe it," she said to Christian, the excitement she'd experienced nearly a decade ago showing on her face even now. "I knew I'd done well on our house, but to be retained professionally…it seemed impossible."

"The proverbial fluke that pushes us in the right direction. If you follow the cue, miracles happen."

"It took me a little longer to see that—thanks to David's opposition. But after I left him, that's exactly how it was. Once I opened my mind to interior design, incredible things happened."

"Miracles."

"Yes, like being here with you." Her hand sought his. They looked at each other and the stupendously beautiful surroundings. For a few minutes they sat, listening to the surge of water hitting the surface of the pool. It drowned out even the shrieking of birds in the jungle behind them.

"Do you think I'd be as excited about interior design if David had just let me do my thing?"

"Why do you think he interfered?"

"I've often asked myself. Part of it was that he couldn't stand it if I had a life of my own. He just wanted me to be an extension of himself. And then I got all these accolades, especially after I finished the Maturins' place. This was different from getting compliments for our renovation; it no longer reflected on him."

"So he made you stop."

"Just like that. I'd finished the Maturin house and was working on a smaller project when he started needling me. One evening he blew up. We didn't need the money, and he'd married me so I could be there for the family. Not him, you see—the family."

"So you stopped."

"I was an obedient wife." Claudia grinned and Christian thought it was a good sign that she could laugh about it. *God, I hope I'll never disappoint her.*

Christian thought about O'Shea. By now, he and his people must be well into preparing for David's disappearance. Earlier, while sitting at the beach, he'd convinced himself that Claudia had enough to cope with. Dealing with the knowledge that David was going to be murdered would be too severe a strain. But just now, when listening to her talk about her married life, he'd tilted in the other direction again. By not including her, wasn't he just another David? Making choices without her…deciding what was best for her? Wasn't he deceiving her if he didn't tell her now, *before* it all took place?

Claudia continued. "I did what he wanted…stopped the design work."

"Until you were on your own again. That took a lot of courage, starting all over again."

"Necessity, Christian. I needed the money and this was something I thought I could do. Then came the job at the Drakes…John's office and library, you know. I'm still not sure whether they gave me the job because they felt sorry for me. They're real sweethearts, those two. They were my guardian angels before you came along."

"We should write them a postcard when we get back to the mainland."

"A postcard a day! If he hadn't given me that job, my design career would have been dead on arrival."

Christian turned toward her and shook his head. "Come on, Claudia…something else would have happened. You wanted to get back into design and you needed a job. It was wonderful of them to help, but you would have found another project if they hadn't been there."

"Perhaps." She looked at Christian doubtfully, then broke into a smile and put her arm around his neck. "You know what? I love it when you express so much faith in me. You have no idea how good it feels."

I was convinced that Christian would tell Claudia about his decision soon after getting to Malaysia. He, who was so proactive and goal-oriented in every other way. But he didn't.

It would have been easier for him to tell, because he wouldn't have carried the burden of it all alone. Instead, he walked the beach, pained by questions like how David would die, what they'd do with his body, and what police inquiries there would be.

As that first August weekend came near, Christian felt the pressure rise. If he told her now and she disagreed with his plan, there was still the option of calling it off. David was still out there, but at least she'd have an equal say. In another few days, that option would be gone.

"Christ, you promised you'd tell her as soon as you got there," I yelled at him after they returned.

"It's not that I didn't think about it," Christian pleaded. "I thought about it every day, all fucking day long. But the bottom line was always the same. I didn't want to burden Claudia."

"And now you're in another pickle like the one when you told her you'd leave, you idiot." I felt terrible for Claudia.

"I tried to think of it from her viewpoint, Jake, but each time I did that I convinced myself that she didn't want to be burdened. She must have known that something major was brewing…"

"I don't know. Whenever you let your fucking logic take over, bad things happen. But it's happened, so let's leave it at that."

"Jesus, I'm so bloody frustrated…it's not like me, this whole thing."

"How do you mean?"

"I've planned decisions and executed them all my life, for God's sake. I made a fucking career out of it. I can't believe I didn't tell her…" He was racked by guilt; it was better not to argue further.

"You'll get through this, Christian. You're still her knight in shining armor, you know. You've fucked up on this one, but think of all the sacrifices you made. I'm sure Claudia will take that into account when you tell her."

The pictures and maps he'd brought back lay sprawled out on the table in front of us and I picked up a few of the shots. They were scenes Christian had described…enchanting beaches and the magic pool.

I was relieved when Christian started to unfold the map of Tioman Island. But then he stopped and asked me if I'd slept well lately, because he hadn't.

"I can relate."

"It's not the David thing that keeps me up…it's that I haven't told Claudia. If I had, there'd be a logical end to this chaotic first chapter of our lives together. David's gone and we won't have to worry about being roughed up or shot anymore. That's what we need now, closure. But instead I screwed up and there's this thing between us."

"At least you don't feel guilty."

"Guilt, yes, but not about David." He looked at me intensely. "You don't think we did the wrong thing, do you Jake?"

"Don't be silly. There was only one course to take. We both racked our brains, didn't we?" Christian relaxed, but then tensed again, when I added "I do feel guilt, though."

He looked pained, then told me how much I'd risked for him and how sorry he felt that he'd put me through this whole thing. I lit up and we sipped at our drinks silently.

"Why is it you can't sleep, Jake…is it icing David?" he asked after a while.

"It's totally irrational. There's nothing better we could have done for the world than get rid of this slime. All the guy ever did was hurt others."

"I thought it might be hard on you. You're high-strung…more sensitive than I am."

We looked at the pictures. A slice of paradise! I should take a week or two at a place like this.

"So there's been nothing in the papers?" Christian asked.

"Not a single word. But I bet you there will be. It's about two weeks since he last showed up for work. They usually wait a few days before checking airline records, car rentals…that type of stuff. Making sure the guy didn't just decide to fly the coop."

Christian pointed to one of the pictures in front of us. It was a wide angle shot of a beach, a construction site in its first stages and what looked like a lot of outdated equipment.

"This is where it'll all be built…look at it. Six hundred-odd rooms, and Claudia will be in charge of decorating them!"

I was happy for Claudia, but my heart wasn't in it. I sat there, smoking, pretending to listen. He talked about the compound, the room they'd stayed in and Wolfson. At least he had the memories and his pride of Claudia to offset his frustration.

I felt sorry for myself. What did I have? Scenes of murder sneaking into my dreams, keeping me tossing all night. "Tell me again about the phone call," I interrupted.

"Just as I said. Some officer called Claudia to say her former husband is missing. He said they'd called her office and learned that she was in the Far East…could she call them when she was back."

"A constable or a detective?"

"I think he just called himself officer…we listened to the message together."

It was a good sign. They weren't taking it all that seriously.

More or less at the same time we were looking at Christian's pictures, the police rang the bell at Claudia's house. She told me the whole story at the cottage a few days later.

The kids had finished their summer courses and were with us, too. Karen was eager to show off her canoeing skills and occasionally called over to Christian to watch her, while he and Jason were doing something on the shore. I saw them reach into the knee-deep water, then walk back up to the beach, cupping their hands.

"What's going on down there, Claudia?"

"They're digging up clams. Jason's determined to have a clambake. I'm not too hopeful about the results, but they're having fun."

"Maybe they'll taste good, after all. We'll pick a nice white wine to wash them down with and all will be well." I watched contentedly.

"Jake, this whole thing is very difficult for me." Her voice had changed and when I looked at her I could see she was holding back tears. "It's really not fair that you're drawn into this, too, but I'm having a hard time accepting what happened."

"I've been as involved as he was, you know. I was the one who set… "

Claudia cut me off. "You haven't been involved in the same way. It's Christian's not telling me that hurts. It's like a foul-smelling, wet blanket thrown over our time in Malaysia. Even him coming along seems insincere…something done to get a damned alibi. And then there's this other woman, Tila. The fact that she's involved doesn't help any." Her voice was choked. I tried to give her a hug, but she held me off. "We've got to talk," she said. "Get me a Kleenex instead."

She related how Christian had come back from my place and asked her to join him for a walk. She'd suspected that it had to do with David. They'd gone to the edge of the park, where it's furthest from the road and sat down on the grass.

"That's when he told me. I could see he was in tatters…he cried his heart out."

"You know why he didn't tell you earlier, don't you?"

"I know he did it to protect me. But he's starting to have a history of devastating me every time he tries to do that. I just got over the first blow!"

"You're talking about when he wanted to leave you. That was my idea too, Claudia…bad advice, in retrospect."

She started crying again, saying I was as bad as Christian. We didn't understand what David used to do to her…giving her hope, then sending her into a tailspin. Then she calmed down a bit, admitting it was her mistake too. She could have brought up the subject herself, but instead, she'd preferred to talk about cheerful, trivial things. She'd hidden herself in them as much as Christian.

"I don't think he was hiding, Claudia. His dilemma was there every minute, burning up inside him. He told me. But he didn't want it to spoil your time together."

"I understand that, on a logical level. But it still hurts, probably because of the whole emotional baggage I carry with me."

"You know, when Christian talked to me that afternoon, he used almost the same words you just did. He knows what David did to you…the last thing he wanted to do was hurt you."

"That helps a bit, Jake. I'm glad we're talking, you and I." She was dabbing her eyes. "Christian told you about the police, didn't he?"

"Briefly. When we saw each other, they'd only left that message. I only heard about the visit yesterday, when he called about getting up here. Even for that, he used a payphone."

"Do you know the details?"

"No, he said we'd talk about it up here."

"I didn't know that. It's been difficult for us to talk to each other, the last couple of days. Anyway, they came on Thursday evening, when you and Christian were together. Maybe it was a good thing I didn't know anything…"

"You said 'they,'" I interjected.

"Yes, there were two. They wanted information to help them deal with David's disappearance."

"Nothing more?" I started pacing the porch.

"Not really. I asked them what they meant by 'disappearance' and they said that was the best word they could use. David had left his practice one Thursday and no one had seen him since."

"What rank were they?"

"The senior one gave me his card when he left…J.J. Macmillan, Detective Sergeant. I think he introduced his colleague as a Detective Constable, but I forgot his name. The junior one took notes while we talked." Claudia's composure was restored.

"So they *are* taking it seriously…," I said, more to myself than to Claudia. "Did they try to intimidate you?"

Claudia looked at me in a funny, observant way and I knew she thought that this was how I act at a trial.

"I have to ask you this, Claudia. Just now, were you picturing me pacing up and down in court—*sans* cigarette, of course? Or am I totally off the wall?"

Claudia gasped. "That's amazing! Yes, I was…I could see you in your black robe, for a minute…gently extracting information."

"And, as I always like to think of myself, confidently getting to the core of the truth."

"How did you ever know?"

"Intuition is my trade, remember? Anyway, tell me about how they handled themselves…the venerable representatives of the police. Courteous or intimidating?"

"Neither, really. The senior guy, Macmillan, would ask me a question, usually looking down at the carpet, then lift his head and these big, moist eyes would look at me…like the eyes of a cow taking a break from grazing. I'd say yes or no and he'd just keep looking, as though I still had a lot more to say."

The description made me laugh. "Some of these guys are good, aren't they? But you didn't say more than yes or no, did you, Claudia? I can see they found their match."

"Unless *he* followed up with another question. But he didn't ask me all that much…mostly routine things you know."

"Like what?"

"Well, he started out by asking where I'd been and I said Tioman Island in Malaysia, and he just keep staring. Then, after five, maybe ten full seconds elapsed, he asked whether I minded telling him what I did there. And so on. He also wanted to know whether I'd been there with someone and I told him about Christian."

"What did he say to that?"

"Not much. He asked me for Christian's full name and asked the constable to take it down. Then a weird thing happened—he looked up and said, 'The investment banker?' But he didn't carry it off too well. I could tell he'd never heard Christian's name until he came across it in the flight logs or somewhere else…"

"Your travel agent…maybe someone at your office."

"Not the office. I only have one employee—Jackie. I'd be worried if they talked to her. She's so fiercely loyal, she'd make a contest out of it. Anyway, I'd be surprised if Macmillan hadn't play-acted that thing."

"They do that. And not always with success."

"Then he got on to David. Had he ever done anything like that when we were married? Gone away without telling anyone, you know. And did I have any idea where he might be? Next came our marriage…the reason why we'd split. He was polite about it, telling me he appreciated these were personal issues."

"But having to know anyway."

"I can't remember what he said, but you're right—he was

polite, but forceful. In an understated way."

"I love it. Cow-Eyes-Macmillan, the master of understated forcefulness."

I felt relief. Things were finally moving again. Christian had finally told Claudia and the police were on the case. Better to see things happening than to wait.

I asked Claudia if she minded if I got myself a drink. She surprised me by asking what I was having.

"Courvoisier…my usual."

"I need one too, Jake." As she said that, there was sadness in her eyes, but behind it I thought I saw a mischievous twinkle. How beautiful she was!

In the kitchen I wondered why I didn't feel apprehensive about the police. It must be because I was on the side of Christian and Claudia, and the police had become a threat to them. I was thriving on adversity. Good! With a bit of luck, it would help me overcome my guilt. As I rationalized this, I could feel the emotions that had troubled me melt away and my intellect take over.

I stepped back onto the porch, handing Claudia her drink and making sure the kids and Christian were still down at the beach. We clinked and I took a soothing gulp. Then I stuck a Lucky into my mouth, letting the tip of my tongue run over the raw tobacco, before taking another sip of cognac.

"So, where were we? Ah—your marriage. What did you tell them?"

"The truth. The years of abuse…all that. Pretty well the same as Elliott's files would show."

"And then?"

"Then they wanted to know how often David had seen his family. Was there anyone he was particularly close to? It seemed strange that he'd ask me. Why not talk with them directly?"

"How did you respond?"

"Again, with the truth. That I hadn't kept contact with David's family and had no idea if he'd seen any of them since we split. Next, he wanted to know what kind of a relationship he'd had with them during the years of our marriage. I told him not an easy one and he wanted details."

"Once they're on to something, they keep digging."

"This was the thing he devoted most time to. He absolutely wanted to know why it hadn't been easy. He asked questions like 'were people afraid of him?' and 'was your former husband a bully?' and 'would you say he had enemies?'"

"Hard to answer those with yes or no, isn't it? What did you say?"

"I told him, yes, he was a bully, but he could also be charming. As to how many enemies he had, I couldn't know, because my observations of David had been mostly confined to home."

"Brilliant, Claudia. Maybe a bit too sharp for them. You never know what makes them suspicious."

"You think?"

"Looking at everything, you've struck the right balance between saying what a shit David was and not putting him down unnecessarily. You couldn't have done better."

"What will they do next, Jake?"

"I'd predict they'll come back a second time, looking for inconsistencies. And if they don't find any, they'll move on."

"To where?"

"I have no idea. But from their perspective, there's nothing further to be gained with you. You were away in Malaysia on business and took along your friend, a senior executive with an excellent reputation. You left David two and a half years ago and everything in your new life is going well. There's no motive."

So far, so good. We'd made the right decision. The bastard was dead and no one would ever find his body. And without a body, what could the cops do?

After dinner, Christian suggested that we go for a canoe ride. I protested a bit, arguing that he should take Claudia, but they both insisted that it should be Christian and I—the old canoe team. "It's good for me to be distracted…," Claudia whispered to me as we got our stuff together. "Being with the kids is perfect right now."

Christian and I paddled for a while, leaving the jumble of clattering dishes and voices behind us.

"How did the kids react to the police visit?" I asked. "I forgot to ask Claudia."

The sun was close to setting, an orange ball sinking toward the tree line ahead of us, horizontal bars of mauve and grey cloud breaking it up into sections.

"Apparently they arrived just as the cops were leaving. Claudia says the big thing for them was the excitement of having the police come to the house, not David's disappearance. Do you think the police will want to talk to them?"

"I don't see why they'd drag the kids in. Unless they become suspicious of you or Claudia, but I think that's unlikely."

"I'm glad to hear that. Anything that makes things easier for Claudia is a plus right now."

"She told me about your discussion…when you and Jason were busy digging up clams. She's doing well, considering."

"I know I've let her down."

"She understands why you didn't tell her. It's the David thing that hurts."

"What, him being gone?"

"No, the way he treated her. It makes what you did harder, but she'll get over it. You've got to reassure her about Tila, though."

"What's Tila got to do with it?"

"Her help with the boardroom, maybe. I don't know what you told her…"

"Actually, I told her everything. That I had a relationship with her and that she helped."

"And you're asking me what's wrong? You won't tell Claudia what you're up to, but you're drawing in an ex-girlfriend? Come on, that's tough for any woman to accept!"

Christian muttered something about how he needed to be straight with Claudia.

"She also told me about the police visit," I said, trying to make him feel better again. "She thinks she did really well. And you know what? I feel a lot better about the whole thing, too. For me, having the police there is like having David back in the picture. I realized something about myself today—when I have an enemy, my emotions take a backseat. Isn't that strange? You'd think most people turn emotional precisely when they confront an enemy."

"Most would."

"It's my profession…it's taught me to rely on my intellect when things turn bad. Anyway, I think I'll sleep well tonight."

212 PETER C. CAVELTI

We were out on the water for nearly an hour. I asked Christian how he thought they'd iced David and where they'd put his body. I kicked myself for bringing it up, but once Christian started talking, I realized it was okay. We probably had to sort through all the clutter on our minds. Closure was needed, as Christian had said.

"It never much mattered," he responded, "until one afternoon. I'd borrowed the cook's motorbike and went all the way to the Northern tip of Tioman. I ended up at a deserted beach. There was little sand…it was mostly pockmarked, volcanic rock, hard to walk on, even with shoes."

I watched the muscles in Christian's shoulder and back tense, as he completed each stroke of the paddle.

"At that beach, I thought about David's murder. Had I blocked it out because I wanted to keep my time in paradise unspoiled, or was it a denial of what I'd done? Maybe I'd just been practical, because it really didn't matter. Let's face it…whatever we think about David is now irrelevant."

"You think like a cop…or a lawyer. You disseminate every last detail and bring the whole picture back together again. Except, your approach is based purely on logic…there isn't much intuition there." We stopped paddling. The sun had sunk and the sky was now a speckled mess of torn cumulus clouds. "I'm in danger of doing the opposite," I mused, "relying on my intuitive powers too heavily. I've noted that each time I screw something up, it's because I dismiss logical connections in favor of intuition."

"We should start some new line of work together…"

"With our combined talents we'd be the top team. Anyway, as you said, it doesn't matter what happened to David. So don't let it get to you."

"That's what I thought, too, but as I got back on the bike and rode on, it started bugging me again. And then I came to this tiny village and saw a bunch of men crouched down in a circle. I left the bike at the edge of the dirt road and walked toward them. A few of them got up and approached, giving me discouraging stares. One of the younger guys made gestures that I should leave and screamed at me. But then a voice from behind stopped him. The circle parted and I could see an old man, dark-skinned with white hair and thin, grey lips. He just stood there and watched me. His eyes were older than the world. Then he shouted in a high voice and motioned for me to approach. A moment later the circle closed again, with me inside it. And there I was, at a cockfight."

Christian related how the scene turned frantic, with the crowd yelling bets and holding up bills and the two bird handlers continuing with their preparations.

"They held their animals up in front of their faces and took their beaks in their mouths."

"What for?"

"I'm not sure whether they sucked air out of their birds' mouth or blew air into them, or moistened them. Whatever they did, the cocks got a lot more agitated. When the money counting was done with and the birds were ready, the old man gave a sign and the handlers threw their cocks into the dusty circle. The animals paced around, puffing out their chests and turning their heads in those jerky movements, circling and sizing each other up. Then, both animals propelled themselves into the air and threw their legs forward. I only saw a blur, then the birds fell back, only to be picked up and returned to their corners. I noticed a sickle-shaped blade sticking out from one of the cock's legs."

"After a short break, the birds went at each other again, and the handlers withdrew them a second time. Obviously, the object was to separate the two animals after each thrust, so that the fight would last longer. The crowd was now frantic. Had one of the cocks managed to cut the other? I couldn't tell. But after a few rounds, the birds started to visibly tire. And each time they were separated, it took a bit longer before their spirits rebounded."

"How did it end?"

"One bird was badly wounded and limped around. He'd fallen over a couple of times. It was pitiful, but there was something enormously captivating about this dance of death. Then, out of nowhere, the victor fluttered half a foot in the air and thrust his blade into the throat of his opponent. A great cheer rose up. And then the money was paid."

Christian told me how he couldn't shake the image of the dying creature, wobbling for a second or two and then falling on his side one last time. As he rode back on the bike, he kept seeing the blood spurting from the cock's neck and the crimson pool that formed and gradually turned into a large black stain.

Invariably, these thoughts brought him back to David. He was no longer satisfied dismissing David's death from his mind. He needed a version of events he could accept.

As he rode down the west side of the island, he went through possible scenarios. He noticed neither the breathtaking views of beaches and sea, nor the rice fields and hamlets he passed. Had they cut David's throat or shot him through the chest? Or had they hit him over the head with a hammer?

"Whatever it was, I hope they chloroformed him first. Christ, even in my dream I used chloroform, before dragging him to the cottage!"

"And how would they have got to him with the chloroform?" I asked.

Christian had thought it through. "I don't think that would have been difficult," he replied. "The murderer might have climbed out of a van with the Bell logo painted on its side, or he could have been an ordinary looking fellow in a track suit with a Pontiac Sunbird at the curb, pretending to deliver a package."

"And then what?"

"I don't know, Jake. He may have killed him inside his house or dragged him away and dispatched him on some deserted stretch of a country road. I spent hours thinking about this shit. Even about what they did with his body. What do you think professionals do?"

"I imagine the mob's ties with the construction industry would come in handy."

"That's what I thought. Maybe they chop the body up and place each part on a different building site—the head at the base of a bridge pillar…an arm under a freshly poured wheelchair ramp."

"Almost poetic, the way you describe that."

"Very funny. Anyway, those were my grisly thoughts on the way back. I had to get it out of my system."

"What was the conclusion?"

"I kept going back to the chloroform. What happened afterwards didn't matter. So that's what I clung to. It's a crutch, but it helped."

Our discussion left me uneasy. Christian had found a way to deal with David's murder, but I hadn't. But we were getting too close to the cottage to talk and, besides, we'd exhausted the topic.

As we returned to the cottage, silently pulling our paddles through the water, my thoughts kept returning to David. They drowned out everything else. If there were tree frogs on the nearby shore or loons calling to each other, I didn't hear them.

The police did show up again.

When Macmillan's assistant phoned for an appointment, Christian had just left for the cottage. Claudia asked if they could come early in the afternoon; the children would be out then.

It was raining. Bolts of lightning charged out of a leaden sky and both policemen were soaked when Claudia showed them in.

"Here we are again, Mrs. Talbot," Macmillan mumbled, as he shuffled down the hallway, his shoes leaving puddles on the polished oak floor. "It's Wednesday, September the first, twenty-six days since your former husband was last seen. It's curious that an established professional, apparently lacking for nothing, should simply disappear, don't you think?" He turned and stared at Claudia.

"I suppose it is," she answered. "I won't ask you into our dining room this time…if you don't mind."

"Not at all. In our condition it's best you take us where we do the least damage," Macmillan answered agreeably. "If you prefer, we can take our shoes and coats off."

"That's an even better idea. If you can do that, the dining room's all yours, after all." Claudia liked the way that had come out—assertive but not impolite. *He's not that unaware,* Claudia thought. *I bet he's noticed the mess he made all along.* She watched them fumble with their shoes.

Macmillan chose to sit at the far end of the table, where David's place had been. The constable sat down next to him and opened his notepad.

Macmillan followed up on his earlier comment. "We think it's remarkable that Mr. Talbot disappeared. In fact, we think it's unlikely that he did so voluntarily. What is your opinion?"

Claudia didn't know what to say. "I guess I don't have an opinion. I really have no clue what my former husband has been up to."

"We thought you could help, Mrs. Talbot. That's still the name you use, isn't it?"

"Yes it is." Her words hung in the air for several seconds, as Macmillan looked at her…just looked, waiting for more. Claudia found it disconcerting and, feeling the need to say something, asked her visitors if they wanted coffee. The junior looked at Macmillan and Macmillan declined.

"What do you think we should do to find out what happened to David Talbot?" The detective looked at Claudia imploringly.

"I don't know. I suppose the people who know best what he was up to are his staff. They see him every day, don't they?"

"*Saw* him, Mrs. Talbot, *saw* him. And that's what worries us. You see, we think your former husband may have been murdered."

"Murdered?"

"Yes, murdered. And we thought you might tell us more about it. You see, we understand from the clinic's receptionist, a Ms. Nyman, that you came to see your former husband not long ago and threatened to kill him."

"Are you suggesting I killed David…is that what you're saying?"

Macmillan waited a few seconds, waiting for her to say more, his eyes glaring. "Not yet, Mrs. Talbot. Not yet. Or should we?" He stared again.

Claudia was no longer calm, but she felt more composed than

she would have thought possible. She'd expected nothing like this from Macmillan. Was he just bluffing—trying to see if, against all expectations on his part, she'd stumble into something? Or was he taking her visit to David that seriously? *I guess it depends on what the damned receptionist said.* "No, of course not," she said after a long pause.

"Of course not what, Mrs. Talbot?"

"Of course you should not suspect me…wasn't that your question?"

"What about the receptionist's testimony? Let me see…." Macmillan held his open hand toward the constable and the junior officer placed a folder in it. "This is a copy of the testimony we obtained from Miss Nyman. I'll read the last part of it—you are free to review it all, if you want."

> **Samantha Nyman**: I then heard Mrs. Talbot's voice rise, as if she was very angry, but being on the phone I couldn't understand the words. I terminated the call and got up, thinking I should check if everything was all right. As I came down the hall I could hear everything. She said she'd kill him.
>
> **Det. Sgt. Macmillan**: Tell us what was said. Exactly the way it was said.
>
> **Samantha Nyman**: Okay, I'll try. She said she'd kill him. Sorry, she said I'LL KILL YOU. I REALLY MEAN IT. And then Mr. Talbot replied HOW WOULD YOU DO THAT? And then she said I'LL FIND A WAY. I'LL FUCKING KILL YOU.
>
> **Det. Sgt. Macmillan**: Are these the words that were actually used?
>
> **Samantha Nyman**: She may have said it slightly differently, but that's what she said.
>
> **Det. Sgt. Macmillan**: She being Mrs. Talbot, right?

Samantha Nyman: Right.

Det. Sgt. Macmillan: When you say she may have said it differently, could anything she said differently have changed the meaning, Ms. Nyman?

Samantha Nyman: I don't think so. It was pretty clear she meant it.

Det. Sgt. Macmillan: What do you think Mrs. Talbot meant?

Samantha Nyman: She meant to kill him.

Macmillan handed the document back the same way he'd asked for it—without looking at his junior. "Is there anything you wish to say to Mrs. Talbot. You don't have to, you know." The constable had started to scribble on a notepad.

"What can I say?"

"Well, is it true that you said these things?"

"Actually, it is. And I feel pretty silly when I view it in this context."

"In what context?"

"The context of you investigating David's disappearance. I can see why you're here." Claudia looked up into Macmillan's eyes and held his stare. She wondered what Jake's advice would be right now. Should she keep talking to them? If she didn't, they'd become far more suspicious, so it was probably better to cooperate, at least until they asked her something unreasonable.

It was fortunate she'd had some time to think about the meeting. One thing she'd determined was not to change any facts. If she did, they'd trip her.

"Why did you say these things to your former husband?"

"Well, it's a long story. David had a history of emotional instability. I'd prefer not to get too far into it, if that's all right. You can consult Elliott Wyndham, the lawyer who handled our divorce, for the case history. David abused us, psychologically...the children and me."

"How do you spell Wyndham, ma'am?" the constable asked.

Macmillan shot him a look. "We can get that later," he said sharply. "Please continue, Mrs. Talbot."

He doesn't want me to have time to think, Claudia realized, then, with deliberate slowness, she said to the constable: "Wyndham is W-Y-N-D-H-A-M. Elliott is like in Pierre Elliott Trudeau. Two Ls and two Ts."

She turned back to Macmillan. His expression had changed; she wasn't sure it was amusement or admiration she saw in his eyes. "Anyway, David never forgave me for leaving him. He'd phone me in the middle of the night, threatening me sometimes."

"Did you report that to the police?"

"No, my lawyer thought there wasn't much point in it…you can check with him." Macmillan knew better than to ask why Elliott had said that.

"Please continue."

"Anyway, the time I was at his office…it was because I'd received a threat note regarding the kids."

"From Mr. Talbot?"

"Anonymous…it was a newspaper article about a girl that had disappeared. And on the margin, something like WHO KNOWS WHAT COULD HAPPEN TO YOUR CHILDREN had been typed."

"Can you produce the letter?"

"No…it's embarrassing. When I went to confront David, I threw it on his desk. And when I left I forgot it."

"Don't you think, Mrs. Talbot, that that's a strange way to have handled things?"

"Like I said, I'm embarrassed. But I lost my composure."

"In what way did you lose your composure?"

"I asked him about the letter and he wouldn't answer. So I blew up at him and told him if he touched my kids I'd kill him."

"So Ms. Nyman's testimony is correct?"

"Yes it is."

"Did you follow up on your threat, Mrs, Talbot?"

"Are you kidding?"

"No, I'm not kidding. I'm conducting a serious investigation into the possible murder of your former husband."

"I'm sorry...no."

"No what?"

"No, I didn't follow up on my threat. There were no more problems with David, and then I went away."

"To Malaysia."

"Yes, to Malaysia."

"What would you have done if Mr. Talbot had threatened you again?"

"Frankly, I haven't thought of it." Then she noticed the intensity of Macmillan's stare, and this time she added something. "Probably met with Elliott Wyndham." She was proud of herself.

When Macmillan said he'd finished with his questions, Claudia was surprised.

"So what happens next?"

"Well, at this stage we're still only making inquiries. No formal decision has been made to classify your former husband's disappearance as murder. But we're considering it, Mrs. Talbot. And if we did that, you'd probably be a prime suspect, at least as things stand now." Macmillan was kneeling, fiddling with his laces, as he said this.

"I'm what?" Claudia's composure was shattered. She'd thought the meeting had gone reasonably well.

The detective got up. "*Would* be, Mrs. Talbot, *would* be. There's no reason for you to conclude anything right now, although I'd appreciate if you let me know of any plans to leave town."

"Of course," was all Claudia could get out, as she let the officers out.

She waited behind the closed door for a few moments, breathing deeply and closing her eyes, then ran upstairs where she threw herself on the bed. "Shit, shit, shit!" she yelled to herself, then broke into sobs.

Claudia called me from a pay phone, saying it was imperative that we meet.

I'd put aside my morning to look through some case studies my research clerk had printed out, so getting away wasn't difficult. I asked her to come to the TD Centre, one of Toronto's office complexes. We'd meet on the twenty-sixth floor of the north tower, the one nearest King Street. Why did I suggest the twenty-sixth? It was the only floor I knew; my accounting firm was headquartered there. "I'll wait outside the elevator. Let's say exactly an hour from now. Make sure you carry a briefcase, or whatever it is you take with you when you go out to see clients."

I walked around the tall, black building for a while, then, five minutes before the appointed time, I went inside and took the elevator up. I prepared myself for a wait and hoped my accountant wouldn't come to the lobby as I was standing there. God knows what I'd tell him. But Claudia was on time. She gave a big sigh when she saw me.

I told her we'd go for a ride and then talk. I waited until a ding announced the arrival of another elevator and got in. It was headed down. I pressed fourteen. On the fourteenth floor, home to an insurance firm, we got out and pressed the Up button, then took an elevator to the top floor. I thought the TD Centre had an observation area; maybe that's where we'd end up.

Things turned out even better. There were two restaurants on the top floor. Personnel were milling about in both, preparing for lunch. We picked the less upscale place and I told a waiter that our meeting had fallen through and now we were far too early for lunch. Could we just sit down somewhere and wait?

"Help yourselves," he said. "And make sure you sit by the window…the views are out of this world. I'll bring you some coffee."

Our minds weren't on sightseeing. "What was that all about, Jake…the elevators and all that," Claudia said when we were safely tucked away in the furthest corner of the restaurant.

I explained that was one of the things Christian had learned from our mobster friend. No one could follow you.

After she told me her story, I was glad I'd been cautious. I was immensely proud of her.

There she was, having paid the price for Christian's and my own actions. Not only had she done all the right things in her meeting with Macmillan; she'd also shown enormously good judgment in how she'd contacted me. I told her that.

"I *was* pretty pissed off with Christian, but after they showed me the receptionist's testimony, I realized that I'd screwed up just as much."

"You're too hard on yourself, Claudia."

The waiter appeared with a silver coffee pot. I pulled out my wallet, pulled the first bill that came into my hands and gave it to him, telling him we appreciated his courtesy. It happened to be a twenty and I could see he was startled.

I waited until he was gone. "I think the way you handled things this morning is nothing short of brilliant. Not to call Christian was a great decision. And you struck exactly the right balance between truth and withholding things with this Macmillan guy. We've got to find a way to tell Christian exactly what you said, in case they want to talk to him."

"Do you think they will?"

"Christian and Elliott seem the most logical next targets. I'd say Elliott's a sure bet. Maybe you should give him a call, telling him he may hear from them."

"If they come back, what should I do? I had no idea whether I should answer their questions."

"Jesus, I'll have to check into this…I'm not a criminal lawyer. But I don't think they can use what you've told them as testimony. They use material like that to fuel their investigation. But you know what? I think what you've told them is more likely to take the focus off you than to egg them on."

"So I should talk to them?"

"As long as they stay within reason. If they try to intimidate you, tell them they're going too far. Call Elliott if that happens and tell him you feel they're harassing you. Elliott isn't the man to handle it, but he'll refer you and, in the meantime, say the right things to them."

I asked when Christian was coming back and she said he hadn't decided.

"Call him or let him call you as you usually do. But don't breathe a word of this to him. Not on the phone, Claudia."

The day after our meeting at the TD Centre, Macmillan and his sidekick were at Claudia's doorstep again. This time, they'd given her a mere ten minutes' notice. To Claudia's credit, she accepted nonchalantly. What spirit that woman has!

Macmillan surprised her again. She'd expected him to follow up on her previous testimony; instead he took things in a completely new direction.

"There are a few things we haven't discussed yet, Mrs. Talbot," he said. "We know that your former husband saw some very strange people during the past few months. That is Ms. Nyman's term for them…you remember Ms. Nyman, don't you?"

Claudia nodded, seeing the tight-skirted receptionist slowly disappear down the hallway, her hips tilting seductively as her long legs settled into each next step.

"Well," Macmillan continued, "apparently they showed up without appointments on several occasions, and to the reception-ist's surprise, Mr. Talbot dropped everything and saw them."

"I see." Claudia wondered what else she could say.

"Look, we believe these visitors may be drug dealers. There are also large unaccounted cash withdrawals from his bank account which add to our suspicion. So here is the question: did David have a drug problem?"

"Are you telling me I'm no longer a suspect, then?"

"We're pursuing several possibilities. People lead us to them…people like Ms. Nyman. The first time we talked to her, everything pointed to you."

"Frankly, I don't think your Ms. Nyman likes me a lot."

"It's funny you should say that," Macmillan said dryly. "We came to the same conclusion, which is why we went back to her to do more research. That's how we became aware of the strange visitors."

"I see." Claudia said again.

"So, if I may ask again. Did your husband have a drug problem?"

"I don't think he used drugs when we were together."

"When we last met, you intimated that you left him because he was abusive. Can I ask you what that entailed?"

"Yes, I suppose you can. He had frequent temper tantrums, coming out of nowhere…he had to put someone down, insult them, degrade them. Usually that someone was me. Sometimes it was the children."

"I see. And you don't think that kind of behavior could have been caused by drugs?" Macmillan asked, suggestively. "You know

. . . .

certain drugs do give people the illusion that they're invulnerable…cocaine's one of them. Users will verbally attack their boss, phone someone on whom their business depends and insult them. It's not that you would have found syringes and needles…" He lifted his eyes up to her.

Claudia saw that the Constable had stopped writing and was looking at her, too. "I don't know," was all she said.

Macmillan didn't wait this time. "Of course you don't."

Claudia wondered when he'd bring up Christian, but Macmillan never did. Instead, the detective spent the rest of his visit asking Claudia about David's siblings. Claudia described them as best she could: his eldest sister Judith, married to Julian Ingman, the owner of a mattress factory in Montreal; his sister Becky and her husband Adam Greene, the accountant; his divorced sister Sharon; and David's younger brother Norman, whose wife Jeanette was the heiress to a newspaper fortune. She stressed that she hadn't seen any of them for years.

"You mentioned that last time. You also said they were afraid of him."

Claudia nodded.

Macmillan asked about Sharon, who was three years older than David and lived in Hamilton, and Sharon's former husband. Had David been friendly with him?

Claudia told Macmillan she didn't think so, but she couldn't be sure. She vaguely remembered Sharon's husband. The marriage hadn't lasted more than two years. He'd been a promoter for rock bands. Within a few weeks of the wedding, Sharon had complained that he was never home and that she hated the people he was hanging around with. His name was Jed…Jed something.

Claudia wondered what Macmillan was after. It must have to do with his suspicion that David had used drugs.

She was convinced that drugs hadn't had anything to do with David's abusive personality. Many of his tantrums had occurred at breakfast, and who would use cocaine first thing in the morning. But why interfere with Macmillan's hypothesis? The cash withdrawals he'd mentioned fit right into his theory—a twist that could help her and Christian. What had Macmillan called them…"irregular cash withdrawals?" No doubt that was the money David had handed over to the mob to come after them. God, Christian had acted just in time!

I can tell you exactly when it was that I next saw Christian, because my first encounter with Hugo took place two nights earlier at a gallery opening—a date I'll always remember!

The opening had taken place on the Saturday (the eleventh of September, 1983) and on the following Monday, I phoned Christian at his place in the city. I knew he was in town. Hearing about Macmillan's visits to Claudia had upset him enough that he'd decided to stick around for a while.

There was no answer, so I left a message, urging him to buy the *Toronto Star*, take a look at the front page and call me back. But he didn't and that's why I concluded that he was staying with Claudia and the kids. I dialed Claudia's number and left the same message. Then I went back to work.

Shortly before noon, Christian showed up at the office. He was deeply tanned, even more than when he'd come back from Malaysia, and his hair was bleached light and had grown longer, which gave him a boyish appearance. Even so, I could see that underneath it all he was troubled. He paced around nervously and suggested we get out of my office. He held a copy of the *Star* in his hand.

I proposed that we walk down to King Street and have something to eat, but Christian didn't like the idea. What we had to talk about was too hot for a restaurant.

"Why don't we go for a drive, then? We'll drive along the lakeshore and see where we end up. Maybe we can walk a bit. They've got all kinds of food stands down there, too."

Christian agreed and, as I slipped the car into gear, I again noticed the paper. It sat on his lap and the article I'd phoned him about showed prominently: FORMER BROTHER-IN-LAW DETAINED IN TALBOT DISAPPEARANCE.

We remained silent as I snaked my way down a few side streets until I was heading south on Bathurst Street.

Then Christian talked. "Thanks for leaving the messages. With the frequency I read papers it could have taken days. What do you think?"

"Too early to think anything. The only thing we know is that they've detained this Tomlin guy. Not charged, just detained."

"What does that mean? Is the poor fucker in the slammer or is he just at police headquarters?"

I explained that detained meant he wasn't allowed to leave the station; he was probably in some fairly decent holding cell, being questioned. The police would have to make up their mind whether they wanted to charge him with a crime, or let him go free again.

"Christ, what a mess! Just when I thought I was the only human on earth who could get away with this kind of thing without feeling guilty, all this crap happens. First they make Claudia a suspect—all while I'm sunning myself at the cottage. And now this shit. I can't believe they can fuck up like this."

"That's what the police frequently do: fuck up. But refresh my memory on this Tomlin thing. Remember, I haven't seen Claudia since our meeting at the TD Centre, and last time I saw you, you didn't go into much detail."

"All right. Remember, I told you about them focusing on this drug stuff? They see David as a cokehead. You agreed it might be a good thing for everyone. The unexplained visits from the weirdos at his practice, the large cash withdrawals....Well, Macmillan seemed stuck on David's sister, Sharon. She's the one who got married to Tomlin...but it only lasted a short time. He's some rock promoter."

"Rock music and drugs. I bet they did a scan on everyone in David's orbit. And this guy Tomlin came up positive...probably had a drug charge when he was a teen or something ."

"And they would arrest him on that?"

"These guys are under immense pressure to produce. Which is *why* they constantly fuck up. It's all a big political machine, the criminal division. Some prominent member of society disappears—they'd better produce something. That's how careers get made. And since every detective has a wife who wants a bigger house and a pool, there are plenty of guys who want to be promoted. What's the risk if they screw up, anyway? They stay where they are. You know public servants aren't accountable."

"I can see you have a high opinion of our police force..."

"I think there are lots of decent street cops. And compared to other cities this size, there isn't much corruption. But there's no shortage of unnecessary bungling, mainly because the system promotes it."

We passed a couple of large buildings and a nautical store and finally came to an array of piers and walking bridges. Dozens of yachts were anchored there, their blinding white surfaces contrasting with the vivid blue of the lake behind.

We decided to walk to the end of one of the piers and talk there. We sat down facing the lake, our legs dangling. A few boats bobbed in the distance, their sails billowing in the breeze.

"So what's the bottom line?" Christian asked.

"The bottom line is they're suspecting foul play, just like the article says. They're not buying the idea that David just took a ride. That's bad, because the way they operate they'll keep digging until they've locked someone away or David shows up. And we know the latter won't happen."

"And you think Claudia is off the hook?"

"It looks that way. This is a whole new direction they're going in and, from their perspective, there's more meat here. But they have to substantiate the thing before they can lay charges."

"I feel terrible for the guy. What I don't understand is why they just go and detain a suspect. Obviously, they don't have enough to charge him with."

"They must be hoping that he cracks during the first day or two. Knowing that he hasn't done that, my bet is he'll be free within a couple of days."

Christian stated that if he wasn't freed, we'd have to take some kind of action to get him off the hook. I feared that he was losing his nerve. His assessment that he wouldn't feel guilty about having David murdered had proved correct. What was equally obvious was that his capacity for guilt in general was undiminished.

The bet I'd taken couldn't have been more wrong. Jed Tomlin wasn't let go, but accused of the murder of David Talbot.

The police didn't give the media a lot to work with. The official statement, which was read out at a press conference, asserted that there were strong drug-related links between Talbot's disappearance and Tomlin's arrest. Sizeable withdrawals of cash had been recorded in David Talbot's account and similar amounts of cash had been deposited in accounts beneficially owned by Jed Tomlin. An examination of the reception records at the Talbot clinic and testimony by the clinic's personnel revealed that the suspect had visited Talbot at least twice. Moreover, the authorities had reason to believe that as yet unidentified intermediaries had repeatedly visited Talbot at his clinic prior to his disappearance.

That was it, apart from a reference to the ongoing search for David's body. I was stunned that they'd laid murder charges without having a body!

Christian didn't have to tell me how awful he felt. There were creases around his eyes I'd never seen before and his cheeks seemed to have hollowed.

"I've been thinking of how much I used to feel in control of life," he said. "Remember how we used to say that we'll always project ourselves into the future, rather than letting circumstance drive us?"

"Don't read too much into it. We both knew this was going to be a tense time."

"Yeah, but will things ever go back to normal? It seems that ever since Talbot first crossed my radar screen, I've been off balance."

I've seen the smiling of Fortune beguiling,
I've felt all its favours and found its decay;
Sweet was its blessing, kind its caressing,
But now it is fled, fled far, far away."

ALISON COCKBURN

PART 5

It was summer of 1994 when my relationship with Christian, Claudia and the kids returned to its former intensity. Nearly a decade had passed since David's disappearance. And they were good years for all of us.

For my own taste, they moved much too fast, the way time can pass only during the middle part of life, when professional and social demands converge to create a state of constant pressure and the feeling that we're mere inches away from achieving something great. Later, when we approach our mid-fifties and retirement is both precariously and blissfully near, we realize that a lasting sense of accomplishment is as elusive as ever.

Not that I have many complaints. In 1986 I won the court battle that was to define my career—the one involving the handicapped woman who was wrongfully fired. As they always do when they lose, the bureaucrats kept appealing and frustrating my case. But eventually their efforts were exhausted and I won one of the most cherished plums a lawyer can win: a victory in the Supreme Court, against the government and on constitutional grounds! A flurry of speaking engagements followed and business increased to the point where I had to expand my practice.

Meeting Hugo was another milestone. He came up to me at that fateful gallery opening, because he'd heard of my pending case, which at that time was still more than four years from its resolution.

Hugo opened many doors for me and enriched my life immensely. He was at the top of his profession, much as Christian had been in his and I was starting to be in mine. But unlike either of us, he was a social maven. His days and nights were a constant sequence of networking, or "schmoozing," as he called it. He'd been appointed chairman of the Workers' Compensation Board because of his social skills, and he was set to use his social contacts to hold on to his position as long as he could.

It took me a while to understand Hugo. His quest for power had led him to the chairmanship of an institution whose mandate it was to look after injured workers. Yet there was no one in the world who despised workers more than Hugo. He ceaselessly praised me for keeping up the fight on behalf of my handicapped client, but it wasn't because I defended her rights. It was for the fame and power it would bring me.

When I told him about Christian leaving Global, he thought the idea of walking away from it all ludicrous. Why relinquish control over others when you're finally at the point where it's yours?

As I write this, I realize how strange it seems that Hugo left *me*. Why, if I have such negative things to say about him, didn't *I* terminate the relationship? What was in it for me?

Above all things, he fascinated me. And he showered me with attention. If I had a case in Ottawa, he'd have his secretary phone and make sure I'd get the best room. He was forever scheming how he could advance my career and to whom he could introduce me. And whenever I came to his place, there was a bottle of some prohibitively expensive cognac and an abundant supply of the Cuban cigars I'd recently started to smoke.

Hugo's universe was one of beauty. He wore custom made suits, monogramed shirts and four hundred dollar, hand-stitched shoes. And when he came home from work, he changed into one of his many silk robes. His condominium was filled with art. Not the type of art I liked, but art whose beauty was indisputable.

I now realize that I'd always deprived myself of sensuality. To see it in such abundance took my breath away and temporarily robbed me of my balance. If a decade can be called temporary.

I've often asked myself what Hugo got out of our relationship. Apart from the physical attraction we felt for each other and the advantages of companionship, I suspect he viewed me as raw material, which could be shaped to his requirements. Not right away— I'm far too stubborn and set in my ways for that—but eventually. And Hugo loves the pursuit of a seemingly insurmountable, challenge. That, after all, is what his whole life is.

His first challenge was to teach me beauty—the way he saw it. We had endless debates, and later arguments, about art. While I favored the rawness and honesty of expressionism, he found it vulgar. He called the art I liked—canvasses by Edvard Munch, drawings by Egon Schiele and bronzes by Giacometti—coarse and unrefined. In order to understand beauty, he said, I should learn to love the paintings of the Renaissance and Impressionism, the sculptures of Bernini and Rodin, and Albrecht Dürer's prints.

For quite a while, I enjoyed the rush of these debates, but eventually it became apparent that our word fights were not about art, but values.

Things started to unravel. I found it increasingly difficult to respect him and started accusing him of elitism and snobbery. I predicted that his lack of compassion would make him a lonely old man. That he'd have a wonderful funeral and an impressive obituary in the national papers, but he'd die a spiritual and moral pauper.

My time with Hugo seemed like a visit to another planet. It was as if the charms of sensuality had been lurking out there all along, waiting to ensnare me. When they did, I fell for them head over heels.

Our break-up left me distraught. I thought a lot about myself, as one does when bringing to an end an important chapter of one's life.

I tried to redefine myself, but could come up with only two things: my profession and my sexual orientation. That I even referred to the latter is perverse and only due to the lopsided puritanism of our times.

Christian and Claudia helped me cope. At first that felt strange. The contrast between Hugo's approach to life and Christian's and Claudia's couldn't have been greater. I was embarrassed about having been with Hugo for so long and concerned what my friends would think of me. But they accepted me back as if nothing had happened. I started to visit the cottage again, and Christian and I resuscitated our Wednesday-night-at-the-tavern ritual. What an extraordinary thing friendship is!

Things might have turned out differently if the cops hadn't withdrawn their charges against Jed Tomlin. Their preparations had been so sloppy that, within less than a week, Tomlin's lawyer managed to amass enough evidence to seriously embarrass them.

He demonstrated that the cash deposits, some sixty thousand dollars, had been Jed Tomlin's cut for a concert in Detroit he'd jointly organized with an American promoter. Why the funds were paid in cash and why there had been three different partial deposits remained a mystery, but Tomlin's partner signed the appropriate affidavit and volunteered to testify.

Even more distressing for Macmillan was that the two visits the accused had made to David's clinic, approximately eight months prior to David's disappearance, were on the recommendation of his physician. Tomlin had suffered from neck pains and when they persisted for weeks, his doctor suggested he might try an acupuncturist or a chiropractor. Tomlin remembered his former brother-in-law, which led to the two appointments.

As to the idea that the two thugs who'd visited David worked with Jed Tomlin, his lawyer had little difficulty convincing the judge that it was pure supposition. If the police had proof of any connection, where was it? He called it an allegation almost as ludi-crous as the murder charge itself. If there had really been a murder, it was up to the crown to prove that. Where was the body of the dead David Talbot? Where was the evidence that Talbot hadn't left for Cuba or Brazil because he was having a mid-life crisis? Maybe that accounted for the cash withdrawals.

On the other hand, Tomlin's lawyer had to concede that his client was a cocaine user. Macmillan's team, armed with a search warrant, hadn't come out entirely empty-handed: they'd found just over two ounces of the stuff in Tomlin's wall safe, enough to nail him for trafficking.

In the end, the murder charges were dropped and Tomlin agreed to a guilty plea for possession of an illegal substance. His sentence was 200 hours of community work, but because he'd spent considerable time in custody, it was suspended. Macmillan wasn't officially reprimanded, but it was a good bet that he'd find himself without the support of his superiors.

I don't know what Christian would have done if Tomlin had been kept in detention. I spent as much time with him as I could, worried that he would never tolerate the incarceration of an inno-cent man.

He felt better when Tomlin was vindicated, but then he start-ed to worry about Claudia again. I reassured both of them that it was unlikely that Macmillan would be allowed to keep the case open. Besides, I strongly believed he'd convinced himself that Claudia was not involved. Even so, it took a couple of months before Christian let down his guard. When he did, he seemed filled with new purpose, possessed with a determination I hadn't seen since his corporate days.

I felt free to let myself be completely drawn into my new rela-tionship with Hugo. The David chapter seemed firmly behind us.

The following summer, Claudia and Christian flew to the Cape Verde Islands and got married. When they returned, they invited

. . . .

friends and relatives to celebrate with them at Baltasar Tavares'
Portuguese restaurant where they'd had their first date. What a
party it was!

When we reconnected, it was like before, but better. Within a
year, I stopped thinking of my closeness with Christian and Claudia
as a couple. My friendship with Claudia had become as distinct as the
one I'd had since childhood with Christian. I discussed my disap-
pointment with Hugo with her and she helped with incisive analysis
and prudent advice. To his credit, Christian encouraged this. Quite
frequently, when I talked to Claudia about some intensely personal
experience with Hugo, he discreetly stepped aside.

When retiring, Christian had vowed to live each day the way it
presented itself. That way, he'd not be bogged down with self-
imposed tasks related to who he thought he was, but was free to
find his real self.

Despite these protestations, I always thought Christian would
eventually return to business. Perhaps not to an executive position,
but to something less taxing, like consulting work. Now, more than
a decade later, I could see that this would never happen. He'd found
himself.

At the cottage, a whole new wall of books on art had been added.
The desk in Christian's office had been replaced with a rough table.
Brushes, palette knives and tubes of acrylics cluttered it. And outside,
there were tubs of clay and a pottery wheel. Christian's dabbling had
turned into something more ambitious. When I visited on weekends, he spent at least half the day on his new interest. I imagine that
during the week, he was even more productive.

Claudia stayed at the cottage more often, too. Christian had
built her a small desk in his office and that's where she did some of
her design work. It was wonderful to see the two at work next to
each other. They both did their own thing, but anyone stealing a

glance at them could see that in spirit they were one.

The children were now adults.

Her father's constant reproaches had left Karen badly starved for the approval and affection of a male figure. Christian had arrived in time to prevent critical damage, but he and Claudia noticed how much attention Karen still required. She excelled at school and helped at home whenever she could, but had an insatiable need to share her accomplishments with Christian and earn his praise. Christian was always there for her.

Karen had finished high school and started at York University, when she met Alex. When Karen grew as dependent on her boyfriend's approval as she'd been on Christian's, Claudia started worrying. But her fears that her daughter would be dealt a devastating blow when the relationship ended never came to pass. Karen and Alex got married.

At the wedding, Karen was stunning. Hers was a quiet, graceful beauty, untainted by the bold, teasing dazzle, which is so common. I remember thinking how much Hugo would approve. Here were charm and beauty that would have been appreciated in any age!

I was equally impressed with Alex, who was four years older than Karen. He'd lost his parents in his early teens, which had made him self-reliant and more mature than others his age. He was determined to recreate the family that had been snatched away from him.

I talked to Alex quite a bit at the wedding—and many times since at the cottage—and I've come to appreciate him both for his intelligence and modesty. In countless ways, even physical ones, he reminds me of a younger Christian.

Karen's wedding also allowed me to catch up with Jason, who was now twenty-four and over six feet tall. He made an unhappy impression. He'd brought a dark haired, alabaster-skinned beauty with him, but hardly talked to her.

When the speeches were done with and things started winding down, Christian and I were standing outside, decked out in our tuxedo best, talking about old times. We both held snifters in our hand and I was smoking a cigar.

He asked me if I'd talked to Jason.

"Not very successfully...he seems very withdrawn."

"He's only here because Karen wanted it. We haven't talked for a while."

"How come?"

"He's been difficult for a long time, but it came to a head last Thanksgiving at the cottage. He argued with Alex, pushed Karen around and insulted Claudia. I took him outside and told him I'd take him straight back to town if he didn't behave. For a minute, he paced around, tears in his eyes. Then he told me he wanted to be taken back to the marina. He'd had it with us."

"Insolent little prick..."

"That's what I said. On the boat ride back I told him that he'd become a pain in the ass to have around."

"Good for you."

"Can you imagine? Here's his mother who loves him and is constantly concerned…"

"And you who's given him more attention and support than he could ever have wanted from a father," I pointed out.

"I told him that too."

"And?"

"He didn't respond. Just stared straight ahead into the grey horizon. Which got me really going."

"I'd have thrown the little twerp overboard."

Christian laughed, but I could tell it was because the festive atmosphere and the cognac had mellowed him, not because he found it funny.

"I did better than that. I told him his allowance and tuition payments were suspended until he apologized and promised to treat his family with respect and consideration."

"So what happened?"

"We didn't hear from him and we actually liked it."

"Claudia, too?"

"There were a few tense moments, but she never panicked."

"Did he ever apologize?"

"No, and we never resumed our support payments to him. To his credit, he somehow got himself through university. I told you he finished his master's, didn't I?"

"You did. What's he doing now?"

"He's in the city, working for the *Star*. It's not the greatest newspaper for a career in investigative journalism, but it's a start."

"I see…all those logs and journals he kept when he was a teenager were a tip-off. Where do you think things will go from here?"

"Karen's brokered a ceasefire, but not peace. I imagine we'll see him occasionally. He may even send birthday cards. But I don't think we'll get phone calls or flowers on Mother's Day." There was a bitter edge to Christian's voice that I'd never heard before.

I saw Tila at the wedding, too. She was still at Global Capital. She was having fun, she said, but was starting to understand why Christian had left corporate life. The intensity of her travel schedule and the incessant pressure of having to keep everything running at home base were starting to weigh on her.

Now in her mid-forties, Tila was still extremely attractive. I spent a good part of the wedding festivities admiring her social skills and the look of indisputable competence about her. Her bearing was slightly haughty, just enough so that anyone who felt like going up to Tila thought about it twice. This was a woman who'd approach you, not the other way around. And it made her all the more alluring.

Christian later told me that he'd stayed in touch with her and that Claudia had decided it was good idea to occasionally invite her to the house. But the few times Tila came, they'd both sensed that she wanted to keep her distance.

That's why Claudia was pleasantly surprised at Tila's reaction when she called to ask for advice. It was two years after Karen's wedding and she'd just graduated from York. Now she was looking for a job.

Claudia asked Tila if she could spend an hour with her daughter and give her some insights. Tila embraced the idea enthusiastically and wondered whether Karen could see her the very next day.

She could, and they ended up talking for two hours at Tila's office and then went out to dinner. When Karen returned home that night, it was with an irresistible offer. She'd work at Global Capital for six months. Then Tila would take her for dinner again and they could decide on the next step. If they both liked what happened, they'd talk about her future at the firm. If they didn't, Tila would help Karen find something else. There was only one proviso,

Karen explained. Tila had insisted that her mom and Christian agree to the idea.

Karen loved working at Global Capital. And Tila, despite her busy schedule, took an active interest in her. She soon recognized that Karen was exceptionally creative and had strong communications skills. As to her one weakness—that she wasn't very suitable for any of the functions requiring a competitive personality—there were plenty of other candidates for those.

After it became clear that Karen would stay on, Tila came to their house more frequently. And by the time I started to visit the cottage regularly again, Tila had become a frequent guest there, as well. Once she felt comfortable with me, she became relaxed and communicative. It reminded me of my first tentative discussions with Claudia, which had, in no time, matured into friendship.

Sometimes, when I looked at Tila, I wondered what it would feel like being with a woman again.

Jason's demand to meet with her alone had left Claudia apprehensive. But now that she saw him, she felt better. He looked good!

For a moment, she thought it was his casual outfit; he wore hiking boots, jeans, a colorful flannel shirt and a black canvas jacket. But then she noticed he'd put on weight and picked up some color.

"You're looking great, Jason" she started. "Do you want me to make you some coffee?"

Either he's in his usual, taciturn mood or he's embarrassed by my compliment, Claudia thought. Then she realized he was lost in thought. He sat down and glared at her absent-mindedly.

"Look, Mom, it would be better if you didn't try to make conversation. I'm here to tell you something that won't please you or Christian. Maybe you won't want to see me ever again, after this."

Claudia sat down. "That wouldn't be such a major change, Jason, would it? We hardly get to see you as things stand now."

Jason stared at the surface of the table. He reminded her of David.

"Can I get to the point? I'll say my thing and then I'll get out of here."

"If that's what you want to do."

"Look, I'm writing a book. About Dad. I thought you should know."

Blood rushed to Claudia's head. She expected her voice to fail, but when she heard herself talk, it sounded remarkably normal.

"A book about your father…what could you possibly want to say?"

"Don't bullshit me, Mother. You know as well as I do that he didn't just disappear. That's what the book's about."

Tears welled up in her eyes.

"Jason, listen to me. That was a long time ago. Why do you want to reopen this damned story?"

"Reopen the story?" Jason shouted. "Reopen it? Christ, for me it's never been closed. It's been there every day of my life, at least my adult life. Why do you think I'm such a miserable fuck? Why do you think I studied journalism…*investigative* journalism?"

"Listen to me Jason!" Claudia shouted back, then caught hold of herself. "Let me get some water. You've got to listen, Jason. Please don't interrupt. I promise I'll listen to what you have to say, too."

"I don't want to listen to you!" Jason roared. "I'm going to say my thing and get out of here. Consider it fair warning. I'm doing you and Christian a huge favor."

"Fair warning? Fair warning of what? You're bloody well going to listen to me if I listen to you. Your father was a no-good, sulky, miserable son-of-a-bitch, whose only goal in life was to hurt others. I've restrained myself from saying this to you for far too long, so here it is. You know that's the truth, Jason, you were there. If he didn't abuse me, he came after Karen and you, wasn't that so?"

Jason was bent forward, his elbows perched on his knees and his head clamped between his hands.

"And what happened after I left your dad? Huh? He stole the only money I had left to support you. Then, after he finally ran out of lawyers willing to take on his pitiful case, he was forced to sign an agreement paying for your private school bills and support. Did the bastard ever pay? No. If I hadn't worked my butt off, you wouldn't have had such a cushy life. Have you ever thought of that?"

Jason looked down at the floor, tears running down his cheeks. She realized her capacity to love Jason, or even feel sorry for him, was depleted. "Then Christian came into our lives. He gave me respect, love and support. And he gave you and Karen time, care and guidance. Apart from the fact that he loves you like a father. And what have you given back? Sulky, disrespectful and inconsiderate behavior. And now you want to top it off by reopening this mess and making everyone miserable. If you can't think of me, think of your sister and Christian. You make me sick!"

"All right, you've had your say," Jason exploded. "So *I* make you sick? What about you guys? My father got murdered and you and Karen just keep on going along, as if nothing had happened. Happy as larks in your newly found love of Christian. That's why I left to live with Dad that time....I couldn't fucking stand it."

"And you were back a week later, weren't you?"

"Yes, goddammit! I couldn't stand how unhappy he was, but I could see why. You and Karen...Christ! What kind of a family are you? Dad leaves, life gets better for you by the day. Dad's gone for good, you positively beam, the two of you. Well, I couldn't deal with it as nicely as you, because he was my fucking father. Do you get it?"

"Yes, I get it," she said, her voice more composed. "That's why I never said to you what I told you just now. But he wasn't *my* father, you have to understand. He was my tormentor and the tormentor of my children and when I left him I left all my troubles behind me. Surely you can understand why I didn't mope."

"That's no fucking excuse for murder," he said.

"What are you talking about?"

"The book I'm writing. It'll be about how my father was murdered."

Claudia paused, determined not to give anything away. "How

do you know he was murdered? I thought the police were still try-ing to figure out what happened."

"Yeah, sure. The police. I've been studying how they operate for a while now. Morons at best, dangerous bunglers nabbing the wrong guys at worst."

"But *you* know, I take it…you've figured it all out."

The further north she drove, the more spectacular the scenery became. The stark and cloudless sky, the trees ablaze in pulsating reds and majestic spreads of gold, raced by her, unseen.

Claudia longed to be with Christian. She needed his strength and objectivity, even though she had a foreboding sense that what had happened was hopelessly out of Christian's grasp.

What alarmed her most was what Jason had said about Samantha Nyman. That woman had almost done her in with Macmillan; now she was at it again.

Claudia remembered the boxes she'd been asked to pick up at the police station, when they were through with them. She had to sign for them. David's possessions...notepads, a bunch of pens, a trophy from the golf club, his diplomas and lots of pictures. Pictures of a time Claudia would rather forget. She'd gone through everything, at least twice, before handing it over to the kids. Karen had declined, but Jason had eagerly taken the boxes to his room.

She'd never thought of David's receptionist and lover. Who would have?

The diary…that damned diary, Christian. It's the key to it all. Apparently, he somehow found this Nyman woman. He drove to St. Catharines several times, to see her."

"I bet you the first thing she told him about was your threatening to kill David."

"She hated me…and if she slept with David, she probably felt cheated out of a relationship."

"I thought about that after you called. But that won't get Jason far. The police already dealt with it, Claudia."

"That's not the problem. She gave him a copy of her testimony! When he read it, he got interested in the mystery visitors Samantha referred to. So he returned." Claudia sipped at her tea. "That's when she gave him some of David's stuff she'd kept, including a diary. It's that damned diary I'm worried about. It led him to Eddie Falco."

"*Freddie* Falco, I think. He found him?"

"That's what he said. That's what his investigative journalism training taught him."

"Oh, shit…"

"Oh shit is right. He didn't say much, except that he found Falco. Apparently he told Jason to give you his regards."

"What?"

"Something like: 'Give your step-dad my regards…he may not know my name, but we had a couple of memorable meetings.'"

"I can't believe it…"

"What are we going to do?"

Christian held her tightly for a minute, telling her they'd go for a walk in the woods and talk about something completely different. That would be soothing, didn't she think? Claudia reached up to kiss him.

They found a patch of honey mushrooms. It had been dry for a few days, leaving them past their prime, but they'd still taste great in the risotto Christian planned for dinner.

Back at the cottage, Christian added logs to the dying fire.

"We have to go through every detail, if we're to assess our options." He grabbed pad and pencil and sat down.

"I'm not sure there's more than I've already told you," Claudia said. "The key problem is he found Falco. And now he knows he's on the right track."

"Or suspects it. We don't know if he has anything else."

"He's got the diary with Falco's name in it and the two affidavits...the one about my threat and the other about the visits by these strangers."

"So we don't really know how big a problem we have."

"Why do you think the police didn't follow up on it?"

"What, the diary you mean? They probably concentrated on the receptionist's log and overlooked it. Or maybe they did look at it and simply didn't attribute any importance to it."

"Give me a break, Christian...with a name like Falco pencilled in three times?"

"Falco may just be a minor hood. Maybe he doesn't even have a record. I bet you if his boss' name had shown up in the diary, they would have jumped. Remember the Fiorentino guy? Owner of bakeries, restaurants and nightclubs?"

"Maybe they never saw the diary...maybe Samantha Nyman nabbed it for herself."

"Why would she do that?"

"Beats me...unless she thought it might implicate David."

"Maybe."

"What if Jason finds his way to Fiorentino?"

"I don't think these guys talk much, especially to an investigative journalist. If Falco told Jason anything, Fiorentino will probably put an end to it."

"How do you mean?"

"He'll impress on Falco not to say another thing."

"But we don't know what Falco has already said."

"Did Jason give you any clues?"

"No, he said he found the guy at some strip club and had a nice conversation with him. A nice conversation…that's how he put it. Enough to keep digging."

"Nothing else?"

"Yes, that his research convinced him that David had been murdered. You know how Jason never looks you in the eye? This time he did. Very intensely."

Christian kept taking notes. He'd toss them into the fire afterwards, but having written everything down guaranteed he'd remember each detail.

"You said something about him giving us fair warning. Did you question that?"

"I asked why we needed to be warned. If he really knew something about his father's disappearance, why not go to the police? He said I knew bloody well what it meant. And that a book about David Talbot would appear, containing the gory truth about his murder."

"Then what?"

"It ended. I told him I had no idea of what he was talking about. All I saw was that he'd inflict a lot of pain on those who'd treated him the best. He replied that he'd already made up his mind to publish it. It would make him feel good to have unearthed the truth and, besides, the publisher was very excited about."

"Big bloody surprise."

"That's what I said. Any publisher would jump at a book solving a murder, especially if it made the justice system look bad. And even more so if the author was a young investigative reporter and the victim his father. I told him he could hand in the most outrageous pile of crap and they'd lick it up."

"I bet that had him on his feet."

"He went crazy. Now I was attacking his professional abilities and questioning his journalistic integrity. Before I knew it he slammed the door shut and then I saw him through the living room window running up the sidewalk toward Eglinton, like someone fleeing from a horrid apparition."

"You think he hates us so much?"

"It's funny you ask that. I couldn't help thinking that he was running away from himself."

I saw Christian two more times that October. The first time we met, he told me about the mess they were in with Jason.

"Who's going to publish this stuff?" I asked and he told me McFadden. He didn't know when or what it would say, but according to Jason it was a done deal.

I offered Christian my assistance; maybe I could talk some sense into Jason. Christian declined. He'd got me far too involved with the David thing, he said. No way he'd engage me in this battle.

Then he told me what a wonderful friend I'd been, which should have perked my attention. But it didn't, because I thought he was talking about what I'd done for him thirteen years earlier. It's only now that I know he was talking about the future. He was already starting to miss our friendship.

I asked what he was going to do and he said he and Claudia hadn't talked much about it yet. I suggested if he needed another brain to sort through the options, I'd be there for him. He put his arm around my shoulder and told me I'd had enough.

The last time we met, I made another half-hearted attempt to find out what he and Claudia had decided to do. At one point he said, "I've told you this before, Jake…you do know that you can use the cottage anytime, even when I'm not there. You have both cottage and boat keys, don't you?"

Why was he mentioning this now? The season was just about over.

EPILOGUE

Nothing ever ends.

We all thought our troubles were behind us when David was gone, but things kept spiraling out of control. I thought my relationship with Hugo was at an end, but lately the bastard has been after me again. More than thirty years ago, I told the world I was gay, but lately I'm having second thoughts about that, too.

And some believe that Claudia's and Christian's disappearance marks an end. But I promise that's not what will happen. The story of Claudia and Christian won't end because I can't allow it.

My drinking and chain smoking haven't lessened, and since I started writing I've developed a weakness for late night eating binges. Few things taste better to me now than a double-cheese pizza with pepperoni and anchovies from Stan's around the corner. Hugo would be appalled.

But having gained a few more pounds has been worth it. I've made progress. Only time will tell, but I think I found the key to the riddle and I have no doubt it's because I forced myself to write this account.

Not that I learned anything from the cops. This time it was the Ontario Provincial Police who handled the case. A couple of deer hunters, eating a sandwich at the edge of the ridge above, had seen a badly smashed-up boat near the rocky shore and reported it to the OPP detachment in Parry Sound. Since it was an unseasonably sunny Friday afternoon on Georgian Bay, one of the two police boats was already on the water. It was quickly summoned to the scene.

If it hadn't been unusually calm, the two investigating officers could never have brought their boat anywhere near the hull that sat mostly underwater. Even under these ideal conditions, they had to shut off the engine and use their man-overboard-poles to push their craft between the rocks that lined the shore.

Despite the fact that large pieces of the boat's bottom and sides were missing, the stern was largely undamaged. The drive shaft of the motor had been whacked off, but the rest looked fine. On the left was the swimming ladder, on the right in large blue letters the words FREEDOM and underneath a few sizes smaller PARRY SOUND. They radioed the desk constable in Parry Sound, reporting a few basic facts and the boat's name.

Twenty minutes later, they were called back with instructions to search the nearby area for possible survivors and additional clues as to what may have happened. A small Coast Guard vessel had been dispatched to assist.

It's in the initial stages of an investigation that police work shines the brightest, largely because the reservoir of information available to the authorities is immense. Within a quarter of an hour, the Ontario Provincial Police's desk clerk in town phoned the local marinas and ascertained that the FREEDOM belonged to one Christian Unger and was berthed at Waubuno Point Marina.

The marina's owner, Al Gregory, said he'd wondered about not having seen Christian and Claudia Unger. It wasn't unusual that they were still at their island at this time of the year, but they came into town at least once a week for provisions. He'd ask around.

Then two things happened simultaneously. The OPP desk clerk did a scan on the names Christian Unger and Claudia Unger and an officer was sent to pay a visit to Al Gregory's establishment and take a statement.

The results of the scan revealed nothing about Claudia Unger, probably because her name back then had been Talbot. But what came back about Christian stunned the police clerk. The profile itself was brief, but there were countless references to what had to be voluminous and consequential files. Among other things, they referred to a Claudia Talbot, the suspected murder of her husband David Talbot, and the arrest and subsequent release of Jed Tomlin.

Meanwhile, the constable at Waubuno Point Marina found Al Gregory's family and staff divided as to when Claudia and Christian had last been seen. Louise stuck to her story that it had been two weeks, since they'd been at the marina, but Jeff, the mechanic, said that Christian had asked him to make an adjustment to his boat's carburetor just a few days ago. Al Gregory himself knew nothing specific, but nevertheless took his wife's side.

In the end, the mechanic took the policeman to his service shop. He remembered that he'd been busy putting through his weekly part orders when Mr. Unger walked in. The log showed Wednesday the 13th of November 1996 as the day on which he'd done that.

It was also a matter of record that a major storm had hit Georgian Bay on the weekend of November 16 and 17, and this fact was to play a major part in both the scope of the search-and-rescue mission and the OPP's eventual conclusions.

Coast Guard personnel working both from the shore and on the water searched the vicinity off and on for another week, but discovered nothing further than a badly discolored lifejacket, a torn windbreaker and a woollen watch cap. These items were half a mile upwind from the wreckage, floating close together. They could have belonged to the passengers of the FREEDOM.

Based on these findings, the Coast Guard determined that Christian and Claudia had likely drowned, the victims of a severe storm. The report refrains from theorizing what might have happened, but dryly states that simple factors like running out of fuel or engine failure frequently cause boaters to abandon their vessel and attempt to swim to a nearby island. Doing so is a treacherous enterprise at best; if wind speed or direction is misjudged or choppy waters impede progress, death by hypothermia results.

In its conclusions, the report states a theoretical nine-day margin of error, allowing for the full range of time between Christian's stop at the marina on the 13th and the discovery of the shipwreck on the 22nd. But it identifies the stormy weekend of the 16th and 17th as the most likely time for the accident.

The Ontario Provincial Police came to the same conclusion, but its final report refers to several files completed by the Metropolitan Toronto Police between September and December of 1983 and a series of conversations with Detective Sergeant Macmillan of said police force. The latter is reported to have voiced misgivings about the Coast Guard report, suggesting that possibilities other than a boating accident should be considered.

I have no idea how far the police went in investigating my friends' disappearance, or whether the Metropolitan Toronto Police force ever formally got involved. But in the third week of December I finally got to see Macmillan, the detective Claudia had described to me many years earlier.

When he arrived at my office and settled into one of the guest chairs, he lowered his head so that he could look up at me and asked me whether I knew the Ungers well. I said yes and, much as Claudia had described it, he just kept glaring at me. He did have large, moist cow's eyes; there was no better way to describe them. He must have noticed my smile.

Macmillan asked what I found amusing and I apologized. I

said I'd expected a visit from the police at least two weeks ago.

"And why did you expect us?" he asked, glowering at me.

"It's a fairly logical conclusion, isn't it? After all, Christian and Claudia have had an accident and their bodies haven't been found. I'm their closest friend." Then I went politely on the offensive, which I'd learned a long time ago was the only way to talk to the police. I asked Macmillan what had taken them so long.

"Jurisdictional delays," he said. "Parry Sound is OPP territory, you know." I told him I understood. I'd done some work for their union, so I knew how complex it all was.

He asked me whether I'd been the Ungers' friend when David Talbot disappeared.

"I've been Christian's friend since we were kids. Claudia's since she started going out with Christian."

Macmillan tried to be smart, asking me when they'd first gone out and I told him. "Two or three years after Claudia and her former husband split, I think."

I stayed deliberately vague, even though I knew the date with almost certain accuracy. After all, I was spending most of my nights brooding over the countless spreadsheets of factoids, timelines and personality profiles I'd assembled, which later became the basis for this journal.

"You mean they started going out about half a year before David Talbot was murdered," Macmillan shot back.

"Murdered, Sergeant? I thought you already lost that battle twice over." I looked straight at him. "Lost it rather badly, in fact…tried to lock up an innocent man, didn't you?"

Macmillan didn't respond. I was convinced that I'd never hear from him again. He might pester the kids for a while, but I was certain he wouldn't get anything out of them either.

The reason for my confidence concerning Karen and, particularly Jason, was what had happened a week earlier. I'd invited Christian's and Claudia's friends to a get-together.

When I'd asked Karen and Alex who should come, they'd suggested it should be a very small group. We immediately settled on Tila, a few friends from work (Jackie Hunter and Chuck Fernaux for Claudia, and Melanie Knapp, Christian's part-time secretary), and John and Mary Drake, their neighbors.

When we talked about her grandparents, Karen expressed doubt. She felt they'd treated her mom horribly and been unkind to Christian. Besides, she'd visited there last weekend and talked with them.

Finally, Karen suggested, she'd call Jason and tell him what we'd decided. She didn't think it would be a problem with him.

We met at Baltasar Tavares' restaurant, enjoying robust Portuguese reds and dishes like grilled sardines and pork and clams. It may not have been the same band as when we were there for Claudia's and Christian's wedding party, but the people who entertained us were from the Cape Verde Islands and their tunes were as Christian had always loved them, seductive as the ocean.

We swapped stories of Claudia and Christian and later John Drake said some thoughtful words, occasionally reading from a piece of paper. Mary said she'd loved Claudia like a daughter. A few of us cried.

When we left we were all a bit soused, even Tila, from whom I would never have expected it. Outside, driving snow lashed our flushed faces and a bitter wind blew.

"Christian told me about the harsh weather when he left Tavares' restaurant with Claudia the first time," I said to Tila. For a moment we held on to each other. She cried and I kissed her on the forehead. I wanted her very badly then.

Jackie Hunter, who'd drunk only water, volunteered to take Karen and Alex home. The others hailed cabs. Suddenly, it was only

Jason and I who stood there at the curb. He asked if he could come to my place. He wanted to talk.

We headed down to Queen Street and then walked a couple of small blocks west to my building. He didn't say a thing. When we climbed the stairs, I noticed that he was drunk. Still, the second he sat down on one of my kitchen chairs, he asked for scotch.

I don't keep scotch at my place, so I poured us both a Courvoisier. He took his glass and started wandering around the apartment, glancing at my labor posters and examining my bookshelves. "I wasn't sure you'd want to talk…I mean you guys must all hate me." Then he added: "I really fucked up, you know."

"We know you fucked up, you little prick. You've been fucking up your entire life."

He broke down completely. I watched him for a minute or so, then got up and held him…told him to get his act together and sit down. Instead he walked to the bathroom and puked.

Later, I took him for a walk. We both needed to sober up and say what had to be said. The wind had lessened while we were inside, but the snow fell harder now. It came in thick, heavy flakes, the kind that builds up into a foot or more in a short time and is a bitch to shovel.

"I don't have anything to say," Jason started, "except that I'm so fucking sorry." Then he went on to talk at some length. How much he'd had to be thankful for and how instead of showing appreciation he'd destroyed their lives. And how he'd hurt everyone else in the process. Me. The people who'd come tonight. His sister. How was he ever going to look Karen in the eye again? And how was he going to live with himself?

I put my arm around his shoulder and told him we all fuck up. His was a more monumental fuck-up than I'd ever seen, but there was nothing that could be done to undo it. And nothing could be done to make life easier for those who'd now have to go through life without Claudia and Christian.

But, I told him, there was one thing he could do to make things easier on himself. He could commit his life to their memory…try to embrace their values and beliefs. He could pass on the gifts he'd received from his mother and Christian.

There was no need to be more obvious. No need to tell him to pull his book. I knew that if he hadn't already shredded his manuscript, he'd do so when he got home. And I knew that if Macmillan showed up at his place, he wouldn't learn a thing, except what great people his mother and stepfather had been.

I slept until almost noon the next day and when I got up Jason sat in the kitchen. A pot of coffee was steaming on the stove. He told me he'd seen a couple of books he'd like to borrow. One of them was Adam Smith's "The Theory of Moral Sentiments". I knew he was on the mend.

I haven't seen Jackie Hunter or Chuck Fernaux again, nor have I run into the Drakes. As to Melanie Knapp, I asked her at our evening at Tavares' if she wanted a part-time job in my firm. If Christian had been pleased with her work I would be, too. Besides, I thought I might learn something from her to help me in my search for the truth. Melanie accepted.

I've seen quite a bit of Jason, since I started writing things down. I haven't told him about this book, but he's been coming over once every couple of weeks and we often discuss what we've read.

He's still crushed and I catch myself wondering why I'm even talking to him. Sometimes merely looking at him makes me want to strangle him. But those emotions pass and we go on talking. The last couple of Wednesdays I've taken him along to the tavern. I wonder what Christian would think.

The key to it all lies with Tila and Karen. Ever since our get-together at Tavares', I've suspected that they know more than they let on to. They acted more as if they missed Claudia and Christian than if they mourned them. Every now and then, I caught them looking at each other in a knowing way—the way people who share a secret look at each other.

I would have thought Tila capable of hiding her feelings, but not Karen. Given her love of her mother and her adoration of Christian, Karen should have been devastated.

My suspicions have hardened. In late January, I was granted temporary power to administer Claudia's and Christian's assets, and ever since, Karen and I have met one evening a week at the Forest Hill house. We started out by taking inventory of bank and brokerage accounts, what debt there was and what insurance policies had been in place. Apart from a small convenience account at a bank branch near their house, Claudia and Christian had everything with Global Capital. That gave me an excuse to ask Tila to come, too.

She helped me read statements and decide which investments should be sold, so that we could pay outstanding bills. She phoned the Gregorys in Parry Sound to see what could be done to close up the cottage, collected fees that had been due to Claudia, made sure the snow got shoveled and did a hundred other things.

Before long, our meetings took on ritualistic overtones. Tila and I went through our task list, sharing a desk in what had been Christian's home office, while Karen and Alex struggled with dinner. Later, we all played cards or just talked. I don't think any of us would have wanted to miss it.

Jason never visited the house. He probably felt he didn't deserve to be there or feared Karen didn't want to see him.

After consulting with Tila, I suggested that Karen and Alex give up their rented apartment and move into the house full time. They could pay the same rent they'd paid to their landlord and we could apply it toward the expenses. I promised I'd discuss it with Jason, knowing that he'd like the idea. It would help him deal with his guilt.

Christian's records were in impeccable order, which helped. Increasingly, Tila and I had time to talk about things other than Claudia and Christian. We got away from the serious stuff and teased each other and shared laughs. A couple of times, I left the house feeling that she wouldn't have minded seeing me more often and alone.

When I started writing, I wasn't sure if I could trust Tila. I thought she still hadn't got over Christian and I couldn't imagine that she liked Claudia. The past weeks have changed my mind. I now know that she still loves Christian, but has long accepted Claudia as his mate. Claudia's trusting her to become Karen's mentor changed things. Her admiration for Claudia grew to affection and, eventually, love.

One night when we met at the house, Alex couldn't make it. Karen was cooking and Tila and I were upstairs in the office, talking about what we'd have to do at tax time, which was getting close.

Later, at the dinner table, I asked Karen and Tila how things were at Global Capital and they talked about the project they were working on.

I didn't listen too carefully, but instead reflected on how well things were going for Karen. Alex had gradually replaced Christian and Tila had stepped into her mother's shoes. She was adorable in her concern and love for Karen.

We were halfway through the soup when I suddenly realized I had a chance to ask the two of them a question. Alex not being there provided the opportunity.

"What about Christian's offshore money, Tila?" I said. "Are you looking after that, too?"

I tried to keep my eyes on both Tila and Karen, hoping to see a scene I'd witnessed in courtrooms a hundred times: the two of them trapped, looking at each other in alarm and then, realizing that I'd noticed, their eyes nervously darting around the room before seeking mine.

But nothing like that happened. I could tell my question had stunned them, but if they were hiding something, they'd carefully rehearsed their response and now executed it to perfection. Tila slowly raised her steel-grey eyes up to mine, held my interrogator's glance for a long second or two, and said: "What offshore money?" When I looked over at Karen, I thought she'd blushed, but even of that I couldn't be certain.

I backed off, but that doesn't mean that I gave up hope. I'm convinced that Karen and Tila are in contact with Christian and Claudia. Call it intuition.

I've been wondering why Tila and Karen should be the chosen ones. Why not me? I didn't have to think for long, though. The logic in doing it this way was unmistakable.

Of those left behind by Christian and Claudia, Karen needed

and deserved to know the truth more than anyone. She'd support-ed her mother and stepfather with unwavering loyalty and also depended on them the most, despite her marriage to Alex. And Tila? She had to know because she was Christian's and Claudia's source of money.

That didn't explain why I couldn't have known, too, but I trusted Christian sufficiently to have made the right decision. Perhaps he just didn't want to involve me, as he'd said to me in the tavern; perhaps there hadn't been time to talk to me. Christian might have thought that it would prejudice my acting as the execu-tor of his estate, or he might have had a dozen other reasons.

What matters most is that I now find a way to make contact and, in two or three years, join Christian and Claudia wherever they are. Maybe once Tila informs them that I suspect they're alive, Christian and Claudia will want to communicate. But communication alone won't satisfy me. The kind of dialogue that would be required, sparse and extremely cautious, is not my cup of tea. Perhaps that's been Christian's reason for keeping me out of the loop.

The only thing that will satisfy me is a reunion. For a week or two every year, on holidays. Or, as I've considered for the past few months, forever. I won't leave what's here while Christian and Claudia's location remains a secret, but if they agree to me joining them, I'll drop all this without a second thought.

Consider the alternatives. If I hang around here too long, I'll be stuck with the company of my soon-to-be retired colleagues from the legal profession. I can well imagine them in their advanced years: bored and boring, but as obnoxious and conceited as they were during their working life. If I get lucky, I'll have luncheons at the club with frail, crusty judges. Or, to liven things up a bit, I'll accept the odd invitation to the glitzy mansions of long-forgotten union leaders, although few of them will be around. The ones who don't die early usually end up in Florida.

I'm not made for that. Thanks to Hugo I've seen how the social scene works, and thanks to Hugo I'm cured of it forever. No, my new ambition is to get out of here. To be with my friends. The people I understand and who can relate to me.

Tila and Karen are the ones I have to watch. Eventually, one of them will book a flight to one of the destinations I've singled out: Malaysia or Mexico. It's where Claudia designed resorts and where she and Christian spent quite a bit of time. I considered the Cape Verde Islands, as well, but I dismissed the idea, because they're far too small to disappear in.

I can't expect Tila or Karen to do it blatantly. I'm sure if the place is Cabo San Lucas, they'll pretend to go away on business to L.A. or San Diego and drive a car down to Baja. Or if it's Malaysia, they'll fly to Hong Kong or Singapore and buy a second ticket there. I'll wait and watch, convinced that my intuition and patience will lead me to success.

My dreams carry me away. When I lie awake at night, I imagine a beach hut on some magnificent shore, not far from the hut in which Christian and Claudia live. We have long sunrise walks, quietly marveling at the changing sky and water. And at night, we visit each other and have rousing discussions. Our faces are lit up by kerosene lamps and a few feet away the breaking surf picks up bits of moonlight.

There aren't any loons crying or midnight canoe rides, as at the cottage, where I always imagined we'd spend many of our spring, summer and fall evenings. But there are compensations.

It's warm, and as we get older we cherish the thought of perennial summer. And I'll escape from the hundreds of things that keep me captive to this rat hole. I'll be free! What was it that the Sheik Raizuli said at the end of *The Wind and the Lion*? "Isn't there one thing in your life that's worth losing everything for?"

Every now and then, I think that Tila would like such a life, too. I've caught her looking at me a few times—the kind of look that says maybe there's more to me than she thought. I don't know if I'm right, but it's another reason why I'll keep a close eye on her.

If she likes me as much as I've grown to like her, maybe we can both get away. I'd have to lose some weight, I suppose, and cut back on my drinking.

I'm not sure whether Tila will enjoy the noisy debates I'll have with Christian in the evenings. We'd have to find out, as we did with Claudia.

But I can see her reading with me in the afternoons, outside our hut. Occasionally she spies a crab poking its periscope eyes out of the sand and side-stepping its way to the next hole. She nudges me and we both put down our books and look on.

Or a couple of kids walk by and wave at us and we wave back. And then we watch the surf erase their small footprints, bit by bit, until nothing is left.

AUTHOR'S NOTES
AND
ACKNOWLEDGEMENTS

PETER C. CAVELTI

. . . .

All novels are, to an extent, autobiographical. The part of this story that's related to my own life is Georgian Bay. I started *A Dangerous Remedy* at my cottage near Parry Sound and I ended it there. All other aspects of this book are fictional.

I've often looked at other novelists' acknowledgements and wondered why it was necessary to thank so many people. Now I know. Non-fiction books, like my works on economics and social issues or my dissertation on the speeches of South Sea Chief Tuiavii, required meticulous research. But once that was done, the rest was easy. A novel, I've learned, is a living thing. Characters evolve and, in turn, take on a life of their own. The challenge is to let them do so. None of my original scenes survived without being altered several times. And when I thought I was finally there, a friend told me that all I had to do now was "make every line sing." I found it to be an intimidating process.

Here, then, are the people without whose help this novel wouldn't exist. Suzi Leonard helped with proof-reading and kept track of contextual details; Katja Pantzar provided invaluable insights into the finer points of style; and my friend, psychologist Jim Weaver, gave his professional advice. The indefatigable Sam

Hiyate helped me improve dramatic tension and introduced me to the fine art of "pruning," a process that cut the manuscript in half. He was there at every critical juncture, gently guiding me one moment and driving me mercilessly the next—but never without the type of enthusiasm only Sam is capable of.

Thanks also go to Stephanie Rayner for her unwavering friendship and objectivity; fellow author Larry Gaudet for his encouragement and support; editor Marjorie DeLuca for her valuable help with pre-publication work; my friend graphic artist Richard Moore for working closely with me on the design of my book; and screenwriter Laurie Riley for believing in my story and making *A Dangerous Remedy* into a screenplay.

Finally, I'd like to extend my sincerest appreciation to Caroline—for reading through countless drafts, helping me develop and refine plot and structure, challenging me when needed and last, but not least, for being my wife and best friend.

GEORGIAN BAY, SUMMER 2004